She Who Finds a Husband:

New Day Divas Series Book One

She Who Finds A Husband:
New Day Divas Series Book One

E.N. Joy

www.urbanchristianonline.net

Urban Books, LLC
78 East Industry Court
Deer Park, NY 11729

She Who Finds A Husband: New Day Divas Series Book One
©copyright 2008 E.N. Joy

ISBN- 13: 978-1-60162-875-6
ISBN- 10: 1-60162-875-7

First Printing February 2010
Printed in the United States of America

10 9 8 7 6 5 4 3 2 1

This is a work of fiction. Any references or similarities to actual events, real people, living, or dead, or to real locales are intended to give the novel a sense of reality. Any similarity in other names, characters, places, and incidents is entirely coincidental.

Distributed by Kensington Publishing Corp.
Submit Wholesale Orders to:
Kensington Publishing Corp.
C/O Penguin Group (USA) Inc.
Attention: Order Processing
405 Murray Hill Parkway
East Rutherford, NJ 07073-2316
Phone: 1-800-526-0275
Fax: 1-800-227-9604

Dedication

How can I not, first and foremost, thank my very inspiration, God Almighty? Before I even put pen to paper with the New Day Divas series, I'd heard many a pastor stand in the pulpit and say, "God has a sense of humor." Well, I learned that to be true first hand when I allowed God's Spirit to dictate each and every word of this story. I'm now a believer: God, you definitely have a sense of humor, and I know my readers will appreciate seeing that side of you.

Acknowledgments

To my husband, Nicholas (Bang) Ross. "Where's the books?" is the question you have posed to me for years. "As talented as you are, you should be spittin' out books left and right; two or three books a year," you'd say. I'd grit my teeth and go to my prayer room and tell God on you for not understanding how busy I was with other people's stuff; my wonderful authors on the Urban Christian imprint, my talented clients for whom I serve as agent, the ghostwriting projects I'd committed to, and my own one book I was trying to squeeze out in between it all. God set me straight and told me to quit masquerading my complaints as prayers, and get to utilizing the talents and gifts He'd blessed me with. Here I was telling on you, but yet I was the one who got in trouble. Go figure. Nonetheless, my comeback to you is, "Here's the books . . . *New Day Divas* five book series. Bam . . . in your face (LOL). Love you, hon!

Carl Weber, had you not called me and pitched this idea, telling me you felt I was the perfect author for the task of introducing this type of series to the Urban Christian line, I don't know if I would have ever brought these Divas to life. Yes, I had notes upon notes of character ideas and storylines just for this type of project that you knew absolutely nothing about when you placed that call to me. So when I got your phone call, I knew it was nothing short of confirmation from God that it was time for me to gather up all those scribbled on envelopes and scrap pieces of paper, and bring this vision into manifestation. Thanks, Boss! Between my husband, you, and God, I guess this series was bound to come forth.

Chapter One

"So just how long had he been sleeping around on you anyway?" Paige asked, almost in a whisper, as if the other women who were in the room weren't already tuned in to the conversation. Paige intensely sat on the edge of her chair in anticipation of Tamarra's response.

"Fifteen years," Tamarra responded through gritted teeth. If the evil expression that was taking over her usually kind and inviting oval shaped face wasn't proof that her flesh was rising up inside of her, then her hands that slowly curled into fists sure were.

"Fifteen years?" Paige repeated. "Oooh, child, the devil is a liar."

"The devil ain't have nothing to do with it," Tamarra begged to differ. Her oak with a gloss finished complexion began to turn red. "Unless devil is another name for that thing down his underwear that he couldn't seem to keep in his pants."

After holding back a chuckle, Paige asked, "How did you find out? I mean, how in the world does a husband tell his wife that he's been cheating on her for fifteen years?" It wasn't as if Paige didn't already know the story. It was just that the more she pressed whenever Tamarra was telling it, the more new pieces of information she'd always learn.

"Oh, it wasn't that coward who told me. It was his fourteen-year-old daughter who showed up on our door step one day looking for her daddy. Her daddy who just happened to be my husband. And there was no denying that she was Edward's child. The girl was his spittin' image. So if this was my husband's four-teen-year-old child, and we'd been married for fifteen years, then surely that meant I was her mother, right?" Of course that was a rhetorical question that Tamarra didn't expect anyone to answer.

The women in the room looked at one another in disbelief. If what Tamarra was saying was accurate, then that meant that Tamarra's husband had been cheating on her for practically the entire fifteen years of their marriage.

Tamarra looked around the room and could read the expression on the women's faces loud and clear. "Yep, that's right. That sucka had been cheating on me for the entire fifteen years of our marriage. The mother of this daughter of his happened to be his high school sweetheart, with whom he'd had a relationship with for years. It was supposedly one of those on again, off again, and then back on again things." She folded her arms and rolled her eyes. "Looks like I must have hooked him when they were off, and just as soon as I said 'I do,' they got it on again . . . I mean, they were on again."

"Unbelievable," Paige stated, making a tsk sound. Although upset, due to her deep dimples that donned her cheeks whether she was smiling or not, it was hard to tell just how upset she really was.

"I mean, at first I thought I was going crazy when that child stood at my door telling me that she was my husband's fourteen-year-old daughter," Tamarra said. "I really thought I had lost my mind; that I'd had a child all these years ago and couldn't remember. For a minute there, I could vouch for the feelings Mary must have felt when she learned she was pregnant with Jesus. Only in my case, there was no immaculate conception. I knew how I would have gotten pregnant and who the daddy would have been, but I just didn't remember being pregnant." Tamarra paused for air, shifting her size twelve bottom in her chair. "I stood in that doorway pondering, trying to recall the nine months of carrying this child in my womb and the hours of labor. But then reality set in, and I realized that this was no more my child than the man on the moon."

"I just can't believe after all those years the child got the courage to show up on your doorstep like that," Paige said.

"Oh, Little Bo Peep didn't just make her way there on her own. Her mother put her up to it, I'm sure. Yeah, I'm sure that wench orchestrated the entire thing. I'd bet the farm she was probably parked around the corner somewhere watching the entire scene play out; taking me for the fool I was. A fool who had no idea that not only had her husband fathered a child by another woman, but had been playing an active role in the child's life. Paying child support. Going to school functions and dance recitals."

"Lord, have mercy." Paige shook her head in empathy. Her slicked back ponytail bobbed with each turn of her hair. Had her skin not been so chocolate brown, she might have even turned red with anger. She had never been cheated on by a man, not that she knew of anyway. Neither had she ever been married. But she could only imagine the pain her friend sitting next to her must have felt to find out that the man she had been so faithfully committed to for all those years had been living a lie.

"Oh, the Lord had mercy all right. He had mercy when I waited at the door for Edward with a big, black frying pan and got to wailing on that no good husband of mine." Tamarra shook her head in disbelief. "I still don't know how he came out of it with only a mild concussion. I mean, I'd watched Madea's Family Reunion enough times to know how to swing that frying pan just right to put him in a three day coma at least. Yeah, the Lord had mercy on him all right; that rotten, dirty, son of a—"

"Sister Tamarra!" Doreen shouted as she stood up from her chair that nearly tipped over from her abrupt movement. "Now I know you're hurt and all about what your ex-husband did to you, but child, need I remind you that you are in the Lord's house?"

Tamarra looked around the room as if to re-familiarize

herself with her surroundings. For a minute there, she had for-gotten that she was in the church classroom where Wednesday night Bible Study was held. Perhaps it was the fact that it was Fri-day and not Wednesday, or the fact that they were in the church classroom instead of the modest sanctuary that made Tamarra forget that she was in God's house.

Doreen, affectionately called Mother Doreen by the members of New Day Temple of Faith, sat back down as she profusely tried to fan away the sweat beads that were now form-ing on her forehead. Her olive colored skin was now shining like the North Star. She pat down her salt and pepper ear length hair that she wore in a roller set as if Tamarra's near slip up had caused it to stand up straight on her head.

Mother Doreen was a petite, calm, and passive woman, always the voice of reason; so even just the hint of any negative drama or excitement got her girdle in a bunch. And the first sign of Mother Doreen's uneasiness was always the sheet of perspira-tion that showed up on her forehead like a pimple the day before prom or school picture day.

"Oh, I'm sorry, Mother Doreen." Tamarra accepted the tissue that Paige handed her and quickly wiped away the lone tear that rested in the bottom lid of her eye before it could even think about falling. "It's just that it hurts so bad. I mean, I know it's been almost a year since my divorce was final, but it still hurts just like it all happened yesterday." Now tears weld up in both her eyes, but she was sure to blink them into the tissue, leaving no evidence that tears were ever threatening to flow.

"Now, now, sweetheart." Mother Doreen stepped away from her chair and walked over to Tamarra. Tamarra was five feet eight inches tall compared to Mother Doreen's four feet eight inches. So Mother Doreen was practically eye to eye with Tamara even though she stood and Tamarra was seated. "I know it hurts, but you got to let go. You got to let go and let God. All this pain, hurt, and anger you're carrying around is binding you up. And anything that binds you is intended to keep you from God. We don't want that, now do we?"

"I know, Mother Doreen, but I swear on everything I want to be angry now and repent later." Tamarra sniffled. "The sun goes down, but my anger doesn't go down with it. I just don't know what to do."

"Then it sounds to me like I need to pray for you. You know what the Word says; the prayer of the righteous availeth much."

"You can pray for me if you'd like, Mother Doreen, but I've been praying for myself, and it still hurts." Tamarra didn't sound too confident in the power of prayer right about now, although whenever she was called on by the pastor to come up and pray for church members during altar call, she could pray down the wall of Jericho. Yet she felt as if her personal prayers regarding her own situations never made it to God's ears.

"I know how you feel, baby, but prayer works," Mother Doreen assured her, very confident in her ability to pray for others. She wasn't the church intercessor for nothing. "I'm a witness that prayer works. I was married to my Willie for almost thirty years. We had a strong, loving marriage, but we had our share of marital issues as well. And it was prayer that brought us through till death do us part." She looked up. "God rest my Willie's soul." She drew an invisible cross across her heart with her index finger and then continued. "I had to pray through the lying. I had to pray through the cheating. I had to pray through the gambling, the drinking . . . " with each issue Mother Doreen called out, for the first time ever, the women could see the flesh rising up in her. And once she noticed that her hands were now balled into fists, she could see it too. "Oh, dear." Mother Doreen began to fan herself again. "Maybe somebody else should pray for you," she said while patting Tamarra on her shoulder, and then walking back to her seat and sitting down. "And maybe they should pray for me too while they're at it."

Not being able to take much more of the scene that was playing out before her, Deborah Lucas rose to her feet. "Oh for Pete's sake," she said under her breath while throwing her hands up. She then said out loud, "I'll pray. I'll pray for everybody . . . God help us all." Deborah sighed heavily.

It wasn't that Deborah didn't want to pray, it was just that she was tired of always ending up being the one that had to pray. This was usually because the women had made themselves weary with reflecting on their past relationships, versus looking forward to the future relationships God may have in store for them. But Deborah should have been used to it by now. The New Day Singles Ministry's first Friday night of the month meetings always ended up being more of an ex bashing session in which the women ultimately found themselves praying and repenting for their words and thoughts. But it was easy for the conversations to stray from words of encouragement to discouragement regarding men, namely the men the women had been in a relationship with. This was because there were no men in the room to object.

In the Singles Ministry's nine months of being in existence, there had been no male members to join. This left an ample amount of time for the women to share their relationship war stories and compare their battle scars; to determine whose wound was the deepest and yuckiest. They discussed things they more than likely wouldn't have discussed had there been men present.

Although Deborah had a few relationship war stories of her own, she never put her business out there like some of the other women did. She didn't want to make herself look stupid, or in her opinion, let the other women know that she was stupid. She had to be stupid in order not to suspect that the last three men she'd dated had been cheating on her. But in hindsight, she could see everything just clearly. Clear enough to know a cheat when she saw one a mile away, or let her tell it, "smelled one" a mile away. Because in her opinion, she could smell a dog before she could see it. And according to the fictitious Book of Deborah, verse 1 . . . all men were dawgs! So with that belief buried in her heart, she always expected the worst from men. But with that same belief system in place, it was up in the air whether or not she'd know a good man if she saw one, or better yet, if God sent her one.

Deborah stood, all five feet seven and a half inches of her medium build frame, at the front of the classroom. She was positioned beside the podium that Pastor taught at every Wednesday. "Everybody, please stand." After the women did as they were asked, Deborah began to pray. "With heads bowed, eyes closed, and all minds clear, saints, let's pray."

Deborah led the dozen or so women into an anointed prayer. She asked God to forgive the women for any impure or unrighteous thoughts and comments, and to touch the women's hearts that they may be able to forgive the men in their past relationships that might have hurt them. She also asked God to place a man of God in the women's lives that was after His heart first, and then the women's. After she closed the prayer, the women clapped, and then hugged before sitting down and resuming their meeting.

"Now, ladies, can we get back to the business at hand?" Deborah said as she pulled her notebook out of her Bible bag, then stood behind the podium. She flipped through her notes from the previous meeting. "At the last meeting we discussed having a singles dinner, but we ran out of time before we were really able to discuss it in detail. I personally like the idea, and I'd like to suggest—"

"No offense, Sister Deborah, and I don't mean to cut you off," one of the women spoke up, "but look around." Deborah's light brown, slanted eyes looked around the room that was full of women. "What good is it to have singles events when there ain't anybody but us women there? I don't know about the rest of y'all, but I'm going to tell the truth and shame the devil. I joined this ministry to meet me a single man. Heck, that's what I thought the Singles Ministry was all about; the singles hooking up and connecting. If that's not the case, shoot, I wouldn't have canceled my membership to that online dating network."

The woman sat back down to a crescendo of "Amens."

"She's got a point," Paige added. "We plan stuff, and then it's just us women who participate. The last time I checked the Bible, that sort of thing was an abomination, if you know what I mean." Paige's comment was followed by some laughter and comments of agreement. "Besides . . . a dinner? Come on. Do I look like I miss that many dinners that I need to put one down on my calendar?" Paige was making reference to her plus size figure.

When Mother Doreen saw that Deborah was starting to become agitated, she interjected before any drama could jump off. "Now, ladies, the entire purpose of this ministry is for the support of the singles in this church. Which reminds me, I need to get the bylaws typed up so I can give you all a copy. Then the purpose and vision will be clear in black and white. But in the meantime, remember that the church is not, and has never been, a place where you come to find a man."

"And just where was it again that you and the late Willie met?" Paige asked with her thick, long eyelashes fluttering over her big, brown eyes. She knew darn well she recalled the story Mother Doreen had told about how she and her now deceased husband had met.

"Well . . . uh . . . at church," Mother Doreen stammered. "But when I went to church. I didn't set out to find no husband. I set out to find the Lord. I just got blessed with both. Because spite all the issues me and Willie had to endure in our marriage . . . " She looked up. "God rest my Willie's soul." She drew an invisible cross across her heart with her index finger, and then continued. "My marriage with that man was a blessing. I wouldn't trade those years of my life for the world." She looked at Tamarra. "And I know if you look back on your fifteen years of marriage, your good outweighed the bad, and you wouldn't trade it for the world either."

"No, not the world," Tamarra partly agreed, "just a little island off the coast of Mexico with enough tequila for me to forget that low down dirty dog of a man ever existed." Tamarra shook her head. "And thank goodness we never had any children together to remind me of that dirt bag."

The comment Tamarra had just made stung Deborah

for her own personal reasons. Reasons that were between her and God. She quickly recuperated and just shook her head, her shoulder length sisterlocks dancing with every movement. She wondered if she'd be needing to pray for these women all over again.

The women began to murmur and mumble, mostly in support of both Paige and the other woman's earlier remarks about what they perceived as failed singles events.

Deborah cleared her throat to get the women's attention. "If you ladies would have let me finish, I believe my suggestion would have covered your concerns regarding male participation in the singles events." Deborah was able to keep from shooting daggers at the women with her eyes before proceeding. "I was going to suggest that even though we can't seem to get the single men at New Day to join the Singles Ministry, we can still invite them to the dinner. That might break the ice and even get a few of them to become members."

The women began to nod and chatter in agreement of Deborah's suggestion. Finally, a breakthrough, Deborah thought a moment too soon.

"Where were you thinking we should have the dinner?" another woman asked.

"Oooh, The Olive Garden has that bottomless salad," Tamarra suggested.

"But Red Robins has those bottomless fries," Paige countered.

"Weren't you the one who just made a comment referencing your weight?" Tamarra reminded her friend.

"Yeah, and now I can't wait to eat," Paige chuckled. She was never one to diet, and complaints about her weight were far and few in between. She knew that if she didn't like her size, she could do something about it. But being "big boned" pretty much all her life, she'd accepted the fact that she was a lifetime member of the big girls club with a platinum card.

"How about we have the dinner at—" The women in the room spoke amongst themselves, throwing out the names of their favorite restaurants as suggested locations to hold the dinner.

"Excuse me," Deborah interrupted, once again clearing her throat. "I was thinking that we could have the dinner right here at the church, in the fellowship hall."

The women eyeballed one another and nodded.

"Hmm, now that doesn't sound bad either," Paige said. "My cousin has her own catering business, Integrity Catering. I know she'd give us a good deal on catering the event."

"Now you know good and darn well I do catering for a living," Tamarra huffed. "You just trying to be funny. Besides, why would you want to have someone outside the church cater when God has everything we need already in this house?"

"I wasn't trying to be funny," Paige stated. "I just figured you'd want to relax and enjoy the dinner instead of preparing it." Paige rolled her big eyes.

Those all too familiar sweat beads began to dance about Mother Doreen's forehead. It was now Deborah's turn to intervene before these meetings ended up giving the sixty-something-year-old woman a heart attack.

"I was thinking that we women would prepare the food and invite the men," Deborah explained.

An instant hush swept over the room, and the women stared at Deborah as if she were standing naked before the Lord . . . literally.

Tamarra stood up and put her hands on her hips. Her fingers wrapped around her toned waist. "I wish I might even think about slaving in the kitchen for a bunch of men who don't even find us worthy enough to come fellowship with us for a night. And it's just one evening out of the month. Oh, but I'm sure they'd come out to eat our food."

"Yeah, I bet if that mini skirt, low cut shirt wearing Lorain was a member of this ministry, the men would flock here in droves," one woman added. "The way they dang near be salivated over the woman is just shameful."

"Guess our skirts ain't short enough and v-necks ain't v

enough, like that Jezebel spirit possessed Lorain's," another complained. "Guess we all can't be spiritual divas like good ol' Sister Lorain." Her tone was laced with sarcasm and a hint of jealousy.

"Then she be having the nerve to run to the altar every dang on Sunday and fall out in the Spirit, showing every ounce of her—"

"Ladies," Deborah interrupted. "We're getting off track again. And in addition to that, we're starting to sound like the children of Israel with all this murmuring and complaining. We're always talking about how we want the Lord to use us, but now we won't even let Him use us to cook a meal for some members of our own church."

"Not just members; the men," Tamarra corrected.

"Ya heard?" a young twenty-something woman stated. "And my momma told me don't cook for no man but my husband. That's almost just as bad as giving up the milk for free without making him buy the cow."

"And the men at this church probably wouldn't appreciate it anyway," Tamarra continued, rolling her eyes. "Trust me, I've been a member for nine years. I know how these New Day men are."

"Let them cook for us," Paige suggested. "Ain't nothing wrong with a man cooking for a woman. Besides, just in case one of these men at New Day is my future husband and God just ain't revealed it to me yet, I don't even want him to get the impression that I'm going to be cooking for him all the time. I need me a man who's gonna take me out to dinner. I ain't trying to always be in no kitchen."

"You could have fooled me," a woman said under her breath, just low enough so that Paige didn't hear her, but the woman next to her could. The two of them shared a private chuckle.

Mother Doreen just shook her head. Listening to these women talk, it was no wonder they were all single. It may not have been scripture, but Mother Doreen was a strong believer in

Chapter Two

"Now I didn't mind slaving over my stove the last four hours cooking up all that fried chicken and macaroni and cheese for these men to eat," Tamarra said to Paige as they made their way back to the fellowship hall. They were returning from retrieving serving utensils from the church kitchen. "But I didn't say anything about serving these men."

"Yeah, Mother Doreen and Sister Deborah know they pushing it," Paige attested. "I'm just going to keep mine real; I ain't old school. I'm not into making sure no man's dinner is on the stove when he gets home from work when I have been working just as long and just as hard as he has all day. If not longer and if not harder. Then I got to turn around and make sure I pile the food up on his plate too. Child, please." Paige sucked her teeth. "I remember watching my mother do that for my father every night. She'd fix Daddy's plate first, then me and my brother's. By the time she'd fix her own plate and sit down to eat, Daddy would want seconds. So she'd get up and fix him another plate. To this day I don't ever remember my mother eating a hot meal. You feel me?"

The clicking of Paige's sassy three-inch Mary Jane pumps matched her sassy attitude. As a matter of fact, Paige's entire personality rang sassy. Twenty-seven years old, never married, never engaged, and no children, she was a pretty good catch for men. With her beautiful, deep chocolate skin and deep dimples, she had caught quite a few; more than she could count on both hands.

That's why she never bought into that concept of skinny women having better luck at finding a man than plus-sized women. She carried herself with so much confidence. And when it came to dressing, she made sure her clothes fit appropriately, complimenting her full-figure. She looked her best when she felt comfortable. And when she was comfortable, rays of radiance surrounded her, attracting many men. Several of them had even been pretty good catches, but for some reason, Paige always managed to find a flaw in the men she dated.

Paige felt that these flaws were immediate cause for dismissal. After all, she was a child of the King, and God certainly wouldn't have sent her flawed merchandise. So she was content with dating as many men as need be in order to get to that perfect man God had for her.

"Now I am old school when it comes to having dinner ready and serving up my man's plate and all that," Tamarra stated, "but like the young sister said at the meeting, only when he's my husband. A husband who's bringing home the bacon so that I can fry it in the pan and put it on a plate. That's one thing I can say about that no good ex of mine; Edward made good money, and he wasn't stingy with it. I didn't mind cooking his food and preparing his plate because he tipped well." Both Tamarra and Paige laughed. "Anyway, ain't nary one of these men my husband for me to be fixing their plates. But I'ma let the Lord use me however He wants for now. But you best believe Sister Deborah and Mother Doreen are going to hear my opinion about this."

"I guess I can go ahead and let God use me without complaint," Paige shrugged, "but if they want seconds, they're getting up off of their behinds and fixing it themselves, because I'm eating me a hot meal."

Paige and Tamarra made their way back into the fellowship hall where everyone was waiting for the food to be blessed by Mother Doreen.

"Before I bless the food," Mother Doreen started, "I'd like to first thank the members of New Day Temple of Faith Singles Ministry for planning this wonderful event. I know God's heart is so pleased at how you all came together to see to it that it was a glorified event in His eyes. For those of you singles who have yet to join the ministry, we thank you for receiving our invitation. We hope that the fellowship you engage in tonight will encourage you to want to become members of the ministry, where we support, encourage, and even hold one another accountable. Because Satan has so many weapons he tries to attack the single saints with, like the spirit of lust. And to know that we have sisters, and hopefully some new brothers, there to touch and agree with us in prayer, we can send those demons to flight. Amen?"

"Amen," the thirty-five persons in attendance declared.

Mother Doreen blessed the food and the hands that prepared it, then the festivities began. Every one dug in and looked to be enjoying the food and the company. It blessed Mother Doreen's heart to see how the dinner had come together so well after getting through all the bickering. Once the prospective date had been set on the church calendar and the pastor had approved the idea, she and Deborah worked together almost daily to make sure that the event went on without a hitch.

Of course there were a few glitches when two women both signed up to bring corn pudding. They fussed about who had signed up first. Mother Doreen resolved the matter by convincing one to make fried corn instead. Once that matter was water under the bridge, there came the issue with the Church Program and Newsletter Ministry failing to list the dinner in the Sunday program for two weeks straight. But it was now obvious that hadn't affected the successful turn out.

All singles had been invited to attend, whether they were actual members of the Singles Ministry or not. And when several RSVPs were received from singles who weren't members, including ten men, the members were hopeful that the ministry would grow . . . with more men, of course. Nonetheless, the turnout could be counted a success.

"So, Sister Tamarra," said Maeyl, a gentleman who served on the New Day's Tape and Sound Booth Ministry. He swallowed a forkful of macaroni and cheese before continuing. "You made this mac and cheese, huh?"

"I sure did. It's my great grandmother's recipe. My husband . . ." Tamarra caught herself, then cleared her throat. "My ex-husband used to love it."

"Well, I don't blame him. I'd marry you for your cooking skills alone. And if we ever did get a divorce, I'd have to sue for alimony in the form of a pan full of macaroni and cheese every month for the rest of my life."

Tamarra tried her best not to blush. She was never one to like showing her emotions. That's why she always prayed to God before going to the Singles Ministry meetings that her emotions wouldn't get the best of her, but it never seemed to work. For some reason, no matter how many times she told herself that she was going to keep her lips sealed and not share with the group, she always managed to discuss her past marriage. Whenever she did that, it was next to impossible for her to talk about it without getting emotional, whether the emotion was hurt, pain, or anger.

Tamarra had always felt that God's purpose for her was to be an encourager and to uplift others. When someone else was in need of encouragement, the Holy Spirit always gave her just the right words to say or pray. So if anyone ever saw her broken down, how could she expect them to believe in the words she was saying to them?

"I surely appreciate the compliment," Tamarra stated, not looking up at Maeyl.

"It's no compliment; it's the truth." Maeyl was feeding Tamarra compliments the same way he was feeding his mouth forkfuls of food.

"Thank you." This time Tamarra looked at Maeyl. His almond shaped brown eyes stayed glued on his plate and not on her as she had expected they might be. He was devouring the macaroni and cheese as if it were the only food on his plate. From the looks of it, he couldn't have cared less about Paige's honey glazed ham she'd bought from the Honey Baked Ham store. Never mind Mother Doreen's baked chicken or Deborah's mashed potatoes and gravy and all the dishes others had bought or home made. No; he only had eyes for Tamarra's macaroni and cheese. Now if she could get a man to only have eyes for her.

"You're welcome." Maeyl still didn't look up from the plate, confirmation to Tamarra that his compliments toward her food was genuine and that it wasn't some slick way to try to flirt with her, although she definitely wouldn't have been offended by a little flirting.

Maybe life after her ex-husband was wishful thinking. She'd given him her best years. What did she have left to offer another man anyhow? She was a size six when she had married her husband, and now she was a size twelve. She was a toned size twelve, but twice the size nonetheless. But she felt like half the woman. Everyone always told her that the average size for a woman was twelve, but she didn't want to be average. She wanted to be the size that had caught her a husband in the first place. Why had God let her waste all those calories on that cheating man?

"Anytime, Maeyl," Tamarra eventually replied to Maeyl's last statement under her breath with a tone of defeat. "Anytime."

Seeing the disappointment on Tamarra's face, Paige, who was sitting right next to her witnessing the exchange between Tamarra and Maeyl, lovingly patted her friend's knee. When Tamarra looked up at her, she winked. Tamarra let a smile cross her lips, signaling to her friend that she was okay.

"It's time for the drawing," Deborah said as she stood in the center of the room with a basket in her hand. Deborah looked stunning with her locks pulled up atop her head. She normally wore them down. The nice floral dress was a change from the pantsuits she usually wore to church.

Upon everyone's arrival at the dinner, they were each given a raffle ticket. This was an idea Mother Doreen had come up with. Another member had suggested they charge one dollar for the tickets to raise money for the next singles event, but Mother Doreen considered it to be too close to just outright gambling. And after the years she had dealt with her deceased husband's gambling addiction, she didn't want to have nothing to do with anything remotely close to gambling.

Deborah pulled out the first ticket and read off the last three numbers on the ticket. "Seven seventy-seven."

"That's me!" a woman called out as she came forward to claim her prize. She wore a little black dress similar to the ones the all female group, En Vogue, used to wear.

"Congratulations, Sister Lorain," Deborah said as she handed her an envelope. It was all Deborah could do to hide the expression on her face when she saw Lorain in such a revealing outfit. Perhaps some of the members of the Singles Ministry were right. Maybe if tight clothes, make-up wearing Lorain did join the Singles Ministry, then men would join as well. Deborah shook her head at the thought. God would have to have a crazy sense of humor to use Lorain in that capacity. Surely He had another purpose for Lorain in His kingdom. "Three fifty-seven," Deborah called out after pulling the next, and last raffle ticket. There was no response. "Three fifty-seven," Deborah called out again, still to no response.

People started to mumble, chatter, and look around. None of the guests had left yet, so they knew the owner of the ticket had to still be there.

Tamarra and Paige double checked their tickets, neither one of them having the number that had just been called.

"Going once . . ." Deborah called out.

Tamarra looked over at Maeyl who still had his face buried in his macaroni and cheese. She nudged him. "You might want to come up for air and check your ticket," she told him.

"Huh?" Maeyl asked with a puzzled look on his face.

"Your raffle ticket." Tamarra held up her own to show Maeyl what she was referring to.

"Going twice," they heard Deborah say.

"Oh." Maeyl pulled his ticket out and showed it to Tamarra.

"You've got it," Tamarra told him, and then looked to Deborah. "Three fifty-seven! Brother Maeyl has it."

There was applauds by some, and from those hoping they'd get another chance at winning, there were moans.

"Come on up, Brother Maeyl," Deborah ordered, "and get your twenty-five dollar gift certificate to the Olive Garden."

Maeyl got up from his plate and went to retrieve his winnings. He then returned back to the table where he finished off his macaroni and cheese.

Once the guests had gotten seconds, some even thirds, some of them began to leave, but not before Mother Doreen invited all who weren't already members to join the New Day Singles Ministry. For those who were already members, she passed out the bylaws that she had finally managed to get typed, with the help of Deborah.

While several members began to clean up, others gathered their pots, pans, and containers.

"Let me get the door for you," Maeyl said when he saw Tamarra heading toward the door in order to take her pans to her vehicle. "As a matter of fact, let me take those for you."

"Oh thank you, Brother Maeyl." Tamarra was happy to have her hands free as she gave him the pans and led him to her Jeep Cherokee."

It's my pleasure."

Tamarra opened her back hatch, and Maeyl placed the pans inside. "Thanks again." She closed the hatch.

"No problem, Sister Tamarra. After all, it's the least I can do for the woman responsible for that delicious mac and cheese," Maeyl said as he turned and headed to his own car. He then stopped in his tracks. "Actually, there is something else I can do." He pulled out the envelope Deborah had given him that held the Olive Garden gift certificate, and handed it to Tamarra. "Here you go."

"Are you serious?" Tamarra was excited to receive the gift certificate to her favorite restaurant. She graciously accepted it.

"Yes, I'm serious. It's all yours," he told her, and then paused. "Under one condition."

"Let me guess." Tamarra smiled. "I have to make you a pan of my macaroni and cheese?"

"No," Maeyl said, "the condition is that you take me with you."

Maeyl might not have been able, all night, to take his eyes off of his food long enough to look at Tamarra, but he was definitely looking at her now. And Tamarra was looking at him right back.

As she admired this six foot tall, medium build man with a bald head, goatee, and bronze colored skin, she wondered why she'd never noticed all of his appealing features before. Maybe because she had never really looked at him before. She'd never seen him outside of church service and Bible Study, and during those times, she'd always kept her eyes on Jesus. But now, as she gave Maeyl the once over, she prayed Jesus was nowhere near to discern the thoughts that were all of a sudden going through her mind. Thoughts she hadn't felt about a man since her ex.

Before that spirit of lust that Mother Doreen had just prayed away a couple of hours ago could attack Tamarra right there in the parking lot, she replied to Maeyl, "Next Saturday. The Olive Garden. Me and You. I'll meet you at seven." She then jumped in her jeep and sped off. "I got away from you this time, ole spirit of lust," she said out loud. "I just hope I can keep running fast enough.

Chapter Three

"Everything Literary, how may I help you?" Deborah asked as she answered her cell phone, which served as her business phone as well.

For the past three years, Deborah had run her own literary agency in which she was a one-woman show; editing, literary consulting, and some agenting. Deborah had learned a great deal about the literary industry during her own literary endeavors after writing a book of her own. She had contacted every publishing house editor she'd learned of in her library and Internet research. She'd also worked with a couple of professional, and very expensive, editors to perfect her writing. Even after taking some editing and grammar courses at Malvonia Community College, Deborah still never managed to get her book published. But as a result of her three-year endeavor, she learned enough information about the literary industry and the entire editing and publication process to start her own consulting business.

It started off with Deborah sharing the mistakes she'd made and the things she'd learned with online literary groups she had joined. The information she provided was priceless for those she shared it with, ultimately even landing a few of them book deals that launched very successful literary careers. One day, an author who had landed a book deal as a result of the information she had shared, sent Deborah a "thank you" card. Inside the card was a monetary token of her appreciation. That's when Deborah realized her knowledge was worth something . . . money.

She registered the name "Everything Literary" and got a P.O. Box as the official mailing address. She had a website designed that listed the services she offered, and now three years later, she had worked with over one hundred writers and had at least a dozen authors who used her editing services on a permanent basis. In addition, she had five authors for whom she had agented lucrative book deals.

So even though her own manuscript was collecting dust in her home office file cabinet, all of the hard work she put into trying to get it published still benefited her, as well as a few others, in the end. She didn't mind that she had made tons of mistakes and wasted tons of money so that other people didn't have to. With the way business was booming, she was being paid back for her losses ten fold.

"Yes, I'm calling to speak with a Deborah Lucas please," the male voice on the other end of the phone stated.

"This is she," Deborah replied at the baritone voice that sounded as if it were intentionally trying, too hard as a matter of fact, to sound sexy and sophisticated.

"Hi, Deborah. My name is Chase. Lynox Chase."

Deborah rolled her eyes up in her head. She hated when men tried to do the *"Bond, James Bond"* thing. It was such a turn off. She sniffed. "Hello, Mr. Chase. How can I be of service to you?"

"Well, I was referred to you by a fellow author. See I've written this wonderful erotic thriller, if I don't say so myself," he bragged. "It's been edited and everything by a professional editor. Twice. Both my friend and the editor raved over the story and are certain major publishers would be fighting over adding it to their production schedule. But the thing is, as you know, most publishing houses won't even look at my work without an agent representing it. And that's where you come in. Now my friend tells me you are a Christian . . ." This guy wasn't coming up for air. "So I hope the fact that my work is erotic won't offend you and deter you from representing me."

"Mr. Chase, I'm not that easily offended."

"Great, because I'd love for you to represent me."

"Not so fast, Mr. Chase. Before taking you on, I'd need for you to send me the first four chapters of your manuscript as well as a synopsis and cover page with all of your contact information," Deborah told him. "You can send it to my attention at P.O. Box—"

"Well, actually, Deborah . . . you don't mind if I call you Deborah, do you?"

Deborah huffed, and she didn't remove the receiver away from her mouth when she did it. Game recognized game. And although this guy may have very well been interested in getting her to represent his manuscript, she could tell by his undertone that he might have been interested in a lot more. She sniffed as if she was sniffing out the scent of a dog . . . or in this case, a dawg.

"Deborah is fine, Mr. Chase."

"Well, Deborah, I happen to live in Columbus, Ohio, which is only a few miles from Malvonia. So we're sort of like neighbors. I thought it might be better if we met for lunch somewhere and had a sort of business lunch."

"What do you mean by *sort of?*" It was time to call a time-out in Mr. Chase's game. "Either it is or it isn't."

"Pardon me. I didn't mean to imply that our meeting would be anything other than professional. I'm serious about my work, *Mrs.* Lucas."

Who was this guy fooling? She'd just given him permission to call her by her first name. She knew he was now deliberately using her last name as a fishing expedition. "It's *Miss* Lucas." Deborah laughed inside at his attempt to find out whether she was married or single. But she had to be honest with herself; something about Mr. Chase was intriguing. And if being even more honest, she was somewhat flattered. Even still, she sniffed.

"My mistake, Miss Lucas. Nonetheless, I really think you would be interested in representing my work. Again, like I was saying, I'd love to meet you in person since I'm pretty much in

the same city." Now the more Mr. Chase spoke, the more serious he sounded, slightly toning down the deliberate charm. "It
doesn't have to be for lunch. It can be at the library, your office,
you name it. I just want to pitch my vision and goals regarding
my work to you. I've often been told that I do much better in person than on paper when it comes to pitching myself. Of course,
my written work speaks for itself."

Deborah appreciated the sincerity that she could now
sense in Mr. Chase's tone. Her timeout must have given him
time to reconsider his next play and the team he was up against.
With that being said, and letting her guard down just a dash,
Deborah stated, "Lunch will be fine, Mr. Chase. I'm free Thursday and Friday of this week."

"How about Thursday at noon?"

"That works for me, Mr. Chase. We can meet at Max and
Erma's on Pleasant Drive, if that's not out of the way for you."

"Trust me, I've come so far along now in this process, I'd
drive a hundred miles if it meant getting my work published."

"Then, Mr. Chase, I'll see you in two days." Deborah
ended the call, and then wrote down her date . . . her meeting
with Mr. Chase.

As she wrote, something inside of her told her that she
should have insisted on him following her regular submission
policy of mailing his work, but toward the end of her conversation with him, Mr. Chase seemed to be just as sincere about
his work as some of her best clients. Perhaps she'd lowered her
guard just a dash too much and too soon. She hoped that he really was as sincere and passionate about his work as he'd led her
to believe, and for his sake, he'd better hope that he was too.
Because many had come before him trying that same thing;
pretending to be an author after seeing her attractive photo on
her business website.

Her long eyelashes that many assumed were fake because
they were so long, and her neatly weaved sisterlocks that graced
her shoulders always called for a double take. She had a medium

brown complexion like the singer, Chilly, in the group TLC. And for some reason, people always asked her what she was mixed with. She'd made a mental note several times to research her ancestral history, but had never gotten around to doing it as of yet.

Deborah sat at her desk replaying her conversation with Mr. Chase in her mind. After reevaluating the situation, she decided to pick up her cell phone to call Mr. Chase back to cancel their meeting. She'd follow protocol and just have him mail her the submission as she'd initially instructed him to do. She had failed to get his contact information and was disappointed when she looked down at her caller ID and saw that he had called her from a private number.

"Oh, well." She harrumphed. Even though it went against her better judgment, she wouldn't stand up the future self-proclaimed Pulitzer Prize winner. She'd show up at the so-called business lunch.

Deborah stared down at the phone and sniffed again. Yep, this time she could smell him, just like always, before she'd ever even see him. Dawg. Well groomed, though. Maybe too well groomed. Even to the point where, perhaps, this time, she could be wrong. "Nah," she said out loud while scrunching her face.

Deborah stared at the meeting information she'd written down. "Mr. Chase, you'd better hope you really mean business. If not . . . let the games begin!"

Chapter Four

"Two tickets to *The Family that Preys*," the gentleman said to Paige as she stood inside the ticket booth of Marcus theatres. "The eight o'clock show, please." He must have noticed how Paige was gazing over his shoulder in an attempt to see why he was purchasing two tickets when he appeared to be alone. "She's not here yet. The person I'm waiting for," he answered her unasked question.

Paige smiled, thinking she'd better be careful and guard her thoughts, as this guy appeared to be a mind reader. "That will be fifteen dollars." She handed him the two tickets.

"Thank you," the gentleman replied after paying for the tickets with exact change. He then stepped aside to wait on the person whose ticket he was in possession of.

Ten minutes passed by when Paige looked at her watch. It was 7:45 P.M. Fifteen minutes and she would be off work, and as far as she was concerned, eight o'clock couldn't get there soon enough. She hated working the ticket window, especially on a Tuesday evening, any weekday for that matter, when business was slow. Working the ticket window reminded her far too much of her earlier, non-management years with the theatre.

As the manager of the Marcus theatre Pickerington location, which was about a forty minute commute from Malvonia, she often felt that those duties were now beneath her. Last week, to Paige's dismay, an employee had quit. Paige had been forced to cover her ticket window duties until she could hire another employee in her place. In Paige's one year of being a manager, this was the first time anyone had quit without the standard two-week notice.

Ordinarily Paige loved her position, but she'd been complaining about her recent duties to Tamarra since having to do them. Other than that, Paige had no other complaints whatsoever about her job.

A few more patrons came to the window, and Paige painted on a smile as she served them. Once the small line disappeared, she groaned before looking at her watch again. "Yes!" she said in a hushed tone. "Just five more minutes, and I'm out of here."

A smile crept across Paige's face. At eight o'clock she would be a free woman. Free to go home, cook her a Lean Cuisine dinner while she took a shower and got nice and comfy in her PJ's. After doing that, she'd sit down and watch some reality show re-runs. She looked out the ticket window, and her smile slowly evaporated. Although she was excited for eight o'clock to arrive, it looked as though the gentleman outside the window wasn't.

The man who had purchased those two tickets a few minutes ago still stood outside, pacing as he repeatedly looked at his watch every few seconds. He looked as though he wished either eight o'clock would delay itself for a little longer, or his date would put a move on it.

Paige tried to play it off when he caught her staring at him. An embarrassed expression covered his face as his light skin cheeks reddened. Paige figured the poor man now wished that he had never even told her that he was expecting someone to show up and relieve him of that second ticket; especially now that it appeared as though this person was going to stand him up.

"Three tickets to the next viewing of *The Women*," one of three young women who stood in front of the ticket booth requested.

Paige turned her attention to her task at hand. She

had just completed the transaction when the door behind her opened.

"Hey, boss. You ready to break this joint?" Norman asked. She must have been too busy waiting on the women to see him enter the theatre.

Just then, Paige realized that there, in deed, was one other complaint she had about her job. One of her employees. Norman.

Norman entered the ticket booth appearing more than anxious to relieve Paige of her ticket counter duties. Paige should have counted that as a blessing, but she knew his anxiety was self-serving and had nothing to do with his desire to rescue her from the Lion's Den. That was her nickname for the ticket booth. She knew that the real reason for his excitement lay in his readiness to flirt with the women who came to the ticket counter in hopes of getting a phone number or two.

Norman loved when what he called "chick movies" were playing at the theatre. That meant chicks would be coming in droves. He'd never gotten more phone numbers in his life than when the movie *Sex and the City* was playing. Now he was aiming to beat his personal best with the movie, *The Women*, starring Jada Pinkett-Smith.

Norman had worked for the theatre for four years, which was one year longer than Paige had. But when the manager position became available, Paige's skills and dedication paid off more so than Norman's length of time with the company. Norman didn't make a stink about it because he knew that he could sometimes be a slacker. Besides, managerial duties would take him away from all the action that he so looked forward to as he worked the ticket booth.

Fortunately, there had never been any complaints from the customers regarding Norman's flirtatious antics. Actually, some women made it a point to return to the theatre because of Norman. They hoped he would be the one to wait on them and perhaps shower them with a compliment or two that might lift their moods and make their day. Sometimes women needed that type of thing to boost their self-esteem, and a few were even willing to pay $7.50 just to get it.

"I've been ready to get out of here," Paige replied to Norman. No one had to tell Paige twice to get to gettin' as she keyed her code into the cash register that logged her out. She moved aside so that her subordinate could key in his.

"Why are you so ready to get out of here? Got a hot date tonight or something?" Norman teased, bumping Paige's shoulder as he winked.

Paige hated when Norman did that; assumed that just because she was single, she couldn't enjoy the alone time that the single life enabled her. For some reason he thought she had to always be up under some man, and his frequent comments confirmed such. He would often say things to Paige like, "Have a good evening, and don't do anything I haven't done already. Wink-wink." And then there was the most offense one of them all: "So what did you get into last night, or should I ask who did you let get into you? Wink-wink. "

When Paige first started working for the theatre, she had enjoyed chatting it up with Norman over their lunch period and breaks. And his little comments like that had never seemed to bother her back then. She'd simply wink back or smile. With her being single as well as he, they would often laugh until their bellies hurt, sharing their date from the pits of hell stories. Ironically, Norman nor Paige never even thought twice about dating each other. The two had nothing in common besides being single, and it was painfully obvious that they weren't attracted to each other the least bit.

Norman was a tall, skinny, slinky white guy; not that Paige hadn't dated a few Caucasian men before. But she'd always preferred a man who had plenty of meat on his bones, considering she was a thick girl herself; size 16. Norman, too, had dated outside of his race. But they had been blind dates or someone he'd met over the Internet without the benefit of seeing a picture of them first.

That's something Paige didn't do; blind dates or Internet dates. Not even when Tamarra tried to set her up on a blind date with some man she'd met at one of her catering events. Tamarra had sworn to Paige that her sprit was telling her this man was the one for Paige. She based it on everything Paige had shared with her regarding what she didn't want in a man. As much as Paige trusted Tamarra and valued her opinion, a blind date she would not do, especially after Tamarra had only spent a couple of hours at best with the stranger.

But Norman drew the line nowhere. He did the blind date and Internet dating thing on the regular. So Paige didn't know if he otherwise would have willingly dated a minority woman or not. Either way, there was no chemistry or even the slightest interest between them.

"Who's the lucky fella that's got you so anxious to get out of here tonight?" Norman pressed. "Or should I say who is the soon to be lucky fella?" He nudged her with his elbow a couple of times, and then winked.

Paige shot Norman a forced smile, but what she really wanted to do was roll her eyes, exit the booth, and ignore him completely. Maybe then he'd get the hint that the old days were long gone. Not because she was now his superior, but because now she was saved. Her walk had changed, so her talk had changed.

In times like these, she regretted discussing her multiple dates and encounters with Norman. And although she never told Norman that she had slept with any of these men, she never told him that she hadn't. As experienced as Norman was when it came to sex, which he had boasted about on many occasions in their past conversations, Paige couldn't dare allow him to believe that she wasn't just as equally experienced. So she let him assume and insinuate things about her without correcting him. Now she wished she hadn't.

Paige had been saved thirteen months now, and as hard as it sometimes was for her to walk her Christian walk, it seemed even harder for Norman to remember that she even had a Christian walk. She always felt like she was the one to blame for Norman not being mindful of her Christianity. The words from one of her pastor's past messages would often bring about this doubt. *"You shouldn't have to wear Christianity on your sleeve. You shouldn't have to run around telling people you are a Christian. People should be able to look at you and know that you are a Christian. God said He made us in His image. Well, do you look like your Father?"*

It was obvious that Paige didn't look like a Christian or Norman wouldn't be so forgetful about it. She made a mental note to call up Mother Doreen and ask for some guidance about that. She'd been a Christian longer than anybody she knew. Surely she'd encountered her share of Normans.

Paige grabbed her purse and keys and instead of the normal, "Enjoy your shift," she'd usually give Norman, this time she said, "Have a blessed evening," leaving Norman standing there looking as though she was speaking a foreign language.

"Yeah, okay." He snickered. "Hopefully God will bless me by putting it on one of these beautiful women's hearts who are heading this way to give me their phone number. Umm, umm, umm." Norman licked his lips.

Paige shook her head as Norman went to work with his smooth operator skills on the two women that approached the ticket window. "God help him," she said under her breath as she closed the door behind her.

Before heading to her car, Paige stopped off into the ladies room after contemplating whether or not she could control her bladder until she got home. Not. Exiting one set of the glass double doors, Paige waved at Norman as she walked by the ticket booth on her way to her car. He replied by tapping his top shirt pocket, which meant it held one of those women's phone number, if not both knowing Norman.

"Oh, excuse me. I'm so sorry. I was too busy waving at my co-worker, and I didn't see you," Paige apologized to the gentleman she'd just run smack into.

"Don't worry about it. I guess you're not the only one who doesn't realize I'm standing out here." The gentleman exhaled, then looked down at the two tickets he held in his hand. He then looked down at his watch as if catching that movie with the person he was waiting for was a lost cause.

"No, show, huh? Your date that you've been waiting for is a no show?" Paige rubbed it in unintentionally.

"Looks that way." He looked down at his watch for the hundredth time, and then scanned the parking lot.

"Maybe you should try calling her," Paige suggested.

"Nah. It's getting late. Besides, I guess I should be used to this by now." He shook his head and let out a deep, exasperated breath. "Have a blessed one," he told Paige as he headed toward the parking lot.

"You have a blessed one too." As Paige watched the man walk away, she wondered how in the world any woman could stand up such a fine specimen as himself. Sizing him up to be about six feet tall, two hundred thirty pounds of muscle with wavy hair that made him look as though he had Indian in his family, Paige thought this man had to be God sent.

She thought about stopping him in his tracks and offering to view the movie with him, as Paige had hardly been one to shy away from men. Bold and no shame in her game, she was always the aggressor when it came to getting her man. If she was ever going to finally give up the dating game, find her a husband, and settle down, she couldn't just sit back and wait for one to show up on her doorstep. Otherwise, she'd be a member of New Day's Singles Ministry until her hair grayed.

By the time Paige figured she'd go for what she knew and offer to be this gentleman's date for the evening, he was already in his car. "Now chasing a man down, tapping on his window and all that. Desperate, I'm not," Paige told herself, then walked a few cars down to her own vehicle.

Once inside her car, Paige started the engine and turned on her Jill Scott live CD. In addition to gospel music, she loved neo soul, jazz, and some R&B artists like Maxwell. She put the car in reverse and backed out as she sang along with Jill. All of a sudden, Paige slammed on her brakes when she noticed a shiny, black Escalade behind her. "Oh no," she mumbled. She realized that she was so busy singing to the CD that she hadn't even looked out of her rearview mirror to make sure no cars were coming before backing out.

Nervousness filled Paige when the driver's door to the Escalade opened and the owner approached her car.

"I'm sorry . . . again," Paige said to the driver, rolling her window down. "That's the second time tonight I didn't notice you, huh? Guess I'm not doing much to salvage what's left of your ego." Paige put her hand over her mouth, although it was too late; those somewhat insulting words had already escaped. "I'm sorry, that came out wrong."

The gentleman smiled. "No need to apologize. I was just checking to make sure you were okay. You slammed on your brakes pretty hard."

"Yes, I'm okay. Thanks for asking though. And again, I'm sorry."

"Well, since I know your name is Sorry, I suppose I should tell you mine. I'm Blake." He held out his hand.

"I'm—"

"Sorry," he finished her sentence. "I know; you've told me a few times already."

Paige smiled at this gentleman's cleverness and play on her words. Heck, he might even give Norman a run for his money.

"My name is Paige. I'm Paige Robinson," she stressed, shaking his hand while staring in his eyes. "And yes, I'm okay."

"I know, you told me already, but I'm glad you're okay. Be careful, Paige," he told her as he began to walk off.

"I will," she promised him. Paige watched out of her side view mirror as the man headed back to his vehicle.

Suddenly, he turned around and walked back toward

her. "I know this might sound crazy, but I have two tickets to a show that's playing in there." He pointed toward the theatre. "No need to let the tickets go to waste. You seem like you have a lot on your mind with the way you keep trying to run me down and all. Perhaps you would enjoy a relaxing movie."

"You said that you have two tickets. I'd only need one," Paige teased.

"Well, I was thinking I'd use the other. I mean, we could leave an empty seat in between us so that it wouldn't be like a date or anything. I know a woman of God such as yourself wouldn't want to give out the wrong impression. Like my pastor always preaches; avoid the appearance of evil."

Blake stood there while Paige took in his words. *Woman of God*, she repeated in her head. *He called me a Woman of God.* Then she even thought back to just a couple of minutes ago when he'd told her to have a blessed evening. Sure he could have said good evening to any other woman, but to her, a woman whom he recognized as a woman of God, he said blessed evening.

Paige couldn't have tried if she might to conceal the huge grin that stretched across her thick lips and chubby cheeks. God had sent this man to remove the doubt that had been plaguing her about not having the appearance of a Christian. This man had clearly seen that she was a Christian without being told; without her wearing it on her sleeve. This man obviously knew who God was and what God looked like, and he had seen Him in her. This could only mean one thing; that he, too, was a Christian. She relied on her childhood saying—it takes one to know one—as confirmation.

Paige pondered over whether this entire occurrence could also mean one other thing; something much bigger than the current revelation she'd just received. But she decided that she'd pray on all that stuff later. For now, she had a movie to catch. And a fine looking man to catch it with.

Chapter Five

Deborah had barely made it inside the door of Max and Erma's when a man approached her. "Deborah? Are you Deborah Lucas?" The gentleman walked up to Deborah with an extended hand.

As handsome as the man standing before her was, most women would have probably claimed to be Deborah Lucas whether they really were or not. There this brown skin, average height gentleman with a tight fade stood before Deborah. The hypnotic cologne he wore lingered in the air. Deborah didn't recognize it, as she didn't make herself familiar with male colognes. He wore a black Sean Jean suit that looked custom made to fit every arch of his sculptured body, yet Deborah was unfazed.

Deborah, just like she did whether she was meeting a male or female client, had prayed, anointing her head with blessed oil. And right now, according to the Bible, He who was in her was definitely greater than he who is in the world; because her spirit man had total control over her flesh. She wasn't the least bit interested in having anything to do with this man other than reading his manuscript.

Had she not prayed and anointed herself, she could have very well, like many women before her, she figured, been putty in this man's hands. But that wasn't at all the case. Deborah had the gift of discernment. She had that gut feeling before she even walkedout of her front door that she would need to be as tuned in as possible to what her spirit man might try to convey to her about this man.

"Yes, I'm Deborah. Mr. Chase?" Deborah held out her hand."

"The one and the only. But please, call me Lynox."

"Shall we grab a table, Mr. Chase?" Deborah asked, looking him dead in his eyes.

"I hear you, Deborah." Lynox chuckled at Deborah's insistence.

The two walked up to the hostess's booth and was immediately led to a table toward the middle of the restaurant.

"Uh, can we sit somewhere else? A booth or something?" Lynox asked the hostess as he scanned the restaurant. "How about there?" He pointed to a booth far off in the corner.

"Sure, not a problem." The hostess picked up the menus she had already set on the table and led the couple over to the booth.

Deborah followed. She sniffed, knowing that not even the most expensive cologne in the world could cover up the scent of a dawg's—

"Your waiter will be right with you," the hostess stated before walking off.

A few moments after Lynox and Deborah were comfortably seated, their waiter then came over and took their drink and lunch orders. Lynox ordered the famous Erma Burger with fries and asked that a glass of strawberry lemonade be prepared for him, even though it wasn't a regular item on the menu. Deborah ordered a glass of water with lemon wedges and a house salad. Although she was hungry and could have devoured an Erma Burger, she planned on doing more talking-getting down to business and less dining.

"So where's this masterpiece of yours?" Deborah said just as soon as the waiter walked away from the table. She purposely left no room for idle conversation or chit-chat.

"I thought you'd never ask." With a huge grin on his face, Lynox cracked open the briefcase he'd carried into the restaurant with him. He pulled out what appeared to be an entire ream of paper and dropped it in the middle of the table. "Voila!"

Deborah couldn't help but chuckle. "Are you serious?" Deborah pulled the manuscript over to her side of the table. "What is this? Five hundred pages?" She created a fan with the corner pages, flipping through them. "Unless there's a four-eyed white kid casting spells in this book, the first thing you're going to have to do is cut this book down."

"I know it's intimidating; all those pages. But trust me, there is action, excitement, and drama . . . oh yeah . . . and sex, on every single page. Plenty of sex." He winked. Deborah sniffed.

"Well, today, during lunch, I'll let you tell me a little bit about the book and what your inspiration for writing it was. And I'll just take the first four chapters with me to read, and if I'm interested, I'll request the remainder of the manuscript." Deborah flipped through the stack of papers in order to get the four chapters she'd need.

"Please, just trust me on this one." Lynox put his hand atop of Deborah's in order to stop her from taking four chapters only. "Save me the postage and just go ahead and take the entire manuscript with you now. It's really just that good. As a matter of fact . . ." He removed his hand off of Deborah's when he realized that she wouldn't look up from his hand touching hers until he did so. " . . . I'll be quiet for the next few minutes while you read the first chapter. You'll see what I'm talking about. I know you hear this kind of thing all the time; everyone thinks they have the next bestseller, but trust me, I, Lynox Chase, really do."

The waiter interrupted by setting their drinks down, and then letting them know that their food would be out shortly. Once the waiter left, Deborah looked at the huge manuscript, gave Lynox the this-better-be-good look, picked up the first few pages and began to read them.

After reading only the first three pages, she forgot all about Lynox even being there. The story was intense from the very first line. It was thought provoking from page two. The characters were alive and breathing on page three. She had yet to have stumbled over one grammatical error or misuse of the English vocabulary. She was absolutely flabbergasted. The author of this work, the man whom she deemed somewhat conceited and arrogant that was sitting across from her, had backed up his every word. Deborah was now coming to the conclusion that Lynox wasn't conceited or arrogant, he was simply walking in confidence with authority. He knew he'd authored something special. And now she felt honored that he'd chosen her to represent his work.

"Here are your entrees."

Deborah jumped, startled by the waiter's quick return; too quick of a return as far as she was concerned. She didn't want to eat again until she'd finished every single page of Lynox's book.

"It's good, huh?" Lynox said as the waiter walked away. He could tell Deborah was enjoying the work by the way she ignored the waiter when he'd asked her if there was anything else he could get for her.

"As a matter of fact, Mr. Chase, I think I owe you an apology." When Deborah was wrong, she wasn't afraid to admit it. "Your work surpasses anything I've ever read before. If the rest of this manuscript is just as well written and interesting as what I've read thus far, I'm liable to create a bidding war among the publishing houses over the manuscript of a first time author." Deborah smiled, thinking inside how Lynox's manuscript could be the ticket to the vacation home in Maui that she's always wanted.

"I told you so." Lynox, once again, had no issue with exercising his confidence with authority. "Now I know it's hard to do, but put the manuscript down and eat your lunch. It might get cold."

Deborah looked down at her salad, and they both laughed. She laughed. She didn't sniff. She laughed. Without even realizing it, she began to loosen up. Her guard came down even more. The next thing she knew, half her salad was gone and she'd shared her story with Lynox about how she'd gotten into the literary business. Lynox, in return, shared with her what inspired him to begin writing.

Before Deborah could even stop herself, she was laughing uncontrollably at remarks Lynox was making that just a few minutes ago she would have deemed as arrogant. The more he spoke, the more confident he sounded. This confidence suddenly took on an attraction all by itself.

While Lynox spoke, Deborah thought about how, for the first time in a long time, she could be wrong about a man. This Lynox character didn't seem so bad after all. But just to be sure, she sniffed. *Ummm*, she thought as she inhaled his intoxicating cologne.

"So I see you're not wearing any rings." Lynox pointed to Deborah's empty ring finger on her left hand.

"Does that mean you're not married?"

"I guess so," Deborah replied. She looked over at Lynox's bare ring finger on his left hand and turned the tables. "I see you're not wearing any rings either. Does that mean you're not married?"

"Married?" he chuckled. "Who has time for women period, let alone a wife, when you're penning something with more pages than the Holy Bible?" Lynox laughed.

Deborah laughed along with him. "Yeah, I guess you're right. But, and pardon me if you take offense, you just don't seem like the type of guy who would lack female companionship."

And it happened just like that; the conversation went down a road Deborah didn't foresee allowing herself to be taken down, let alone be in the driver's seat.

"It's been hard. But I've been married to this woman right here for the last year." Lynox tapped the manuscript. "It just didn't seem fair to expect a woman to play second fiddle to what some would have deemed as a hobby or extracurricular activity. So it's been quite some time since I've dated."

"I know what you mean," Deborah sympathized, pushing her locks that she'd just had tightened the day before behind her ear. Her modest diamond earring now showed. "That's how I am when it comes to my work. I like very little interference."

Lynox leaned in to the center of the table. "Looks like we have a lot in common, Miss Lucas."

With Deborah's guard now completely down she replied, "Looks like we do, Lynox."

The next few seconds were awkward as Lynox sat there staring at Deborah. He admired her perfect cheek bones and perfectly rounded nose. He usually went for the woman with a little bit more meat on her body, but he was pleased by all 135 pounds of the woman who sat before him.

Deborah decided to clear her throat and excuse herself to the ladies room. She didn't have to use the bathroom, but she knew she needed to go pray . . . again.

"If you'll excuse me, I need to go use the ladies room." Deborah wiped her mouth with her napkin, and then stood up.

"Oh, no problem," Lynox said, standing as Deborah walked away.

Once in the bathroom, Deborah went into a stall and let out a deep breath. "Lord, in the name of Jesus, send down your power," she prayed under her breath. "Send down your strength. I need it now more than ever to hold me back from doing something I have no business doing with somebody I have no business doing it with. Please, Lord, provide some type of interference right now in the name of Jesus. Amen."

Deborah stopped praying when she heard someone enter the bathroom and turn on the faucet. She flushed the toilet although she hadn't used it and exited the stall. She walked straight over to the sink and turned on the water faucet as well.

"Sister Deborah?" the woman standing next to her at the sink stated.

Deborah looked up at the woman standing next to her and recognized her to be Helen, a fellow New Day church member. And also a member that Deborah had always made it a point to avoid at all cost.

"Uh, hi, Helen," Deborah spoke, then immediately cast her eyes away from Helen.

"Fancy seeing you here." Helen turned off the water, then grabbed a paper towel.

"Yeah. I'm, uh, here on business." Deborah washed her hands as if they were covered in mud. She scrubbed and scrubbed as steam from the blazing hot water poured down on her hands.

Helen noticed the steam from the running water.

"Is that hot enough for you?"

"Huh?" Deborah looked up at Helen. She had no idea what she was referring to.

"The water." Helen nodded toward the sink. "It looks scalding."

Deborah hadn't even realized until Helen pointed it out that she hadn't turned on any cold water. As if the stinging pain from the heat was just taking effect Deborah pulled her hands from under the water.

"Here you go." Helen handed her a paper towel as she turned the water off.

"Thank you."

"You're welcome."

There was silence until Helen spoke again. "Well, anyway, it was good seeing you. See you at church this Sunday?"

"Uh, yeah, sure," Deborah said as she tossed the paper towel into the trash container. Deborah then hurried past Helen who remained in the bathroom to freshen up her make up. She felt like Mother Doreen there for a minute as she made her way back to the table, wiping the visible beads of sweat from her forehead.

"Is everything okay?" Lynox asked, observing Deborah's flushness. He stood as she sat down, then he rested back in his seat.

"Oh, yeah. Everything is good."

"Good." Lynox reached across the table and took Deborah's hands into his. "Now where were we before you ran off to the bathroom?"

"Lynox!"

A ringing voice startled Deborah and Lynox, and probably half the restaurant as well. It was the same voice Deborah had just heard moments ago, only now it was more pierced and louder.

"Lynox Chase," Helen sneered, giving him the look of death. "So this is why you couldn't have lunch with me?" Helen nodded her head toward Deborah without taking her eyes off of Lynox.

"Uh, Helen," Lynox stuttered. He then looked over to Deborah in embarrassment. "Helen this is—"

"I know darn well who this is," Helen said, cutting him off. "But what I want to know is what you're doing here with her? Let me guess. She's the reason you don't return my calls?"

Deborah couldn't hide the look of embarrassment as the restaurant patrons turned their attention to her table. This explained why Lynox hadn't wanted to sit at the first table the hostess had led them to. He was too nervous about one of his women spotting him. Looks like sitting off in the corner hadn't faired too well either.

Figuring it was time to step in and see if she could calm the mad, black woman down, Deborah decided to speak up. "Look, Helen. This isn't what it looks like," Deborah tried to intervene.

"Oh, I know. It's just business." Outlining the venom in Helen's tone was sarcasm.

"Excuse me, Deborah," Lynox said to Deborah as he stood up. "Let me go take care of this, and then—"

"Oh, you don't have to take care of this." Helen ran her hands down the length of her size 14 curvy body. "Trust me, this gets taken care of, and you won't be the one doing it anymore."

"Look, Helen, I don't appreciate you trying to insinuate—"

"I'm not trying to do anything," Helen said, cutting him off.

Lynox was becoming agitated by Helen's loudness and rudeness. "Fine then," he said as he sat back down. "I didn't want to do things like this, Helen, but you've left me no choice. I mean, you said it yourself; I declined your lunch invitation. I haven't returned any of your calls. Couldn't you take the hint? Do I have to be Vanna White and spell it out for you?"

The reaction Helen gave to Lynox wasn't one he was expecting. And he almost went into shock when the strawberry lemonade splashed all over his suit. Lynox jumped when the cold liquid hit him, soaking up his manuscript as well. He picked up the wet pages and shook his head. He then looked down at Deborah with pity. "It's obvious we're not going to be able to take care of the business we came here to take care of," he said to Deborah regrettably. "Perhaps we can schedule some other time to meet."

Whatever was the look Deborah shot Lynox as he gathered his things and walked away. She wished she would have walked out with him. Anything rather than be left alone with Helen.

"Really, Helen, you've got things all wrong," Deborah explained. "Lynox's and my meeting was strictly business. I don't know how well you know Lynox, but he's an author. And it's no secret that I'm—"

"Funny you should use the word secret, seeming you've got one yourself; and I don't mean your little rendezvous with Lynox." A mischievous grin spread across Helen's lips like butter on bread. But I'm sure I don't have to remind you of anything. Surely you're reminded of it every night when you close your eyes and try to sleep, huh?"

Deborah's lips began to quiver. She couldn't have been any angrier with Helen than at that moment. She was angry that Helen was absolutely right. Not only had Deborah gone through many sleepless nights, but sometimes it was even hard for her to look at herself in the mirror. She was angry that Helen knew this about her.

"But don't worry, Sister Deborah, I won't take your little secret and run with it the way you just took my man and ran with him." Helen looked Deborah up and down. "But don't push me. Like the Bible says, everything in the dark eventually comes to light. I'd hate to have to be the source of that light." Helen picked a tomato out of Deborah's unfinished salad. "Enjoy your lunch." She popped the tomato in her mouth, and then walked away.

Of all people Deborah encountered, it had to be Helen. Perhaps this was meant to be the interference she'd prayed for from God. Next time, she'd have to be more careful of what she asked for.

Chapter Six

Tamarra was feeling pretty good about her scheduled dinner with Maeyl at The Olive Garden. The time of the date was just two hours away. She hoped all would go well, considering it was the first real date she'd had since divorcing her husband. Prior to now, she'd only given two other men the time of day. One was a guy Paige had convinced her to ask out. It had taken Tamarra an entire month to build up the courage to approach the man. Unlike Paige, Tamarra had never had to exercise her women's liberty—times have changed—what's good for the man is good for the woman tactics. But Paige had assured her that it was a new day, and unless she wanted to spend the rest of her life wallowing in her past failed marriage, she'd better get with the times.

Mother Doreen was old school and had voiced her opinion against women being the aggressor in a relationship. Being the supportive person that Mother Doreen was, she had suggested to Tamarra that if she were going to ask a man out, then she couldn't think of a better place for them to go than to church.

So Tamarra decided to take both the advice of her now best friend, Paige, who she'd only known for a little over a year, and the advice of Mother Doreen, a woman she'd known since walking into New Day Temple of Faith nine years ago. She asked the man to accompany her to Sunday service, promising they'd go to lunch afterward. Tamarra even put the cherry on top of this women's lib thing by offering to pick up her date.

Whoever told Mother Doreen that church was the perfect place for a Christian to ask a non-Christian to go to for their first date should have asked somebody; somebody like Tamarra. It turned out to be a disaster. Tamarra should have foreseen as much on the drive over to the church. She compared their ride to church that morning to the ride Damien, the little boy in the movie *The Omen*, took to chruch.

At first Tamarra thought he was just nervous about their date when sweat began to pour from his forehead. The same way sweat shot from his pores, so did his questions about church.

"They don't make you stand up and speak when you're a first-time visitor do they?" he asked, loosening his tie. "Is it Communion Sunday? Does your church use real wine? I could use a drink." Chuckle. Chuckle.

Tamarra assured him that New Day was very welcoming and that he'd feel right at home. She thought that would make him feel more relaxed, but the questions kept coming and nothing she said seemed to comfort him.

By the time they arrived at church, he looked like he'd done a few laps in the pool with Michael Phelps. He was drenched in perspiration. Tamarra had made a mental note once she got to know him better to suggest to him a stronger antiperspirant as she tried to ignore the stench being released from his armpits.

During service, at a time when the spiritual realm was high thanks to the anointing of the praise and worship team, a cell phone went off. Even though Tamarra closed her eyes and said a quick prayer that the ringing cell phone belonged to anyone other than her date, she wasn't so lucky. Lo and behold, she opened one eye only to see her date shutting off his cell phone. And there it was. His Caribbean themed ring tone had breached the Spirit.

Needless to say, their lunch was nixed. Eventhough her date had tapped her on the shoulder during the reading of the announcements and told her that he was going to the bathroom, and then never returned, she wouldn't have gone out to lunch with him anyway. As far as Tamarra was concerned, he'd done her a favor by keeping her from losing her Christianity. She had already made up in her mind that she wasn't going to waste the four-dollar gallon of gas dropping him off back home. She'd had every intention of leaving his butt right there on the church door steps, chalking it off as the worst date ever. With that being said, her date with Maeyl could only be better.

In preparation for her date, Tamarra stood over her bathroom sink and ran some water on her hands. She then ran her wet hands through her hair, which she wore short and natural. She reached underneath the sink and pulled out a bottle of foam setting lotion and put a few pumps in her hands, then scrunched her hair. The natural curls began to tighten. Voila! That took care of her hair. She'd already showered and she didn't wear make-up, with the exception of lip gloss to keep her lips moist, so her next step was getting dressed.

Just before stepping into the shower, she decided on a mustard colored linen skirt and tunic outfit with matching ankle strap sandals. She slid into her clothes, then walked over to her dresser so that she could accessorize. An hour later, she was ready. With a half hour to spare before she had to leave her house to meet Maeyl, she decided to go to her special prayer place.

After her ex-husband had their roomy two-bedroom home built, Tamarra had immediately secluded off a corner in her finished basement and turned it into her special place of prayer. Not that God couldn't hear her prayers wherever she was. There was just something about this designated place that made her communion that much sweeter.

Tamarra prayed that God would go before her on this date and prepare the atmosphere. She prayed that God would send His angels to go fight off anything that might try to taint her time with Maeyl. She also prayed that if Maeyl was a devil in disguise like she'd surmised her last date to be, that He'd make it so that Maeyl didn't even show up to meet her. After closing her prayer, she grabbed her purse and keys, then headed toward her evening's destination, confident that God had answered her prayer even before she had finished it.

Once Tamarra arrived at the restaurant and fifteen minutes later was still waiting in the front lobby area for Maeyl to arrive, she guessed God had answered her prayer and made it so that Maeyl didn't even show up. She didn't know whether to be pleased or upset. Pleased that God had kept her from experiencing any heartache that falling for Maeyl might have brought on, or upset that God didn't at least allow her to get a free meal out of the deal first.

"Why'd I have to go and ask God to do that?" Tamarra chastised herself. Her pastor had warned the New Day congregation on more than one occasion not to ask God for something or ask Him to do something if they really didn't mean it. Tamarra questioned whether she'd really meant it.

Another fifteen minutes went by, and Maeyl still hadn't arrived. She didn't need God to come down and show Himself in a burning bush for her to get the message. Maeyl wasn't coming.

"You leaving us?" the hostess asked Tamarra as she headed out the door.

"Yep. Have a good evening," was all Tamarra said as she exited through the doors. Heading to her car she heard someone call out her name.

"Tamarra! Tamarra!" the voice called, sounding out of breath.

When Tamarra turned around she saw Maeyl, bearing a bouquet of flowers, doing a light jog toward her.

"I'm so glad I caught you." Maeyl was out of breath once he caught up with her. "I hoped I'd find you here."

Tamarra shot him an indignant look. "Why wouldn't you have found me here? This is where you were supposed to meet me a half hour ago."

Maeyl took a deep breath and then spoke. "I was at the Olive Garden on Hamilton Road. I'd forgotten all about this new one they built on 256. I don't get out of the Malvonia city limits too often. I didn't even know it was open yet until the waiter at the one on Hamilton suggested you might be here after I sat and waited on you forever. I'd gotten us a table and everything at the other one. I thought about calling you on your cell phone, but I didn't have your number. I didn't want to call and ask someone from church because well . . . you know how it is when some church folk get to talking."

Tamarra smiled, Maeyl's first sign that she might forgive him.

"Apology accepted." Tamarra's stomach grumbled. Instead of being embarrassed by the loud noise, she decided to make light of it. "At least my head accepts your apology. I can't speak for my stomach. But it sounds like it's speaking for itself." There was another chuckle from Tamarra followed by one from Maeyl.

Maeyl was relieved, and so was Tamarra. A night that just a few minutes ago neither one of them thought would be, actually was. And Tamarra felt in her spirit that it was going to be a good night indeed.

"Shall we?" Maeyl extended his arm for Tamarra to grab hold of his elbow.

"Yes, we shall." Tamarra smiled as Maeyl led her back into the restaurant.

"Oh, I see you're back with your date," the hostess said to Tamarra.

"Yeah," Maeyl replied for her. "I had to keep the lady waiting. Couldn't make it that obvious of just how much I've been looking forward to tonight."

Although Maeyl was addressing the hostess's comment, Tamarra knew he was speaking directly to her.

"Right this way," the hostess said after grabbing two menus and leading the couple to their table.

After Maeyl and Tamarra were seated, their waitress came over and took their drink orders. The forced conversations that some couples experienced on first time dates were nonexistent in Tamarra and Maeyl's case. They talked so much that when their waitress came back to take their dinner orders, they weren't prepared because they hadn't stopped talking long enough to look at the menu. When the waitress came back the second time they each ordered their entrée and continued their conversation where they had left off.

"So do you have any brothers and sisters, or are you an only child?" Maeyl asked Tamarra.

After hesitating for a moment, Tamarra replied, "I'm an only child." Tamarra immediately felt convicted. Her and Maeyl's first date could be the beginning of something good. Too bad she was starting it out with lies. But in her own heart, she felt justified in her reasons for lying about being an only child; reasons she hoped that all the people she'd lied to thus far would never find out about.

Chapter Seven

"Pastor know that sermon was preached today!" Paige said after the pastor gave the benediction and excused the congregation.

"Didn't Pastor preach though?" Tamarra agreed as she gathered up her purse and Bible bag.

Paige scanned the sanctuary. "You know, I didn't see Sister Deborah here today," she pointed out. "And she never misses a Sunday."

"Hmm. Me either." Tamarra proceeded to scan the sanctuary as if, perhaps, Paige might have overlooked Deborah. Right before her eyes made their way back to Paige, she noticed Maeyl in the sound booth with his assistant. A huge smile spread across Tamarra's lips when he looked up and noticed her.

Maeyl's hands seemed to be busy fiddling around with equipment, so instead of waving, he gave her a wink and a nod. Tamarra nodded in return, and to keep from blushing, she quickly turned her attention back to Paige, who was shooting her a strange look.

"What?" Tamarra asked Paige, shrugging her shoulders.

Paige had a peculiar look on her face as she let her eyes fall from Tamarra, to the sound booth, then back to Tamarra again.

"What my foot, young lady." Paige said, now scooping

up her belongings from off the pew. "You got some 'splainin' to do, Lucy." Paige gave her best Desi Arnez impression from the *I Love Lucy* show. "And I have a feeling it ain't for the Lord's ears to hear, so come on." Paige grabbed Tamarra by the arm and escorted her out of the church. Once in the parking lot, she began to drill away at her friend. "Now what was all that?"

"All what?" Tamarra played dumb as she walked to her car that was parked two cars away from Paige's. She clicked the remote to unlock the doors, then removed her thyme green brimmed hat that matched the suit and pumps she was wearing. She laid it on the driver's seat while she stood outside the door talking to Paige. "Whew, this August heat gon' make me have to reconsider wearing church hats in the summer." She patted at her short, moist hair.

"Don't play with me, Sister Tamarra," Paige warned. "I flunked kindergarten because I do not play. Now forget about that outrageous hat collection of yours and tell me what the jacks is going on with you and Mr. Sound Man in there." She pointed toward the church.

Tamarra chuckled. "All right, already," she gave in. "Maeyl and I went on a date."

"A date? You went on a date with Brother Maeyl?"

"Shhh." Tamarra put her index finger to her lips and looked around to make sure that no members walking to their cars were within earshot. "We might as well have stayed in the sanctuary if you were going to broadcast it like that."

"Oh, my bad," Paige apologized, lowering her tone. "But when did all of this go down? I mean, how? I've never even seen you two interact, so when did this man get a chance to ask you out on a date? Oh, let me guess, you took my advice again and asked him out? See, girl, I told you there isn't a thing wrong with a woman asking a man out on a date. That last incident with you and what's his name was just a bad fluke. But—"

"Will you shut up already, and let me tell you the dang on details?" Tamarra interrupted a speed talking Paige.

"Oh girl, I'm sorry. It's just that I can't believe that God has just been moving in both of our lives as far as relationships go. All in the same week at that; He's put someone in my life and yours. I mean, can you believe . . . " Paige's words trailed off once she realized that she was busted. She, too, was guilty of engaging in a date without sharing the details with her friend.

Although Paige and Tamarra had only been friends a little over a year, one would think they'd been friends forever. Trust between the two was formed almost instantaneously. The way Paige had connected with the woman almost ten years her senior, she was sure God had placed Tamarra in her life as her very own counselor.

Growing up, the only person Paige had to confide in was her younger brother, and there was only so much a girl could tell her brother that was two years younger than she. Paige's mother never had time to give mother-daughter talks because she was too busy catering to her husband.

Although Paige and her brother's father had been a wonderful provider and a strong head of the family, she often resented him for taking up so much of her mother's time, leaving her to have to learn things that a girl's mother should teach her, on her own. Paige felt that her father expected too much from her mother and that her mother darn near ran herself ragged to make sure that all of his expectations were met. He was bossy and unappreciative of her mother's time is how Paige saw it.

He expected her mother to keep the house clean, make sure the lawn was watered, meals were prepared to his daily preference, take care of the kids at home and show up for school functions as well as get them to dentist and doctor's appointments, and do laundry. This might not have been so bad had Paige's mother been a stay-at-home mom, but she wasn't. She worked full-time and paid half the bills. So Paige never understood why her father's list only included taking out the trash and cutting the grass. The least he could do was pay all the bills since he was working her mother like a Hebrew slave.

Paige had made it up in her mind a long time ago that when she found herself a husband, he'd be nothing like her father, which explained why she had dated so many men. The first sign one of the men gave that he held a trait of her father's, he was cut off. Deemed flawed.

Tamarra had often told Paige she wasn't giving these men a fair chance, but Paige always countered with, "God shows me these things speedily so that I can get rid of the losers speedily without becoming attached."

Tamarra didn't agree, of course. She would always reply with, "God is a God of second chances, so He at least expects us to operate in the same manner." As much as Paige valued her good friend's opinions, she never took heed to that one.

"Well, if it ain't the pot calling the kettle black," Tamarra shot at Paige after hearing her slip up about God placing a man in her life. "You hounding me about keeping my date with Maeyl from you, and here you are holding out on me. So spill it. Who is he, what's his name, and more importantly, how do you know God sent him?"

Paige cleared her throat. The same smile that had been on Tamarrra's face when she made eye contact with Maeyl just a few minutes ago was now on her face as she thought back about her movie date with Blake.

"His name is Blake," Paige confessed. "He's in the real estate profession, and I just know in my spirit it was a divine set up that he came into my life."

"Keep it coming," Tamarra insisted.

"I just met him a couple of days ago, but I feel like I've known him a lifetime. The same way I felt when I first met you."

"Don't try to butter me up now that you're busted."

"Seriously," Paige stated. "I was destined to meet this man, Tamarra." Paige had the most sincere look in her eyes as she explained to Tamarra how she came about going to see the movie with Blake. "So what do you think?" Paige asked Tamarra. "Do you agree that this man could possibly be the one? Sent from God?" Paige's tone was more than genuine and so was the look on her face as she waited for a reply. If there was ever a time when Paige couldn't trust her own instincts, she truly valued Tamarra's all the same.

Tamarra had been saved since she was twenty-five, and had been committed to church since then, which is why Paige was so drawn to the older woman. As a babe in Christ, Paige wanted to connect with someone who could mentor her; who could help wean her from spiritual milk to meat. What Paige really admired about Tamarra was that she wasn't one of those people who thought that just because she was saved she had an automatic go-straight-to-heaven pass. Tamarra made every effort to walk in the Word and not only be committed to the church, but first and foremost, to be committed to the Lord.

Paige would often, and still did on occasion, call Tamarra up and ask her to explain certain scriptures of the Bible. Tamarra knew the Word like the back of her hand it seemed, but in all humility, Tamarra would admit to Paige that it was the Holy Spirit giving her revelation of the Word at the very moment she'd spoken it to Paige. Either way, Paige knew that God was using Tamarra to help her in her own walk.

"Either way it goes, I'm happy for you, Paige," Tamarra concluded. "I mean, you made it through one whole date without finding a flaw. But then again, that was a date in the dark, in the movie theatre where you can't talk to each other anyway."

"So do you think he could be my husband; placed right there in my lap by God?"

Tamarra thought for a minute, and then shrugged. "I don't know. Go on a date with him in a well-lit place where the two of you can hold a real conversation, then ask me."

"Well, that will be sooner than you think. I'm having lunch with him on my day off this week." Paige smiled. "I guess that prayer about God placing men in our lives that Sister Deborah prayed at the last Singles Ministry meeting worked." Just then her smile faded when she remembered something. "But enough of us talking about these new men in our lives like we're back in high school or something. We need to do a drive by to Sister Deborah's and see why she wasn't in church today."

"Yeah," Tamarra agreed in a worried tone. "It's not like Sister Deborah to miss church on a Sunday, especially the first Sunday. Communion Sunday. If everything was all right, she'd be here."

"Which can only mean one thing," Paige concluded. "Something's wrong."

Chapter Eight

Deborah sat up rocking in her bed with her knees to her chest and her arms wrapped tightly around her legs. She couldn't get rid of the pounding in her head, a pounding that was a result from crying all morning long.

"The Lord is my Shepard; I shall not want. He maketh me to lie down in green pastures: He leadeth me beside the still waters . . ." Deborah had been reciting Psalm 23 ever since early this morning when she decided not to go to church.

Fully dressed in her Sunday's best, Deborah had every intention of going to New Day Temple of Faith to get her praise on when she awoke this morning. But that nagging voice in her head had chased her around the house while she got ready for church, and it kept hurling insults at her about being a phony and fake Christian hiding her sins. That voice had finally broken her down and convinced her that the last place a wretch like her needed to be was in church. The stench of her past sin would stink up the place.

Now here she sat, rocking back and forth like she belonged in a loony bin somewhere, reciting the same Bible verse over and over while staring off into a daze. She'd hoped that her voice would drown out the one that had been taunting her, but it had yet to work.

"That stupid Helen!" she ranted right in the middle of walking through the valley of the shadow of death. "I wish she were . . . I wish she would just . . . why did she ever have to step foot in New Day in the first place? That was my church! My church! And now here she comes tainting the life I've built there. Here she comes digging up the bones I've buried. How dare she. Who does she think she is?" Deborah despised the day that the Lord had made just a few months ago when Helen showed up at New Day.

By now Deborah was out of the bed pacing back and forth in anger. Somewhere between walking in the valley of the shadow of death and not fearing any evil, she'd decided to shift blame from herself to Helen. Never mind the actual act that she had committed four years ago, the act that Helen obviously had found pleasure in dangling over her head. Helen had no right to all but threaten to reveal her dirty little secret. It was Deborah's secret. Who was Helen to try to take ownership?

Once again there was pounding. Deborah jumped back in bed in the same position, only this time she covered her ears with her hands in order to drown the pounding out.

"The Lord is my Shepherd; I shall not want," Deborah started again. Her lips were fixed on the scripture, but her mind was fixed back to the very day she had been reminded of the heap of dirt she'd swept under the rug.

Deborah loved when Pastor assigned her an altar duty, be it reading the announcements or assisting during altar call. But her favorite had always been the welcoming of first time visitors. It did good for her spirit to welcome first time visitors and encourage them to keep coming back to New Day. Pastor had even shared with Deborah on more than one occasion how some visitors who were now regular members said that one of the reasons they came back was because of the warm, sincere, Holy Ghost welcome they'd received from Deborah.

All along Deborah had just thought she was doing a simple assignment weighing low on the totem pole compared to the pastor's assignment of delivering God's Word. It reminded her of something Mother Doreen would say to members when they'd complain about an assignment they received from Pastor, such as door greeter. *"You never know what part of the service is going to minister to someone, so never deem one assignment too small and you too big to do it."*

But on one particular Sunday a few months ago, Deborah would have given anything to be the door greeter. That way she would have seen the enemy coming and braced herself.

"Here at New Day Temple of Faith we always like to acknowledge our first time visitors," Deborah had said that day in the pulpit. "We know it's not by accident that you are here to praise, worship, and fellowship with us today, but it is by God's divine order. You are supposed to be here with us, and we don't take you for granted, as we take no blessing from the Lord for granted. And you, first time visitors, are indeed a blessing."

"Amen." The congregation was in complete agreement.

"So at this time, can I ask all first time visitors to stand, state your name, and have a few words if you'd like?" Deborah had asked as she scanned the room while five new faces stood.

With Malvonia being a small town, five new visitors was awesome. Most people liked to travel to one of the larger churches in Columbus just to be around new faces and to get out of the small city. Usually the visitors at New Day weren't from outside cities, but instead, newbies to the town of Malvonia. Pastor said that God was omnipresent, in other words, He was everywhere, and it didn't matter that residents of Malvonia went outside the city to fellowship rather than attend one of the two churches in the town. Pastor felt that as long as they were going to church, that was all that mattered. God looked at their heart and their walk, not what church they belonged to.

"We welcome each and every one of you," Deborah had said to the last of the five visitors she'd seen stand at her invitation. "Just know that here at New Day Temple of Faith we have a loving pastor who is here if you ever . . ." Deborah's words trailed off when she heard members shouting something to her.

"You missed one."

She was finally able to understand what the members were trying to tell her; that another person had stood without her noticing.

"My apologies," Deborah said with a warm smile as she scanned the room to find the person she had skipped over. Her smile suddenly faded as if she'd just swallowed a peeled lemon when her eyes landed on the oversight. How she could have missed this particular visitor, she still doesn't know to this day.

"No need to apologize," the female visitor said. "Like the Word says, the last shall be first and the first shall be last." She winked.

The way the woman spoke, that underlying sassiness, and that wicked wink answered the question that Deborah had floating in her head, which was, *I wonder if she remembers me?*

This woman, who later introduced herself as Helen, remembered Deborah all right; just as well as Deborah had remembered her. If only Deborah hadn't been so noticeable that day when the two had originally met. If only she hadn't stood out. But no, thanks to her accomplice, no one in that place that day would ever forget Deborah's face, and Deborah would never forget that day. And Helen had showed up to make sure of it.

Chapter Nine

"She's not answering." Paige looked back at Tamarra after knocking on Deborah's door.

"Here, let me try," Tamarra said, slightly bumping Paige out of the way as she proceeded to pound on the door.

"Did you used to work for five-0 or something?" Paige asked, referring to the way Tamarra had just pounded on the door like she was the police.

"Girl, no, but this ain't my first drive by either. You can't come play pitty-pat with the devil. You got to beat the devil down to let him know you mean business."

"What makes you think the devil has anything to do with Sister Deborah not being in church today?"

"If I recall, Sister Deborah was supposed to fill in to do the first time visitor's welcome. Pastor originally had Mother Doreen down to do it, but she had a family emergency and had to go see about her ill sister in Kentucky. I'm almost certain she asked Sister Deborah to fill in for her."

"Hmm, you may be right. Because only the devil himself could keep her from that assignment," Paige stated.

Tamarra pounded on the door again. "I wish we could see in that garage of hers; to see if her car is in there."

"I can call her." Paige pulled out her cell phone and began to dial. Tamarra stared at Paige, waiting to see if she was going to engage in a conversation with Deborah on the other line. "No answer." Paige shook her head. "Let me try her cell." When

Deborah's cell phone went straight to voicemail, she hung up the phone.

"Come on, Deborah. Answer the door before the buffet line at the Golden Corral gets a mile long." Tamarra pounded on the door once again.

"You a mess, woman of God," Paige chuckled.

"Girl, you know I'm right. We go there almost every Sunday after service." Tamarra looked down at her watch. "And right about now is usually when it gets stacked up in there. But never mind me and my grumbling belly; I just pray my sister is okay in there."

"Um, hmm, yeah right. Don't try to clean it up now, woman of God. You know good and well—"

Just then the two women heard the door locks jiggling, and then saw the door open. They hadn't anticipated the vision that awaited them on the other side of the door.

"Well, hello, Sister Paige . . . Sister Tamarra." Deborah smiled as she stood in the doorway looking back and forth from one woman to the next. "What brings you by?"

Tamarra and Paige looked at one another, each one signaling for the other to speak because neither knew what to say. The two felt like complete fools standing there expecting the worst but being greeted by the best. They'd expected to see Deborah in her house coat, puffy red eyes, or even looking hung over with a remaining stench of alcohol as a result of some cabaret she'd attended the night before. Some sign of backsliding or visible evidence of a stronghold that had kept her from coming to church today. Those were some of the scenes Tamarra had grown accustomed to over the years of doing drive bys. But that wasn't the case at all this time around.

Deborah could tell the two women from her church were dumbfounded; that she'd given them something they hadn't expected. She'd presented herself to look holy and acceptable unto the Lord. Like everything in her world was A-okay, although her insides begged to differ.

That pounding that had been in her head all morning was mistaken for the recent pounding on her front door. Once Deborah realized that the pounding wasn't in her head but one story below her in her split-level home, she raced to her bedroom window only to see both Tamarra and Paige's cars pulled up in her driveway.

"Haven't they ever heard of calling before coming by?" she'd complained to herself, but then realized that her upstairs cordless phone hadn't been charged and that on Sundays she never turned on her cell phone until after church service was over.

Deborah raced over to her full-length mirror and straightened out her clothing. She put on her shoes, and then went into the bathroom. She pulled out a hair twisty from her bathroom drawer and put her locks up in a ponytail. She then ran back into her bedroom and over to her dresser where she retrieved a pair of turquoise clip-on earrings to match the turquoise, black and white pantsuit she was wearing. After thirty-two years, Deborah still feared the little pinch of the earring gun used to pierce ears. To this day she still wore clip-on earrings.

"I'm coming," Deborah said, knowing her two uninvited guests couldn't hear her as she raced downstairs to the door. Now here she stood in front of them looking like her marvelous and wonderfully made self. "Is everything okay?" she asked Paige and Tamarra, turning the tables.

"Oh, uh, well, uh," Paige stammered, searching for words.

Tamarra knew it was time to jump in. "You weren't in church today, Sister Deborah. We were worried. You had welcome duties today, and we know how much you look forward to that assignment. We knew that nothing but the devil or death could keep you from it. It's obvious it's not the latter . . . although you do look casket good if I don't say so myself."

Deborah chuckled. "Well, thanks for the compliment. The minute I saw this suit, I knew I had to have it."

There was a moment of silence.

"So anyway," Tamarra continued. "You didn't attend church today."

"Yes, I did," Deborah stated. "I just didn't go to New Day. One of my clients invited me to her church, Power and Glory Ministries over in Reynoldsburg. She dances in the dance ministry there and invited me to see her minister in dance. It was awesome. You know that church goes crazy for the Lord. They be running around the place and everything. They say if folks can get all radical and scream and shout at the football games and basketball games, then they can definitely give the Lord some radical praise." Deborah had tried her best to recall the visit she'd made to the church over a year ago and make it sound like it had been just yesterday, or in her case, just today.

"Yeah, I heard you can go there on any given Sunday and expect to encounter a move of God," Paige stated. "I'll have to go visit one day."

"Yep, like Pastor always says," Deborah stated, "it doesn't matter where you go to church, as long as you do go to church." On that note Deborah had almost dared the women to question her any further regarding her Sunday whereabouts. "I'll have to call Pastor, though, and apologize for neglecting my altar duties. I'd honestly forgotten all about Mother Doreen asking me to fill in for her."

"I'm sure Pastor will understand. We're just glad to see that everything is all right," Tamarra stated. She looked over to Paige as if to ask her if there was anything she wanted to add.

"Uh, Tamarra and I are on our way to grab something to eat. Would you like to join us?" Paige threw in.

"Oh, that's okay. I've already whipped a little something up for myself. But thanks anyway," Deborah declined.

"No, problem," Paige said as she and Tamarra headed back to their cars.

Deborah watched the women's backs and let out a deep sigh of relief. "Thank you, God," she looked up and said, giving

Him credit for being able to get rid of them without incident. How could she have told them why she really wasn't in church? What in the world would they think of her? But then again, what if God had sent them there for her to tell them? Maybe sharing her hurt, pain, guilt, remorse, and shame with someone would help her get through. Just maybe . . . .

"Tamarra, Paige!" Deborah called out, swallowing hard, trying to force the words she needed to invite them back out of her mouth.

Both women turned around in unison. For a minute there Deborah thought she saw a gleam of hope in their eyes. A gleam of hope that told them that they weren't crazy after all. That the Holy Spirit had, in fact, led them over to her house in order to save her; save her from herself. Save her from her past.

Deborah wanted so badly to invite the women back. She wanted to beg them to come back; miss a meal on her behalf and just sit and listen while she bared her soul to them. But she couldn't get naked before them. No. She had far too many unsightly bruises and scars. She hadn't even been able to get naked before the Lord, who already knew the ugliness of the wounds.

"Yes, Sister Deborah?" Tamarra asked, snapping Deborah from her thoughts. "Did you want something?" She paused and took a couple of steps back toward Deborah. "Did you need something, my sister?" Tamarra had made her last question in somewhat of a pleading tone.

"Uh, I, uh just wanted to say thank you for being so concerned as to drive all the way over here and check on me. Enjoy your dinner." Deborah quickly closed the door. She pressed her back up against the door and looked up to the heavens with tear-filled eyes. "Please hide me, oh, Lord. Hide me."

Chapter Ten

"So I saw you come back into the theatre last week after you got off work," Norman said to Paige as he entered the ticket booth. Today he had come in an hour earlier than he was scheduled in order to relieve Paige while she interviewed a couple of prospective employees.

"What? What are you talking about?" Paige asked, puzzled.

"Well, if you've forgotten about Mr. Movie Man already, then I guess he didn't have anything worth remembering, huh?" Norman winked and elbowed Paige in the arm.

"Mr. Movie Man?" Paige thought for a minute, and then realized that Norman must have been referring to Blake. "Oh, you mean Blake."

"Is that his name? At least you remembered it. I know how those one-night stands can be."

"Blake wasn't a one-night stand," Paige defended.

"Oh, then there was something memorable about him. It's amazing what a man can do to a girl in a dark theatre. Trust me, I know."

"Look, Norman, I know back in the day you and I used to talk about everything. But things have changed now. I'm—"

"My boss now." Norman finished her sentence with a slight attitude. "Oh, I get it. You got a little promotion, and now you can't associate with the little peons anymore. And you're supposed to be a Christian. Tsk. What is that in the Bible about staying humble?" Without even giving Paige a chance to respond, Norman continued with his rant. "Well I guess in all of your Bible Study sessions you missed that one. But you don't have to worry about me conversing with you anymore, *Boss*. You're way up there on the totem pole now. Got a new title, making a few extra dollars. Too good to rub elbows with the little guys now."

Paige wanted so badly to just sit Norman down and explain to him that her position as his superior had nothing to do with the fact that she was choosing not to engage in such conversations with him as she had done in the past. "Look, Norman—"

"Oh, what are you going to do now? Write me up for insubordination? Well, I apologize, Boss. I beg that you'll let me off this time with just a verbal warning. I promise this will be my last time ever saying two words to you again."

Norman appeared to be so hurt and offended that Paige almost felt sorry for him. After all, Norman wasn't that bad. He wasn't a bad person. Once upon a time Paige had honestly looked forward to her conversations with Norman. But things had changed. She had changed and, if the conversations didn't glorify God, she just didn't want to be a part of them. But how could she get Norman to understand that? Deciding not to say anything to him at the moment, but to pray on it instead, Paige grabbed her things and exited the booth while Norman proceeded to help a customer.

Norman's little fit hadn't been all bad, Paige thought in her attempt to see the glass half full. "At least he called me a Christian." She smiled as she made her way to meet her prospective new employee.

"So how has work been going?" Blake asked Paige as the two sat in a family-owned café in Malvonia with a name that reflected such: Family Café.

"Work is great," Paige answered. "It's the people I have to work with that are the problem." Paige picked up her Reuben sandwich that was cut in half and took a bite.

"Is someone giving you trouble?" Blake had a concerned look on his face as if the school bully had stolen his girl's lunch money, and he had every intention on meeting him at three o'clock after school to retrieve it.

Paige chuckled, flattered by the protective stance Blake was taking on her behalf even though he'd only known her a couple of weeks. "No, Blake, it's nothing like that."

"Then what is it?" Blake ate a spoonful of his chili.

Paige didn't care how famous the café was for its chili, for the life of her, she didn't understand how people could still eat it during the hot summer months. Her father would have had a fit had her mother tried to serve him chili anytime other than late fall and winter. Paige smiled. The glass was half full. Blake wasn't like her father in that respect at least. So far she'd have a good report to give to Tamarra.

"Well, it's just that there is this employee of mine named Norman." Since Paige hadn't gotten around to talking about her issues with Norman to Mother Doreen, she figured she'd give it a stab with Blake. He'd been so easy to talk to about everything else. "Back before I became his supervisor we used to—"

Blake put his hand up to halt Paige's words. "Pardon me for the interruption, but I'm a strong believer that when two people are in a relationship, details about their past relationships, unless detrimental to one's health or something, shouldn't be discussed. So if it doesn't bother you all the same, I'd prefer not to hear about Norman or how you dated him before you became his supervisor."

Relationship, Paige smiled inside. Had she heard correctly? Had Blake just spoken their relationship into existence after only three dates?

For years, Paige had been a firm believer in the dating game. She felt people needed to date several people in order to see what all God had to offer. She'd heard church members bad mouth reality shows such as *The Bachelor*, finding nothing holy about a man dating dozens of women at one time in order to find the perfect one for him. But Paige begged to differ and would always use the book of Esther to back up her belief. "If King Ahaseurus hadn't dated all those women that ultimately led him to finding Queen Esther, what in the world might have become of the Jews?" Then of course someone always had some smart aleck un-Christlike comment such as, "Well, I don't know, Sister Paige. You'll have to ask Hitler about that one."

In spite of others' opinions, Paige felt that dating was necessary and never put her eggs all in one basket by being exclusive with one man. But this time she felt different. This time it wasn't about her putting all of her eggs into one basket. It was about her putting all of her faith in God. Not just her faith, but her trust as well. She was going to trust God and believe that what she and Blake were on more than just a date. They were on a path to a relationship, as he'd just so eloquently put it.

"Norman and I were never in a relationship, Blake." Paige blushed. "What I was going to say was back before I became his supervisor we used to always talk about life; being single, dating and what not. But back then I wasn't saved, so the conversations were . . . how can I put it?"

"Uncensored?"

"Yes, exactly," Paige confirmed. "And now that I'm saved, Norman just doesn't get it."

"Get what? The fact that you don't do the things you used to do and say the things you used to say? So now, you pretty much don't have anything to converse with Norman about because he's still where you were?"

"Exactly!" Paige's eyes lit up. First he'd finished her sentence with the exact word she was searching for, and now he was reading her spirit as if it had been communicating with his spirit.

"And let me guess," Blake continued, "this Norman fellow probably thinks you're just being all high and mighty because you're his boss now."

"You hit it right on the money, Blake."

"Yeah, because I've been there, done that, wore the T-shirt and drank out of the coffee mug," he explained before taking a sip of his sweet tea. "Before I got saved, I was the typical bachelor. I was a firm believer that the dating thing was the way to go. I mean, after all, look how well it worked out for Queen Esther's husband."

Paige almost choked on her lemon water when Blake said those words. This man was definitely her equal in thoughts.

"You okay?" Blake asked Paige when he heard her swallow hard.

"Better than okay," Paige said, regaining her composure. "You were saying . . ."

"Oh, yeah, the dating thing. Anyway, I never thought it was a good idea to just date one woman, and then jump right into an exclusive relationship with her. But once I got saved, I had to ask myself, what if I felt that same way about God? What if I only dealt with God when I felt like it? How could I possibly expect to form a relationship with Him? So I knew right then and there that the same way God wanted all of me and wanted me to have a relationship with Him, I needed to apply the same principles when it came to women. Now I'm not saying not to date altogether. I'm saying dating multiple women at once didn't make good sense."

"How so?" Paige asked. At first he was driving right down her street, but all of a sudden it appeared as though he was going to drive right past her house.

"Because going back to my relationship with God, God courted me. During this courtship I was able to give God all of me. Now had I been gallivanting around town with other gods, I'd not been able to eventually form the relationship with God that I have now. I wouldn't have had the time to really get to know Him. Not with the distraction of all those other gods. And not with my flesh, of course, trying to see what it could get from one god and which god had more to offer, etc . . . See, the God I serve is my everything, as will be the woman God shows me to seek after. So I feel as though I can still do the dating thing, but just with one woman. Because, God willing, there is the promise that the courtship will eventually turn into a relationship; an everlasting one."

In a matter of minutes, Paige's entire perspective on finding a husband had changed. For the first time ever, someone had spoken to her in such a way to make her look at things differently. Perhaps it didn't take dating several men.

How was it that this man knew everything that was in her spirit? Soul mates, she surmised. If, in fact, Blake was truly her soul mate sent from God, then there was one thing about her that she felt he should be able to deal with. There was so much Blake knew about her without her ever even having to say a word. Hopefully this would be one of them; otherwise, she didn't know how exactly she was going to tell him.

Chapter Eleven

"Deborah, I mean Miss Lucas. This is Lynox. Chase. Lynox Chase."

Deborah listened to what had to have been the hundredth voice message Lynox had left her since the incident at Max & Erma's a month ago. He was persistent. She had to give him that. He'd been calling leaving messages of apology, and that he wanted to explain his relationship with Helen. That it was over. That it was nothing. That it never really started, so there actually wasn't anything to be over. Blah-blah-blah.

Deborah didn't want to hear it. Sure she had no doubt that that manuscript of his was a *New York Times* bestseller all day long, but it wasn't worth it. Obviously, whether Lynox felt the same way or not, Helen was into him. Helen thought that there was something that had gotten started. Something she wasn't fond of it being over with; if it was actually over. Either way it went, Deborah didn't want to give Helen any more reasons to be on her back than she already had. So she deleted the message from Lynox without listening to the rest of it.

Running behind on her day's work, Deborah had about twenty-five more pages of a manuscript that she needed to edit. After she finished that, she had an evening appointment with a prospective client who needed some editing work done. The woman had called just this morning sounding desperate. She was claiming that thousands of dollars had been paid to other so-called professional editors whose skills hadn't been worth the paper the manuscript had been typed on. It was Friday, and the woman would be going on vacation for the next two weeks. She really wanted to have an enjoyable vacation knowing that her work was finally in a credible editor's hands.

"You came highly recommended by a nice woman I met who goes to your church," the lady had told Deborah. "Her name slips my mind, but she's invited me to come visit your church, and I told her I'd take her up on the offer sometime after I return from vacation."

Deborah was flattered, and at the same time, able to put herself in the woman's shoes. She reflected on all of the money she'd wasted on persons claiming to be professional editors, although they were only professional by their own definitions. Deborah felt for the woman and agreed to meet with her.

"I have to get this done in the next hour so that I can start getting ready," Deborah said to herself as she went through the tedious manuscript. She'd taken on the project as a favor to a fellow editor. The other editor had gone through the manuscript once, but knew giving it a second look wouldn't do any good as the story was just awful. She needed fresh eyes; Deborah's eyes.

Deborah never understood why her colleague just took on any and every project that was dropped on her doorstep. Perhaps it was because of that three hundred thousand dollar house she was living in. Barely able to afford the always adjusting mortgage rate, she couldn't be too picky with the projects that came her way. Although Deborah, too, lived in a nice home, she felt that it would be wrong for her to just take on any and every project, knowing she couldn't compliment it in any way. She trusted God to bring forth projects which her skills could enhance, and she made it a point to always read through the projects before taking them on, which is why she'd forewarned the woman she had to meet this evening not to prematurely get her hopes up too high. Deborah told her that she'd only take it on if she felt in her spirit that the manuscript could benefit from her services.

An hour and a half after Deborah declared only having twenty-five pages to go, she still had fifteen more. "I don't care if she is paying me the full three thousand dollars the author is paying her," Deborah complained in frustration, "this editing job isn't worth all the money in the world. Hideous."

She set the manuscript aside, deciding the heck with the last few pages for today. She needed to rest and clear her mind before meeting with the would-be client tonight. The poor grammar, run-on sentences, sentence fragments, misspellings, ten main characters, and six major storylines had taken its toll on Deborah's sanity. And on top of a late appointment, she had to go to the Singles Ministry meeting afterward. Tonight they were going over the by-laws, and she knew with the bunch of rambunctious divas in that group, it was going to consist of a lot more than Mother Doreen saying, "Class, let's all read this together," and then meeting adjourned. No, she was certain a handful of women would have their say, especially considering Mother Doreen was proposing meeting dues to help fund some of the Single Ministry's functions.

Just as Deborah stood up from her desk to head toward her master bath where she would prepare a nice, hot bath with the jet bubbles set on high, her cell phone rang. Deborah walked over to the phone and looked at the caller ID. It was him again. Lynox. She pressed the ignore button and sent him straight to voicemail. Surely after only two rings he'd know she'd purposely ignored his call. Hopefully, just like he'd told Helen, he himself would get the hint.

Making her way into her master bath, Deborah rinsed out the tub and ran some water. She sat on the edge of the tub watching the water spill out the faucet and fill the tub. The sound of the water flowing was soothing. As she sat there, though, for some reason her mind traveled to thoughts of Lynox. The weirdest thing; she wondered what might have come of the two of them had Helen not become a factor. Would their dealings have remained professional, or would they have taken things to a more personal level?

Deborah couldn't deny the man was handsome, professional, confident, and very talented in the literary category. A smile rested on Deborah's lips without her realizing it. Might she have become his manager/wife like so many successful men had appointed their wives to be, such as Sugar Shane Mosley, the famous boxer? Deborah had always admired how low-key and professional Mr. Mosley's wife had been while guiding his boxing career. That's exactly how Deborah would have played her role. She could see it now; auctioning her famous husband's novels off to all the major publishers and auctioning his movie rights to major film companies, even before the books were written.

"Yeah," she nodded with a smile, this time realizing she was smiling. Realizing she'd been fantasizing. About a man. Not just any man; Lynox. "Girl, get it together. That manuscript really is driving you crazy." She chuckled as she turned the water off, turned the jets on, and found herself soaking, cleansing herself. The outside anyway. But if only she could cleanse away what was on the inside.

When Deborah walked into Family Café, she spotted several familiar faces. She waved and greeted as Zelda, the owner's daughter, approached her.

"Welcome to Family Café, Miss Deborah. It's good to see you." Zelda gave her regular huge smile that displayed the gap, which she referred to as a window, between her two front teeth.

"Hello, Zelda. It's good to see you too." Deborah returned the greeting. She liked Zelda and was always impressed by the hard work she put into the family business. It didn't matter what time or what day of the week Deborah patronized the café, which was often; Zelda was hard at work.

Deborah would have preferred to set up her meetings at the library in one of the meeting rooms, but Malvonia's first and only library was still in the process of being built, and the nearest one was in Reynoldsburg. Reynoldsburg was another suburb of Columbus and about a forty-five minute drive from Malvonia. In traffic, it could take Deborah over two hours of roundtrip driving time to meet with someone. On occasion she'd had meetings at the Book Brewery, a family owned bookstore located in Malvonia. Deborah liked the set up, but the store played distracting music that she sometimes found difficult to hold a conversation over. Family Café would do just fine as far as Deborah was concerned. It allowed her to take care of business and fill her belly all at one time.

"You alone today, Miss Deborah?" Zelda asked as she led Deborah to a booth.

"I'm meeting someone, Zelda, so I'm going to need to sit facing the door so that I can watch for them."

"Not a problem." Zelda placed a menu in front of Deborah as she sat her in a spot facing the door as requested. She then placed a menu in the vacant space across from her. "I'll bring you your ice water with lemon while you wait. And it's always good seeing you, Miss Deborah."

"You too, Zelda. Now I'm still waiting to see you over at New Day." Deborah winked.

"Always the evangelist." Zelda smiled back.

Zelda had once been a faithful member of New Day. Her entire family still was. But the youth Sunday School teacher repeatedly kept chastising the children, Zelda's child included. The chastising was done in a manner that was un-Christlike and sometimes even physical. It bothered Zelda that the church didn't really do anything about it, causing her to leave the church permanently. That was a year ago, and Deborah, as well as a few of the other members of New Day who crossed Zelda's path, had been encouraging her to return ever since. Had Zelda been attending church elsewhere, perhaps Deborah wouldn't have been so aggressive, but to her knowledge, Zelda hadn't been to New Day or any other church since.

"Sometimes you just have to let people go," the pastor

had once said about members who leave their churches. "On some occasions, God removes a person from a church because He wants to do something with them. Their calling may not be at the church they are attending, so God wants to shake things up a little to give them a wake up call. Kind of a push toward their destiny."

As far as Deborah could see, God wasn't shaking anything up in Zelda's life at any other church, because ever since leaving New Day, she'd not been fellowshipping elsewhere. So this had to be an exception. Perhaps this wasn't about Zelda at all. Perhaps it was a test to see if New Day would go after one of it's lost sheep. Deborah didn't want to fail the test.

"I'm not going to give up on seeing you back at New Day, Zelda." Deborah smiled as she picked up the menu and covered her face, a sign to Zelda that she didn't want to hear anything else about it.

Zelda smiled, shook her head, and walked away, knowing that her regular customer meant well.

Deborah held the menu up and feigned reading it a few seconds later. She knew that menu like the books of the Bible. When she finally put the menu down, she immediately looked out the window to see if she might be able to recognize her meeting companion pulling up. She didn't know what the woman looked like, but figured she'd be able to recognize a Malvonia outsider who might appear as though they were looking for someone.

"Here's your water, Miss Deborah." Zelda placed the glass in front of her. "I'll be back to take your order once your guest arrives. Hopefully you'll be trying something other than that open faced roast beef sandwich."

"Zelda, now you know I've tried everything on this menu. It's all equally delicious, but I prefer my favorite all the same."

"I know, but like yourself, Miss Deborah, I just thought I'd try to persuade you." Zelda winked and walked away.

Deborah shook her head and smiled as she picked up her drink, held it in both hands and took a sip of the ice cold water. "Mmm," she closed her eyes and said after the refreshing cool liquid made its way down her throat. It was exactly what she needed for a hot summer day. And besides that, Zelda always put just the right amount of lemons in her water. She filled her mouth with more of the drink before she opened her eyes. Without being able to help herself, Deborah spat the water all over the person that sat in front of her. After all, this was the last person she had expected to see.

Chapter Twelve

"Haven't you been getting my messages? You don't know how to return a call?"

"Sorry. I've really been meaning to call you back. It's just that—"

"I know, I know. You're so busy and all."

This was typically how Tamarra's conversations with her mother went. Her mother would call for two weeks straight leaving messages before she'd finally catch Tamarra. Tamarra would apologize for not returning her calls, the excuse being she'd been busy.

"Right, Mom. I've been busy, and I wanted to call you when I could really—"

"Sit down and hold a conversation," her mother finished her sentence with an exasperated tone. "How many years are you going to feed me that excuse?"

"I don't know, Mother. How long are you going to keep buying it?" Tamarra was part joking, part serious.

"Don't get fresh with me, girl. You might be in Ohio, and I might be in Maryland, but I got GPS. I know how to get to you in six hours or less," her mother threatened.

"I'm sorry, Mom. It's just that I'm in the middle of loading up food and stuff for an event I have to cater."

"You need to slow down, girl. I know God gave you the gift to burn in the kitchen, but I hope you ain't spending all of your time cooking and catering, and not spending any time with God."

"Mother, please. I attend church faithfully every Sunday."

"I hope that doesn't mean you're one of those Sunday only Christians."

"It doesn't, Mother. I commune with God daily and am constantly in His Word. I'd be a fool not to be." Tamarra had no idea why her mother was always on top of her about church and God when she herself didn't even go to church and never talked about God moving in her own life. But Tamarra never questioned it. That would mean having to hold a conversation with her mother for much longer than she wanted to. "God is the only person in this world who I can trust. The only person I can turn to and who I know is going to protect me no matter what. He'll protect me when no one else will."

There was dead silence on the line. Tamarra knew that last statement had brought back memories to her mother. She'd meant for them to. Why should she be the only one affected by the memories? Misery loved company. Tamarra's misery deserved company.

Tamarra's mother cleared her throat before saying, "Well, I guess I better let you go."

Tamarra knew those were going to be the next words to come out of her mother's mouth. Every time her mother feared the conversation was going to go in a direction she'd managed to steer clear of for years, she rushed off the phone.

"Okay, Mom. I'll talk to you later."

"Call me and your father sometime. Your father would love to talk to you."

Tamarra shook her head. *My father*, she thought. *Yeah right*. Whenever they did live in the same town, her father could barely look at her. She knew darn well he didn't want her calling, forcing him to talk to her. Liar, Tamarra thought about her mother. But then again, once a liar, always a liar. For years her mother had lived a lie. Their entire family had lived a lie, Tamarra being forced to participate in it, forced to believe it was for her own sake.

"Sure, Mom. Take care. Bye-bye."

"Bye, Tamarra. I—"

And just like clock work, Tamarra hung up the phone before the conversation went in a direction she didn't want it to. No sooner than she hung up the phone, it rang again. Tamarra's heart beat one hundred miles per hour. After all these years had her mother decided to call back and force her to say the words?

"Hello," Tamarra answered.

"Hello to you too."

"Oh, Maeyl." Tamarra sighed, relieved that it wasn't her mother calling back.

"You sound stressed. Is everything okay?" Maeyl asked through the phone receiver.

"Yeah. Well, sure, I guess," Tamarra said as she stacked pans and warmers in the back of her jeep while locking her cell phone in between her ear and her shoulder. "Dang it!" she said when several pieces of utensils she'd had sitting on top of one of the pans hit the ground.

"Not to call you a liar or anything, but it doesn't sound like it."

Tamarra took a deep breath. "No, Maeyl, you're right. I am stressed. I booked two catering affairs for one day. In addition to that, as you know, we have the Singles Ministry meeting tonight at seven. I have to be there because we are going over the bylaws, and you know how that goes. It's speak now or forever hold your peace. If you're not there to have input, then you can't comment on something later. It's just like voting. If you don't go out and vote, then you can't complain about the government leaders."

"Well, what time are your catering affairs?"

"One is at four o'clock. The other is later tonight."

"Four o'clock is just in a couple of hours."

"I know. It shouldn't be but a couple hours long. Only thing is, I forgot to go pick up the uniforms for me and my staff from the dry cleaners so that we'll have them for the second catering event. We'll be okay as long as we don't spill anything on the ones we have while catering the first event. We can't show up in dirty uniforms to the second affair. That would be way too unprofessional."

Maeyl thought for a moment. "What dry cleaners are the uniforms at?"

"Mr. Lawson's," Tamarra answered. Mr. Lawson ran the only dry cleaners in Malvonia. "But he closes at six. It will be too late by the time I finish the first catering affair, and I don't have time to stop before hand."

"How 'bout I help you out by stopping by Mr. Lawson's to pick up the uniforms. I can meet you up at the church so that you'll have them before your second catering affair."

"Could you really? You wouldn't mind?"

"Not at all. Just put your phone on vibrate or something, and I'll text you once I'm outside of the church."

"Oh, thank you so much, Maeyl. You are a life saver."

"Not a problem. I'll see you this evening."

Tamarra hung up the phone feeling good that she had one less thing to worry about. She was thankful for Maeyl. The two had talked on the phone almost every day for the past month. They'd even gone out on two more occasions after their initial date. Although Maeyl was an attractive man, she was so thankful that prayer worked and God was allowing her to see this man's heart and characteristics versus just his physical being. In Tamarra's opinion, Maeyl was the epitome of what's on the inside of a person mattering most.

The fact that Tamarra also exercised some of the dating tactics she'd learned from the Singles Ministry helped her to keep her and Maeyl's courtship on the straight and narrow. Tamarra had allowed Maeyl to come to her house, but only to pick her up. She was impressed when he came to her door to let her know he had arrived, and didn't even allow Tamarra enough time to invite him in to wait, even if she had wanted to. He simply told her how lovely she looked followed with an, "I'll be waiting for you in the car."

Impressed didn't capture how Tamarra felt. Blessed was more like it. She could tell by Maeyl's actions that she was receiving reciprocity early on in this relationship. He respected her just as much as she respected him. With this mutual respect, they each had avoided finding themselves in compromising, tempting positions. But unfortunately, avoiding the mere appearance of evil would soon become something they unknowingly would fail to escape.

Chapter Thirteen

"I'm so sorry," Deborah apologized, embarrassed out of her mind. She looked around Family Café to make sure no one had seen her disgusting act of spitting water out of her mouth onto the person who sat across from her. From the looks of things, she was in the clear. Every one was either too busy indulged in their own conversations or had their faces buried in their delicious entrees.

"That's quite all right." Lynox removed the silverware from the cloth napkin on the table and proceeded to wipe down his blazer. "Seems like every time we meet, I end up with a dry cleaning bill," he joked with a slight chuckle. Any humor he thought might come out of his comment was quickly put to rest when Deborah sat before him with a stone face, not finding anything amusing.

"What are you doing here?" Realizing she'd asked in a tone louder than she wanted to, Deborah looked around once again to confirm that she hadn't drawn anyone's attention. Like Pastor always told the New Day congregation, she had to be careful and mindful of what she was doing and saying at all times because she never knew who she might be witnessing to.

"You know exactly why I'm here. I wanted to apologize in person. I've tried a dozen times over the phone, but you never pick up. I've left you messages, but who knows, you've probably deleted them without even listening to them. This was the only other way I could think of."

Deborah listened to Lynox's words, and then began to dissect them. She sniffed. Eventually she came to the conclusion that she'd been tricked. Bamboozled. That there was no desperate author in dire need of her editorial services. It had all been a set up. Lynox put some woman up to call her and set up a fake appointment knowing all the while it would be he who would show up to meet with her. Deborah's blood began to boil.

"Are you that desperate?" Deborah asked through gritted teeth.

"As a matter of fact, I am," Lynox said without regret. "I refuse to allow what happened a month ago at Max and Erma's to interfere with my passion. My future. My destiny."

"Well, from what I could tell, your true passion came in the form of high heels, lipstick, weave, and an attitude," she spat. "I'm a professional. I don't have time to get caught up in any drama."

"Neither do I, and I haven't been able to rest knowing that you might have gotten the wrong idea about me."

Lynox's words were sincere as well as the look in his eyes. Deborah sniffed. Nothing smelled fishy, but she had fallen for Lynox's façade before, and she wasn't about to fall for it again.

"Didn't I make it clear by ignoring your calls that I could care less about you or your book, Mr. Chase?"

Lynox realized that Deborah was not an easy nut to crack. "Look Deborah—"

"That's Miss Lucas to you," she corrected.

"Miss Lucas, it was evident that during our date at Max and Erma's—"

"Meeting," Deborah made another correction.

"Our meeting," Lynox cleared his throat, "there was something there . . . between us."

"Oh, please." Deborah threw her hand up as if to shoo away Lynox's perception.

"Deny it all you want, but I know something was there. We were only in each other's presence all of an hour, but I know something was there. And I have to be honest and say that I would have loved to entertain it to see where things could have gone."

Deborah could not escape the sincerity of the man in front of her no matter how hard she tried. *Try the Spirit by the Spirit,* was her motto. Well, her spirit was being anything but vexed by Lynox's presence. As much as she didn't want to believe it, Lynox was more convincing now than ever. It was very possible that he was exactly who he said he was.

With Deborah sitting speechless, wrestling with her emotions, Lynox continued. "But all that personal stuff aside, there is still the business aspect of things; the original reason for my meeting with you in the first place." Lynox lifted the briefcase that had sat beside him in the booth and extracted his manuscript from it. "I printed off another copy for you to take. Please just read it, and hopefully you'll see its full potential and reconsider representing me."

Deborah looked down at the manuscript, then back up at Lynox. She shook her head with confusion as she rested her hand atop the manuscript. "Do you know how many big time agents there are out there who'd love to represent this caliber of work? Why are you so fixated on this small town, literally, small town agent?"

"I really feel like God has led me to you."

"Don't you dare use God's name in vain."

Lynox let out a deep breath. "Would you at least just pray on it?" he asked, subconsciously placing his hand on hers, just as he'd done at their previous meeting.

Deborah looked down at the strong, yet gentle, hand that covered hers. The man had asked her to pray on the situation at least, which was something Deborah realized at that moment she hadn't done. She'd been too busy trying to sniff him out for herself and come to her own conclusion. How could she refuse the man a prayer?

"Well . . ." Deborah started. There was still slight hesitance in her voice.

"Please, just pray on it. If God says no, then I'll go away.

But if God says yes . . ." He left that sentence for Deborah to finish on her own.

Without saying a word, Deborah pulled the manuscript to her and stood up, preparing to leave.

"Thank you. Thank you so much." Lynox was ecstatic.

"Don't get your hopes up too high. I still have to pray on this."

"I know. And like I said, I'm sorry about Max and Erma's and Helen. I don't even talk to that woman . . ."

Just hearing Helen's name made Deborah's heartbeat pick up a pace or two. Helen. She'd forgotten all about her. No matter how sincere Lynox was about his work, she had no idea how Lynox might be connected to Helen. Although he'd just stood there declaring that he didn't even talk to her, from the way Helen reacted over seeing the two of them together, that wasn't the complete truth. Complete truth; that was something Helen knew about Deborah; the complete truth about the woman she really was. The woman hiding underneath the one everyone in New Day knew. No matter what God said, Deborah wasn't going to put herself in a position that would land her in a battle with Helen.

"I'm sorry, but I have to stick with my instincts and not get caught up." Deborah tried to hand Lynox the manuscript, but he wouldn't accept it.

"Caught up in what? Me and Helen's relationship?"

Relationship. There, he'd just said it. He'd just confirmed without even realizing it that he and Helen had a relationship. She knew she smelled a dawg and she wasn't about to hang around and step in a pile of you-know-what that he might leave behind. No way.

"Look," Deborah said sternly, once again getting louder than she'd intended. This time patrons in the café did turn their attention toward her. "I said no. Now take your manuscript and find another agent." Again Deborah tried to hand Lynox his manuscript back, and again he refused it, this time by folding his arms in a stubborn stance.

"I'm not going to play games with you, Lynox. All of this has been nothing but a game to you. Arranging this bogus meeting."

Lynox sat there with a look of confusion on his face.

"That makes you a liar," Deborah continued her rant. "And once a liar always a liar. I don't know your real motives and hidden agenda, but you can best believe it's not going to work with me. Here, take your manuscript and lose my number." Deborah threw the manuscript in front of Lynox. It slid off the table and into his lap, pages floating to the floor.

Deborah raced out of the café, slamming into a woman who was entering as she was exiting. "Watch where you're going why don't you?" Deborah spat to the woman as she made her way to the parking lot and into her car.

Zelda stood in the café staring out the window and into the parking lot at Deborah. She shook her head. "And she's got the nerve to be inviting me to church. As if I'm the one who needs Jesus. Hypocrite."

Apparently Deborah had thrown Pastor's message about being careful and mindful of her actions out the window. Now if only those demons that were haunting her would follow.

Chapter Fourteen

"But isn't that what our tithes and offerings are for?" a woman asked, not happy about Mother Doreen's proposal regarding meeting dues. "Why is it that every Sunday we put money in that basket, then every time we want to turn around and do something, we got to give more money?"

"Yeah," another woman who sang in the New Day choir confirmed. "My sister and I just had this same discussion. Her husband had a fit last week when he looked in their checkbook and saw that she had written a check for ninety-six dollars to pay for her new choir robe. She said her husband asked the same thing: 'Why you got a check written for tithes and offering, then the very next check is to purchase a choir robe? Seems like the tithes and offerings would cover that.' And she didn't even have a godly answer for him. So the same thing being brought up right now is only confirmation that all this extra check writing for dues and fees ain't of God."

Deborah washed her hands down her face, and then took a deep breath. *Here we go again,* she thought before standing up from her seat and walking up next to Mother Doreen who was standing in front of the classroom. It was times like these she wondered why she'd ever even joined the Singles Ministry anyway. It wasn't as if she really expected God to join her with a soul mate. Surely God didn't really find her worthy enough to give her a husband, especially not after she tainted her relationship with the man she knew in her heart God had made just for her. The man whose heart she had gone after in the same manner that David had gone after God's. But still, she figured she'd amuse herself with just the thought. Just the possibility . . . .

"Look, Sister Gail," Deborah replied on Mother Doreen's behalf.

It wasn't as if Deborah hadn't had a hectic evening herself. After her blow out with Lynox in Family Café, she felt awful. It wasn't until she was halfway home did she recall all the familiar faces in the restaurant who knew her. She knew there were a couple of New Day members who had probably already blown up Pastor's phone to report how ungodly one of the church's members had behaved. Although Deborah did care about what others thought about her, a part of her wasn't going to dwell on it. "Those people don't know the whole story. They have no idea what I'm dealing with. What I'm going through," she had told herself.

"*Then tell it. Tell them your story,*" her inner voice instructed her. But Deborah had quickly silenced it. And looking out amongst the room at the complaining women who sat before her, surely this wasn't the group she was supposed to share any part of herself with.

Deborah tried to control her mind by forgetting about past thoughts and reflecting on the present, so she continued her spiel to Sister Gail. "For now, why don't we just forget about dues?" Deborah looked to Mother Doreen who agreed with a nod. "Let's just allow Mother Doreen to continue with the remaining sections of the by-laws. If we don't have time to come back to it tonight, then we'll discuss it at a later date."

"Sounds good to me. Thank you, Sister Deborah." Mother Doreen smiled as Deborah headed back to her seat. Before Deborah walked off, they each gave one another a look that was an unspoken commitment to scratch the idea of dues from the list and never bring it up again.

Just as Deborah was about to sit down, she heard a voice say, "Sorry, I'm late."

It can't be, Deborah thought as she took her seat without

looking up for visual confirmation. She didn't want to put the face with the voice.

"It's better late than never. Come on in," Mother Doreen kindly greeted the woman, who was clad in an all white linen outfit. She wore her hair tightly slicked back with a weave bun that rested in the back of her head. "Just find you a place to sit."

Helen stood in the doorway of the classroom, her eyes searching for a place to sit. After a few seconds, her eyes rested on the only available seat in the class room. The seat just happened to be directly behind Deborah.

As Deborah heard and felt Helen coming her way, she could have kicked herself for not setting out more of the couple dozen or so chairs that were stacked up in the back of the classroom. But she knew no matter how many chairs were out, Helen would have made it a point to strategically place herself right behind Deborah.

When Helen sat down, Deborah could have sworn she felt heat on her back where Helen was probably burning a hole right through her with her eyes.

What did this woman want from Deborah? Only time would tell, but in the meantime, Deborah knew it was going to be a *mean* time.

Why now? That was the question that lingered on Deborah's mind as she concentrated more on the woman sitting behind her than the meeting at hand. Why now was her past all of a sudden coming back to haunt her? Terrorize her? Yes, terrorize was a more fitting word. Deborah knew God must have been trying to tell her something. She wished He'd just spit it out plain and clear so that she could move on already. But maybe that was it; that was the message God was trying to get across. Perhaps He didn't want her to move on like she'd spent the last four years so desperately doing. Perhaps He wanted her to face this thing dead on.

"Sister Deborah? Sister Deborah?"

Deborah didn't know how many times the woman in

front of her had tried to get her attention before she finally snapped out of her thoughts.

"Sister Deborah?"

"Oh, yes, I'm sorry." Deborah took the papers that the woman was extending to her.

"Pass Sister Helen a copy of the bylaws."

"Oh, sure. Certainly."

"You okay?" the woman couldn't help but ask. "You look like you've seen a ghost."

"I'm fine," Deborah lied with ease. Lying seemed so easy now. After all, she'd been lying to herself for quite some time. "I haven't seen a ghost." Deborah forced a chuckle before turning to hand Helen the bylaws. *Just the devil,* she thought when Helen locked eyes with her. *Just the devil himself . . . herself.*

After a half hour of going over the bylaws, Helen excused herself to go to the ladies room. She didn't really have to relieve herself. Well, not technically the way everyone else thought anyway. But she did have to relieve herself from that sad group of women that remained in that stuffy classroom.

Once Helen entered the bathroom and saw that the two stalls were empty, she let out a sigh of relief. "Lord, have mercy. What a pathetic group of women they are." She looked at herself in the mirror. "I am too much of a diva for this group." She admired every inch and curve of her size ten frame. "Imagine a group of women having to create rules on how to meet and get with a man." She chuckled. "What's your kingdom coming to, Father?" Helen shook her head as she ran her hands down her body.

She smiled, feeling blessed that she had what it took to get a man; that she wasn't all desperate like she'd always assumed members of any Singles Ministry to be. She knew how to find herself a man, a husband if she wanted one. Of course her husband would have to accept that one little flaw of hers; a flaw she minimized as small but knew that to a man, especially one without children, it could be major. But that wasn't why she'd joined the New Day Singles Ministry anyway. Her real reasons were yet to be revealed, but in the meantime, she'd just have to grin and bear it, and in her opinion, suffer by keeping company with those women she could barely tolerate on Sundays.

"You can do this, girlfriend." She gave herself a pep talk in the mirror. "As long as Miss Deborah in there keeps her secret, yours will be safe too," she reassured herself before exiting the bathroom to rejoin the meeting. "And I'm going to do everything possible to make sure she doesn't open her mouth." *Not even to you, Lord.*

On the way back from the bathroom, Helen noticed some movement outside in the parking lot, which she could see through the clear glass church doors. Afraid someone might be trying to break in one of the members' cars, she crept to the door to go check things out. That's when she saw Maeyl transferring Tamarra's dry cleaning from his car to hers, with Tamarra standing right there next to him.

"Well, well, well," Helen said snidely. "Looks like someone is on the creep. Guess she even left some of her clothes at her little boyfriend's house on the times she's spent the night with him. How nice of him to take the liberty of having them dry cleaned for her and hand delivered. Now that's the kind of man I need," Helen told herself.

Helen shook her head and continued her conversation with herself. "Man, I tell you, these women of New Day walk around here like some holier than thou wannabe divas. All the while, they all got skeletons in their closet, or should I say under their big hats?" She chuckled. "But I bet no one would ever believe it." Just then Helen's phone vibrated. "Phone . . . yeah . . . that's it," she said, reminded that her phone had a camera on it. "They'd believe it if they could see it though."

She had put her phone on vibrate before coming into the church. She looked at the caller ID and said, "You'll just have to wait, Lynox. Right now I need my phone for something more important than hearing your same ol' same ol'."

Helen hit a couple buttons, and then the phone flashed, and right on time as far as she was concerned. Because at the very minute she took a picture with her camera phone, Maeyl and Tamarra had been holding hands with their eyes closed, appearing as though they were going in for a kiss. Helen took several more pictures as Maeyl and Tamarra opened their eyes, released hands, and went in for a hug.

"Everything okay, Sister Helen?"

Helen quickly put her phone away and turned to address the voice that had startled her. "Oh yes, Mother Doreen. I thought I saw something going on out in the parking lot with one of the cars. I was just checking to make sure everything was okay. And it appears as though everything is. But you can never be too sure."

"Yeah, I've told Pastor that with that carryout across the way and all them youngins hanging out, we probably need a security ministry to watch over the parking lot when activities are going on."

"Well, until pastor decides to move on that suggestion, let's just thank God that He has His angels out there standing post. Amen?" Helen said.

"Amen," Mother Doreen said before she turned and headed toward the direction of the bathroom. Talking over her shoulder, she said to Helen, "You better go on and get back in there. They are about to finish up the last section of those bylaws, and you don't want to miss anything. Hopefully you'll decide to become a member and even get the privilege of voting on them."

"I'll get right in there, Mother Doreen," Helen told her before saying under her breath in a menacing tone, "I don't want to miss a thing at all." Helen headed back toward the classroom. A smile rested upon her lips. She'd quickly come to the conclusion that joining the Singles Ministry just might not be so bad after all. With the way things were looking now, she'd be able to kill two birds with one stone. Helen patted her purse where her cell phone rested. "And if these old maids can ever get any men to join," she said to herself out loud, "I just might be able to make it three."

Chapter Fifteen

"You nervous?" Paige asked Blake as he drove down Interstate 70 with her on the passenger side.

"No," he replied without letting two seconds go by before repenting. "I take that back. I lied. I repent. I'm nervous as heck."

Paige laughed. "I knew it." She flipped down the sun visor and ran her fingertips across her freshly waxed eyebrows. They were arched so thin they looked drawn on.

"It's that obvious, huh?"

"You haven't said two words in the last ten minutes."

"I guess I'm just rehearsing in my head what to say to them. It's not everyday a guy gets invited to meet a girl's parents."

"Oh, trust me, my mom and dad are harmless. It's my girlfriends that you'll have to look out for," Paige teased.

"So tell me about your friends. We've been seeing each other for almost two months, and I haven't met any of them yet."

"Well, I really only have a couple. There's a sister from the church named Deborah. She and I aren't tight, but we talk here and there. Then there is Mother Doreen, everybody's spiritual mother. And of course there's my best buddy, Tamarra. My spiritual sister in every sense."

"I'd love to hang out with you and your best friend. Perhaps we can all go out sometime, on a double date or something . . . when Tamarra isn't busy catering an event, of course."

"That sounds nice," Paige agreed, not even realizing she

hadn't once mentioned to Blake that her best friend was a caterer.

"Honey, before you sit down, grab me another roll from the basket. I know I'm going to need another soon to slop up allthis delicious homemade gravy you done made up."

That's one thing Paige noticed her father always did; compliment her mother while he was slaving her around. As if he had to butter her up to get her to do anything for him. Her mother would jump off the Empire State Building if that man asked her to; trusting on everything that God would be there to catch her and save her since she was only doing it out of obedience to her husband. Talk about obedience being better than sacrifice.

"Oh, no problem, Samuel," Paige's mother said gladly, just before she sat back down to dinner, she turned to retrieve the requested roll.

Thus far, her mother had only been able to sit at the table long enough to participate in grace. Immediately after he'd said, "Amen," Paige's father had already started to, what Paige thought was purposely, have her mother miss a hot meal, only to enjoy a lukewarm one. Paige shook her head at the fact that her mother had managed to give new meaning to the term "lukewarm Christian."

"On second thought, you better make it two rolls." Paige's father then looked over to Blake. "Son, you need another one while she's up? I'm telling you, my wife's homemade rolls and this gravy, they go hand in hand."

"No, sir; I'm fine," Blake responded.

Paige's mother placed the rolls on her father's plate, then headed back to her chair to sit down.

"Susie, go on and grab the young man another roll before you sit down." It was as if Mr. Robinson hadn't even heard Blake decline.

"Oh no, really I'm fine," Blake said to Mrs. Robinson, who then took her seat.

"Trust me, son," Mr. Robinson said to Blake, "them rolls will make you wanna slap my mamma. I say my mamma because Susie uses my mama's recipe, and it belonged to her mama, and so on. That recipe has got to be about four or five generations passed down." Mr. Robinson took a bite of one of his rolls. "Delicious as always." He looked to his daughter but was still speaking to Blake. "You're going to have to get Paige to make you up a batch." He paused as if in thought. "Although I don't think this one ever learned how to make these rolls. She gon' be the one to break the tradition."

"Mama never taught me the Robinson family recipe, or any other recipe for that matter." Paige tried to contain the anger she always felt when ever she thought about her younger years as a growing girl. "She was too busy wearing herself ragged waiting on you hand and foot."

Blake cleared his throat just to create a sound that would interrupt the few awkward seconds of silence that had circled the dinner table. "So, Paige tells me that you're retired from the construction business," Blake said to Paige's father.

"Oh yeah," Mr. Robinson said proudly. "Thirty-five years in the business. Now my son runs the company."

"Is that so?" Blake sounded genuinely interested. "A family business. What a blessing."

Paige hadn't told Blake that her family owned a business. She knew he would wonder why she wasn't a part of it. And just as if Mr. Robinson could read Blake's mind, he addressed Blake's curiosity.

"Tried to get Paige here to get involved ever since she graduated high school, but no, she was too highfalutin for the construction business," he joked. "Instead, she decided to use that business degree of hers and sell movie tickets."

Although it hadn't been her father's intention, Paige felt degraded by his comment. Then again, maybe it had been his intention. Paige had watched him degrade her mother with snide little comments such as that for more years than she cared to remember. Someone had planted in this man's mind that women were beneath men. He didn't seem to care how many degrees his daughter had. His son would always rank higher than Paige. He hadn't spent a day in college, but got into the construction business his senior year of high school, working part-time after classes.

"I don't sell movie tickets, Dad. I'm the general manager of the theatre," Paige huffed.

Mr. Robinson gave a puzzled look that went from Paige to her mother. "But honey, you told me Paige met this young man when she sold him movie tickets."

"Well, that's what I was told," her mother confessed, then looked over at Paige for back-up, clarification, or something. "She told me she sold him two tickets, and she ended up going to the movies with him." Mrs. Robinson smiled. "Such a beautiful story." She looked at Blake and winked. It was an expression of approval.

"Yes, I did sell Blake two movie tickets," Paige explained, "but that was only because I'd just lost an employee, so I had to cover ticket sales until I replaced her. But now I've hired someone, and I don't work the ticket booth anymore."

"Two tickets?" Mr. Robinson questioned, not purposely changing the topic of conversation, but nonetheless, doing so indeed. "Why were you buying two tickets in the first place?" he asked Blake. "If you didn't meet my daughter until you got to the ticket booth, then how did you know to buy two tickets? How did you know she'd join you for a movie? Or had you planned on taking someone else?"

Paige watched Blake shift uncomfortably in his chair as they all waited for his answer. Up until now, she honestly had cared less about who Blake was supposed to be meeting at the movie theater that evening. She hadn't even questioned him about it, especially since he'd made it clear that he did not like to discuss past relationships. Leave it to her father to try to stir up confusion in her blooming relationship. That's another reason why she never brought any of her past dates to meet her parents. Well, that and the fact that none had ever lasted this long.

"Umm, these rolls are delicious," Blake said as he quickly stuffed one in his mouth, hoping that with a full mouth, no one would expect him to reply to Mr. Robinson's inquiry. "I think I will have another one." He removed the napkin from his lap in preparation to stand to go retrieve his roll.

"Sit on down, son," Paige's father ordered him. "Susie will get it." He looked at his wife who was about to put a forkful of food in her mouth. "Susie, go get the young man another roll."

Mrs. Robinson dropped her fork and prepared to get up.

"Oh, that will be all right," Blake said before Mrs. Robinson could rise. "I don't have a problem getting it myself."

Paige, try as she might, couldn't keep her lips from stretching into a wide grin. Oh yes, this man was heaven sent all right. He was everything her father was not, which in her opinion meant that he was the perfect man for her.

Before Blake walked away from the table, he looked at Paige's mother who had only one bite of her roll left and asked, "Mrs. Robinson, can I grab you another one while I'm up?"

Mrs. Robinson almost choked. Had this man just offered to serve her? This was a first unless she'd been out at a restaurant and their server was male. "Uh, no, son, I'm fine. But thank you anyway."

The expression on her mother's face didn't go unnoticed by Paige. Too bad it was Paige's man instead of Mrs. Robinson's own husband who had done so, offered to serve her. It made Paige warm inside to be able to witness her mother see that in this day and age, a woman deserved to be catered to just as much as a man did.

Paige smiled as she dug into her food. What a blessing Blake was. He continued to validate why he was the only man she'd ever brought to her parents' home. He was perfect; un-

flawed like all those other men she'd dated that could hardly get
past date number two. But Paige was convinced that Blake was
different, even though during one of the Singles Ministry meetings Deborah had told her many times that if she were waiting
for God to lead her to the perfect man, she would be waiting forever and a day. Well right now, at this very moment, her forever
and a day had arrived. Blake was perfect in her eyes. How could
he not be as he was part of God's divine set-up? God's divine
plan in her mission to find a husband? But beneath it all, her
perfect encounter with the perfect man wasn't so perfect at all.
She'd been set up all right, in more ways than one, and by the
person she'd least expect.

Chapter Sixteen

"Who could have done such a thing?" Sister Deborah asked Mother Doreen through the phone receiver. "And I thought there was a moderator that had to approve all postings to the church website."

"There is," Mother Doreen assured her, "but I don't think everything goes through the moderator first. I think they just have the ability to delete things if need be. Because whoever thought a church website would need to be manned in such a way? I mean, this is just another way the world has turned one of God's creations into something perverted. The Internet is supposed to be a source to do Kingdom work, to spread the gospel, but man has tainted it."

Deborah could visualize Mother Doreen wiping away sweat beads as they spoke. In all honesty, Deborah had pretty much had to do the same thing herself when she got the call from the church secretary about the recent photos posted to the church website on the Singles Ministry page. To see Tamarra and Maeyl in such a compromising position made her blush with embarrassment. She could only imagine how Tamarra must have felt when she saw them.

"Tamarra!" Deborah thought out loud. "Has she seen or heard about the photos?"

"Oh my. I'm not sure," Mother Doreen replied.

"Well, hopefully the website moderator will get those things deleted before Tamarra has a chance to see them."

"Well, they couldn't get a hold of him this morning."

"Yeah, I guess that's why the church secretary called me this morning; thinking either you or I had the capability to remove the photos," Deborah assumed. "Who is the website moderator anyway?"

Mother Doreen cleared her throat. "Uh, that, would um be, Brother Maeyl."

"What? Are you serious?"

"I'm telling the truth to shame the devil. Brother Edmondson used to be the moderator, but just a couple months ago the Finance Committee was going over church expenses and noticed several Internet charges. After making a few phone calls, they discovered that several of those nasty ole' pop-ups were being accepted, and the fees to view the websites were automatically charged to the bill."

"Do you mean those pornographic pop-ups?"

"Those would be the ones," Mother Doreen confirmed. "Pastor asked him to step down from his duties as overseer of the church website and has been counseling him on his porn addiction."

"But his wife, Sister Tonetta, she's so beautiful. I can't imagine him finding a more beautiful woman to look at on the Internet."

"It ain't about flesh and blood, child, need I remind you. It's just one of those demonic things that Satan uses to steal, kill, and destroy. Funny thing is, until Brother Edmondson started spending so much time on the church computer as part of the New Day Computer Ministry, he'd never in his life looked at porn."

"Umph, umph, umph." Deborah shook her head. "Now I'm not that computer savvy. I can write on them, edit, etc . . . , but I know there is a program that disables certain sites from being viewed. There are also pop-up blockers. Why is it we don't have these things in place?"

Mother Doreen took a deep breath. "Once again, dear, who would have thought we'd need to take such precautions in the house of the Lord? I guess Pastor gave church folks the benefit of the doubt."

"Pastor has a good heart, and I know Pastor doesn't like to make waves with folks, but I pray God uses these incidents to show that Pastor needs to walk in God's given authority."

"I hear you, child," Mother Doreen agreed. "When God gives you an assignment or puts you in authority over something, sometimes you can't be caught up in folks' feelings. At least that's what God told Jehu in Kings 1 or 2. I can't recall off the top right now."

Deborah was in agreement with Mother Doreen, but felt, in a sense, that Mother Doreen held some of the same "save face" characteristics that their pastor did. It often showed in how she handled the women in the Singles Ministry. There were times when Deborah just wanted Mother Doreen to jump up and put those women in check on the spot, but she never did, at least not in the in-your-face manner in which Deborah had wanted to see it done.

"I know you're probably saying to yourself, 'If that ain't the pot calling the kettle black,'" Mother Doreen said. "I, too, sometimes don't walk in my God given authority."

For a minute there, Deborah feared she'd spoken her thoughts out loud.

"But that's something I'm working on myself," Mother Doreen admitted. "There's been plenty of times God has told me to go give a word to someone, but the word sometimes seemed so rough and harsh, I just couldn't confront the person with it."

"Well, I'll pray in that area for both you and Pastor, Mother Doreen. But in the meantime, I'm going to try to get a hold of Tamarra. Whether the moderator gets the photos off the website before she sees them or not doesn't really matter. You know folks are going to get to talking and make it seem worse than it really is."

"All right, dear, you stay blessed, because you already are."

"Thank you, Mother Doreen, you too." Just then, Deborah's cell phone rang. She picked it up and looked at the caller ID. It was Lynox . . . again. She rejected the call . . . again. Eventually he'd realize that persistence would get him nowhere with Deborah.

"Oh, Sister Deborah, before I forget, I just wanted to give you a heads up that I gave a woman I met your phone number regarding a book or something. So she'll be contacting you if she hasn't already."

"Okay, Mother Doreen," Deborah said, more concerned with rejecting Lynox's call and focusing on Tamarra's situation. Besides, someone was always giving her number or email address out to the tons of people who had written a book, or wanted to write a book and needed direction. "I'll talk with you later."

Deborah ended the call with Mother Doreen, then prepared herself to call up Tamarra. She said a quick prayer that God would go before her and touch Tamarra's heart and mind so that receiving the news would not weigh too heavily on her.

Deborah dialed Tamarra's phone number. When she received the greeting on the other end of a loud, angry, "Hello!" Deborah knew her prayer had been a moment too late.

Tamarra was seething as she looked at the set of four pictures of herself and Maeyl plastered on the Singles Ministry page of the church website. The pictures made it appear as though she and Maeyl were smooching in the church parking lot. Although in reality they had just been praying, and then leaning in to give each other a godly hug, the person who snapped the photo did it in such timing that it made it appear as though they were going in for a kiss.

Tamarra could tell from the poor quality that the pictures weren't taken by a professional, like a private investigator or anything like that. From the looks of it, it seemed as if they were originally taken from a cell phone or something. Nonetheless, Tamarra was outraged.

"Son of a—" Tamarra caught herself before cursing. Prior to getting saved, she didn't have a filthy mouth, and now that she was saved, she wasn't about to let the devil get the victory of being able to say his cursing demon was stronger than the spirit man in her. No way no how. But boy oh boy did she just want to let one loose.

Tamarra didn't even bother to properly exit the church website and shut down her computer. She wanted those pictures to go away—and fast. She yanked all the plugs associated with her computer out of the wall, jumped up from her computer chair and began pacing across her bedroom floor.

"Why, God? Why is this happening? Don't you think I've suffered enough in my lifetime? Now I'm going to be the talk of New Day for years to come."

Tamarra's rant to the Lord was interrupted by her ringing telephone. "Uggghhh," she screamed as she walked over and pulled that cord out of the wall too. "If that phone rings one more time!" That had to be the tenth time her phone had rung in the last ten minutes, which only meant that the news of the photos were spreading like a California wildfire.

Just ten minutes ago, Tamarra had rudely answered her phone only to find Deborah on the other end. Tamarra felt bad for the un-Christlike greeting she'd given her and apologized, explaining to Deborah that people from New Day who had never called her in the past had been ringing her phone all morning asking her about the photos posted, as if she'd posted them herself.

"Now why would I have done a thing like that?" Tamarra had posed that rhetorical question to Sister Deborah, who surprisingly gave her a response.

"I don't know. Maybe some people think you could have been trying to pull the covers off Brother Maeyl or something. A woman scorned or something. Now I know you better than that, but some people like to write, star in, and direct their own drama series. So they could come up with all kinds of things.

But who knows, Tamarra? Just keep your head up and know that God will take care of everything. Pretty soon, those pictures will be removed from the website, and all will be forgotten."

Deborah had been partly right, Tamarra had concluded. The pictures would eventually be removed from the website, but not from people's minds. And what if someone had copied, downloaded, or even saved the pictures? Those pictures would never go away.

Exasperated, Tamarra collapsed on her bed. This was not the way she had anticipated spending her Saturday morning. She laid there for a moment, thinking about all the phone calls she'd received that morning. "The nerve of people to actually think I would post those pictures to the website." Sure, Tamarra eventually wanted to bring her and Maeyl's relationship into the light, but she didn't want to do so before she knew exactly where the relationship was heading. She and Maeyl, just last week, had even had a similar conversation.

Maeyl felt that the two months they'd been seeing each other had been a long enough test period. He proclaimed that his feelings for Tamarra had surpassed the brothers and sisters in Christ type of connection and was well on its way beyond the "just friends" stage.

"It looks like we're sneaking around by not making mention of our seeing each other," Maeyl had stated to Tamarra as they fed the ducks at a local pond. "When people do things in the dark, it's as if they have something to hide. Well, I don't have anything to hide. Do you?" Maeyl had asked without getting a response. "Everyone is going to know eventually. I'd like to at least have something to do with that. If anything, we owe it to Pastor to at least mention that two New Day members are in a relationship; a godly relationship," Maeyl pointed out. "Besides that, Malvonia isn't but that big." He snapped his fingers. "Heck, there's probably somebody we know here right now that is spotting us."

"Spotting us?" Tamarra had brushed off Maeyl's last statement with a chuckle and shoo of her hand. She then broke a piece of bread from the last slice she had left and threw it into the pond. "You make it seem like we're fugitives on the run or something."

"No, Tamarra." He removed the last slice of bread from her hand and threw it down. He then took her hands into his and looked at her while she stared off at the pond. "You make it seem like we're fugitives. At least that's how you make me feel anyway." Maeyl released her hands, then stood. "I'll meet you back at the car."

Now that Tamarra thought about it, ever since that conversation a week ago, Maeyl had been more distant than usual. They'd only talked on the phone twice and gone out together once. The time they did go out wasn't so pleasant. Maeyl had wanted to go to Family Café, but Tamarra put up a fight, and they ended up having lunch at a restaurant in Columbus. Maeyl knew the only reason why she didn't want to go to Family Café was because they were bound to run into someone they knew, especially someone from church. Though neither one of them expressed their true feelings regarding the matter, they didn't have to. It was clear and evident, just like things were now becoming more clear and evident to Tamarra.

"*Everyone is going to know eventually,*" she repeated the words Maeyl had said that day at the pond. "*I'd like to at least have something to do with that,*" she recalled him saying. No sooner than she recalled those words, she remembered Maeyl telling her during their first date how Pastor had just asked him to temporarily fill in for Brother Edmondson as the church website moderator. Things were indeed clear and evident. Maeyl had obviously been set on spreading the word about their seeing each other, and obviously, he'd had help in doing so; help from someone with a camera.

"So you at least wanted to have something to do with everyone finding out about us, huh, did you ol' Maeyl?" she spat as she stormed over to her dresser drawer in search of something to throw on. "Looks like you had everything to do with it, and if you thought you were going to get away with it, you've got another thing coming."

Tamarra quickly slipped on a pair of jeans and threw on a T-shirt. She was so anxious to leave the house and go confront Maeyl that she didn't even realize she'd forgotten to do something with her hair. It stuck straight up in the air without the usual water and setting lotion she typically used to tame it. On top of that, she didn't notice that her shirt was on both backward and inside out. But none of that mattered to her anyway. She had bigger fish to fry, and from the looks of things, someone was about to get burned!

Chapter Seventeen

Tamarra had knocked on Maeyl's door for the third time, ringing the doorbell twice in between. His car was parked in his assigned parking space in front of his apartment building, so she knew he was home. He'd probably peeked out of the window and saw that it was her and knew why she'd come to his house, so he was hiding behind closed doors like a coward.

"Answer this dang blasted door, Maeyl. I know you're in there," Tamarra said to herself as she beat on the door once again. She had made up in her mind that if she had to stand on that porch and knock until morning, then so be it. She knew he had to come out in the morning in order to go work the church sound booth. He'd never missed a Sunday that she could remember. He was dedicated to New Day; always in position. So she knew that if he wouldn't even allow the devil himself to keep him from his Sunday morning duties, he surely wouldn't let her.

With arms folded, Tamarra stood on the stoop of Maeyl's doorway, tapping her foot. After a few moments, she rang the door bell again, then resumed her stance. After a few more moments, she snapped her fingers. "The back patio," she said to herself. She turned to go around to the back of the apartment complex, and that's when she heard Maeyl's door creek open.

"Tamarra, is everything all right?" Maeyl asked in a panicked tone. "What's going on?" He opened the door and gestured for her to come in.

"You know exactly what's going on, and, no, I'm not

okay." Tamarra stormed into his place. Maeyl kept the door open, a little something he'd learned from Tamarra that she had learned from the Singles Ministry. It was behind closed doors that the devil often liked to present sin to a person; tricking them into believing that the sin would stay behind closed doors. And once again, Tamarra wanted to avoid the appearance of evil; not that it had worked for her up to this point.

"You've been beating on my door for the last fifteen minutes." The worry in Maeyl's voice was sincere. "Please, tell me what's going on."

"If you heard me beating on your door for the last fifteen minutes, then why in God's name didn't you open it? Oh, let me guess; Too busy trying to get your story together?" Tamarra was on fire. Maeyl had never seen her in this rare form.

"Will you calm down?" Maeyl requested. "I was down the basement in my prayer room praying. I don't allow anything or anyone to interrupt my prayer with God. You know that. I don't answer the door or the phone when I'm in sweet communion with the Lord."

"Oh, pahleeeeeze!" Tamarra spat. "If I did happen to buy that line, I'd hope to God that you were praying for forgiveness." Tamarra's eyes watered. "Maeyl, how could you?" She fought back tears of hurt. "I know you really wanted people to know about us; you thought I was hiding you—ashamed of you or something perhaps, but I swear I wasn't. You don't know what all I've gone through, and I just wanted everything to be right. I've been praying about us; you and me. I know how I feel about you, but it's not about me. I've made mistakes before when I made things about me. I wanted this, me and you, to be about God. So I was waiting on Him. I was waiting on Him to tell me to move. But you . . . you just couldn't wait, could you? And now, although things might look good on your end, you might look like the man, the mack daddy, but I look like a fool, a cheap—"

Maeyl caught Tamarra's fists when she raised them. He had no idea what their final destination was, and he didn't want to find out. "Tamarra, honey," he said with such tenderness in his voice, that Tamarra had quickly forgotten how he'd put their relationship on blast in such a manner. She allowed her forehead to rest forward on his chest, exhausted from arguing. She felt drained, so drained she could barely hold her head up.

"Why?" was all Tamarra could say.

Maeyl allowed Tamarra to release several more 'whys' before he spoke. "Tamarra, I honestly have absolutely no idea what you're talking about."

Tamarra looked up into his eyes, and then pushed herself away. "How dare you patronize me like I'm some fool? But if games are what you want to play, then I'll play. I guess all of this was just a game to you in the first place. It had to be for you to do something like this. Just like a man; can't ever seem to get that ego in check."

"If you are going to stand here in my living room insulting me, the least you can do is let me know why."

"The website!" Tamarra finally blurted out. "The pictures; the ones of us—me and you. The ones that you posted on the church website."

"I have no idea what you're talking about," Maeyl said, walking toward Tamarra.

"Oh, just stop it." She pushed past him to the door. "I expected as much from you. I don't even know why I came here in the first place. I don't know how you did it, or if you even had help, but none of that matters now. Goodbye, Maeyl."

"No, Tamarra, wait!" Maeyl called after her.

He started to chase after her, but paused when he realized his feet were bare. He never wore shoes into his prayer room and had yet to slip some on. He didn't have a chance. Once he'd prematurely closed out his prayer, his only concern had been to see who was beating on his door. He could tell by their persistence that they were not going to go away, and their constant banging had stifled the Holy Spirit.

He had planned on resolving the matter that awaited him outside his front door, and then return to prayer, but now his mind was just too consumed. Tamarra, the woman he had actually been praying for and about, was furious with him and he needed to make things right. He looked around for something to slip on his feet, but nothing was in sight. He then barged out the door anyway.

"Tamarra!" he called out as he stepped down off his porch to go after her. "Ouch!" he screeched after stepping on something. He immediately grabbed his injured foot and hopped around on one leg in pain.

Seeing that Tamarra was not going to oblige his request for her to come back and speak with him, Maeyl watched her get in her car and drive off. Unfortunately, so did the church secretary who had decided to pay Maeyl a visit after so many failed attempts to contact him by phone. The church secretary sat in her car. Her mouth dropped when she saw Tamarra come storming out of Maeyl's house in a rush, so much of a rush that she'd put her shirt on inside out. And her hair looked as though she and Maeyl had been doing God only knows what. And then there was Maeyl in his bare feet.

The church secretary clasped her chest in disbelief. When she decided to take it upon herself to drive over to Maeyl's house, she never thought for the life of her that she'd stumble upon a lover's quarrel. If the church thought the mere pictures of the couple were bad, wait until they heard about this.

Chapter Eighteen

"Ain't no devil in hell gonna keep me from my Lord," were the words that played on the radio as Tamarra drove to church.

She'd be a liar if she said that she hadn't thought all night long about not coming to church, but there was no way she was going to let Maeyl feel as though he'd gotten to her with his little stunt. He'd tried calling her house and cell phone a dozen times, but she wouldn't take his calls. Paige, after hearing about the pictures and then going online to see them for herself, tried calling Tamarra several times from work. Tamarra finally did take her call after hearing how worried she sounded. Paige offered to come by her house after she got off work at eight o'clock. She said she had a date with Blake, but could cancel it, but Tamarra told her friend that she'd be fine.

Tamarra was surprised when Paige showed up at her door anyway at eight thirty. She'd cancelled her date in order to be there for her friend. The two talked and prayed well into the midnight hour before Paige finally left, offering to come back in the morning to pick Tamarra up so that the two could go to church together. Tamarra knew it was Paige's way of making sure she went to church, but she assured her that she would be there, joking that she didn't want anybody having to do a drive-by if she didn't show up.

"On top of that," Tamarra said out loud as she drove to church, "I didn't do anything wrong. There's no reason why I can't show my face in New Day. Nope. There is no need at all for me to be ashamed of anything; anything at all." If anybody should feel ashamed, she reckoned it should be Maeyl.

Tamarra pulled up into the church parking lot prepared to go get her praise and worship on and hear the message of God just like she'd done any other Sunday. But just as soon as she stepped foot out of her jeep, she knew this wasn't going to be like any other Sunday.

"They had just done what?" were the words Tamarra heard when she stepped into the ladies room at church.

Because of the memo always posted in the church programs about limiting getting up and down doing church service, Tamarra always made it a point to go to the bathroom before service started. She didn't want to be one of those saints who were always up, being a distraction in the sanctuary.

It was never a surprise for her to walk into the ladies restroom and find a couple of hens plucking away at the latest gossip, but never had the gossip been about her. Tamarra could tell the two women who'd been chatting away had been talking about her, because as soon as she entered and they locked eyes with her, she could see the canary's feathers hanging out of each of their mouths.

"Good morning, Sister Tamarra," one of the women said, who just happened to also be a member of the Singles Ministry. "It's a wonderful day that the Lord has made, isn't it?"

Tamarra held her head up high and replied. "Why it certainly is, and therefore we should all rejoice and be glad in it. I know I am." Without further ado, Tamarra made her way into an empty stall. She closed the door, locked it, and then let out a huge, deep exhale as if she'd been holding her breath the entire time. She then said a silent prayer to God. *Lord, thank you for restraining my flesh so that it didn't rise up and knock their blocks off for talking about me. In Jesus' name. Amen.*

"Humph, I bet she's rejoicing all right," one of the women said as the two women exited the bathroom together. "I'd be rejoicing too after a roll in the sack with a fine specimen like Mr. Sound Man."

Tamarra could hear the women laughing like hyenas as the door closed behind them. Everything in her wanted to go confront them. To shake them and make them listen to the truth. Never mind what their eyes saw. Things weren't what they looked like. But why should she even entertain those two or anyone else who decided they wanted to get caught up in the gossip? People were going to talk about her. That was life. People had talked about Jesus, and God still gave Him the victory over every tongue that had spoken against Him.

"With God on my side, who can be against me?" Tamarra said to herself after flushing the commode, and then going to wash her hands. After drying them she looked at herself in the mirror and repeated once again the words, "With God on my side, who can be against me?"

With restored strength, Tamarra exited the bathroom and made her way into the sanctuary where it had appeared, with all the glares she was getting, the rumors had preceded her. It looked as though she'd gotten the answer to the question she had just posed to herself twice. "Who can be against me?" she mumbled under her breath sarcastically. "The whole church."

Chapter Nineteen

"And they call themselves saved!" Paige spat as she scooped up a mound of mashed potatoes from the Golden Corral Buffet.

"You know what Pastor always says, everybody in the church ain't saved. That's why we have the church. Jesus didn't come to save the righteous." Tamarra walked alongside Paige down the buffet. While Paige's plate was practically full, Tamarra had barely placed anything on hers. After dealing with all of the glares, stares, and whispers from the members of the church today, she didn't feel much like eating.

"I get that and all, but we're talking about the same people who be speaking in tongues, now using their tongues to spread gossip and lies," Paige countered. "I mean, so what if you spent the night at Maeyl's house Friday night? That's your business, as well as what ever the two of you did. That's between you and God. You're my girl, so you know I'm not going to judge you."

The loud crashing noise of the plate hitting the floor startled Paige. Tamarra stood there as if she weren't the one who'd just dropped the plate that was now in a million pieces on the floor. "Spent the night with Maeyl?" Tamarra said to Paige. "Did you just say that I spent the night with Maeyl?"

Tamarra's voice was so loud that other diners who were fixing their plates could hear her.

"Come on, Tamarra, let's go sit down for a minute. We'll

ask the waitress to bring you another plate." Paige slightly tugged Tamarra's arm to lead her back to their table.

Snatching her arm away from Paige, Tamarra said, "I don't want another plate. I want to know why my so-called best friend just accused me of spending the night over some man's house and doing . . . and doing . . ." Tamarra couldn't even get the words out. She lowered her tone and said, "doing *it*."

"Look, Tamarra, I'm not the one accusing you of anything. It was someone from the church who saw you with their own two eyes leaving Maeyl's house Saturday morning with your hair in disarray and your shirt on backward and inside out. What did you expect people to think?"

"I'm not talking about people, I'm talking about you; my best friend." Tamarra paused for a moment as the two women stood in the middle of the restaurant. "Well, what do you think?"

Paige thought for a moment. She wanted to choose her words carefully.

"Forget it," Tamarra said, shaking her head. "What you're not saying says it all." Tamarra walked back over to the table where they had been seated, grabbed her purse from under the table, and made a beeline to the exit door and straight to her car. She hadn't gotten her car door open before Paige came running after her.

"Tamarra, wait!" she called out, almost out of breath. Tamarra stood at the door and waited for Paige to approach her. "Look, I'm sorry."

"For what?" Tamarra wanted her to say it. What was she sorry for? Was she sorry that her friend was going through a scandal of lies and the baring of false witnesses? Or was she sorry that she believed those lies? "Tell me, Paige, why are you sorry?"

"I guess I'm sorry because . . . I don't know, Tamarra. I'm sorry about everything. I'm sorry that you are having to deal with this. I'm sorry that you don't think I'm being a good friend right now."

"That I *think* you're not being a good friend, or that you

actually aren't being a good friend? Don't you get it, Paige?" Tamarra ran her fingers through her short hair. "Those people at New Day can think what they want. They don't know me, but you do . . . friend." Tamarra opened the jeep's door to get in it.

"Hold up, Missy. Don't put this on me just because you got caught leaving Maeyl's place. I mean, I don't know what went on at his place Friday night or Saturday morning or whenever, but I do know that I spent all Saturday night with you and not once did you mention to me that you had been over Maeyl's."

"So just because I didn't give you every little detail of my day's schedule, you think I was over his house up to no good?"

"Well, I couldn't think of any other reason why you would hide it from me."

"Hide? Hide?" Tamarra threw her hands up in defeat. "Why does everybody always think I'm hiding something? First, Maeyl thinks I'm hiding his and my relationship and now so do you."

"Well, aren't you? You made it out to be such a big secret that even I, your best friend, had to pry it out of you. I talk to you about Blake every day. I brought him to the church just last Sunday. You yourself got to meet him, although it was only for a hot second since you had to leave church early." That particular Sunday Tamarra had to leave early for a catering affair at New Destiny for their church anniversary. "But I introduced him to Pastor. Here you and Maeyl are right under Pastor's nose acting like there is nothing going on between y'all. I don't know what you call it, but to the rest of the world, it looks like you two were trying to hide something. And usually people only hide things when they are up to no good. So forgive me, Tamarra. I'm sorry. I'm sorry that for one minute I thought that just maybe you did have something to hide. I confess that much, and I'm sorry."

Tamarra stared at Paige who stood there in a puddle of remorse and frustration. Tamarra couldn't help but think this is the exact same way Maeyl must have felt too. Perhaps she had pushed him to find a way to tell everyone about their relationship. In hindsight, she may have very well brought all of this mess upon herself. There was a slight chance that she'd been using the fact that she was waiting on God to speak to her about her and Maeyl's relationship as an excuse to stand still in her own fears; fears of moving forward. Fears of being happy again. Now not only had her fears affected her, but everyone around her as well. Now how could she turn things around and make them right?

Knowing at least where to start, Tamarra placed her arms around Paige and apologized for her role in all of the confusion. After Paige accepted her apology, Tamarra jumped in her jeep knowing exactly what she had to do next.

Chapter Twenty

Although just yesterday she had been banging and ringing the doorbell like a madwoman, today she hesitated pushing the doorbell. She wondered if he would even open the door if he looked out of the peephole and saw that it was her standing there. She couldn't blame him if he didn't. So she gathered up the necessary courage that allowed her to push the button.

Tamarra stood on the little porch of Maeyl's apartment waiting, hoping that he'd answer the door. A few moments went by and there was no answer. She looked back over her shoulder just to confirm that her eyes hadn't played tricks on her; that Maeyl's car was in its assigned parking space. Once she confirmed that his car was in fact there, she prepared to knock on the door. Just as she raised her fist to make contact, she heard the locks clicking, and then the door opened.

"Tamarra," Maeyl said as if surprised to see her. "Come on in." He opened the door and stepped aside for her to enter.

She couldn't believe how welcoming and warm his greeting was. He was acting like she wasn't the woman standing in his living room twenty-four hours ago yelling at the top of her lungs and swinging her fists. Or the woman who acted as if he didn't even exist while at church today. How could he be so forgiving so fast?

"How are you? Are you okay?" Maeyl asked her, aware of all the gawking and gossiping she had to deal with today at church.

"You know what, Maeyl, as a matter of fact, I think I am okay."

"Good. Because I know there was a lot of staring and whispering going on today at church. Pastor even asked me to come into the office and have a chat this morning before service."

"Oh, my," Tamarra said, digesting the confirmation that she wasn't the only one affected by the situation. She'd come there to apologize to Maeyl for her behavior. She wanted to tell him that she didn't blame him for posting those pictures. Especially after the way she'd tried to force him to keep their relationship a secret as if they were doing something dirty. Now a part of her was beginning to think that perhaps Maeyl didn't have anything to do with the posting of those pictures after all. Why would he want to subject himself and his character to the criticism of the church just to spite her wishes? On top of that, why would he subject himself to having to be confronted by the pastor?

"What did Pastor say to you?" Tamarra asked him.

"Well, I was asked about our relationship, of course."

Tamarra swallowed. "What did you say?"

"The truth. The clean truth, which is what I wanted to do all along."

Tamarra put her head down in guilt. "And what did Pastor say?"

"Pastor thanked me for clearing things up, but wished we hadn't added to the situation by being so secretive. Pastor felt that our secrecy alone gave people reason to doubt our intentions."

"What else did Pastor say?" Tamarra asked, wondering if their pastor had come flat out and asked if they were taking their relationship to an ungodly level as the pictures insinuated.

"That's about it. The church secretary knocked on the door to let us know the leaders were waiting in the conference room for morning prayer. Pastor is supposed to be calling me this afternoon to talk more about the situation."

Tamarra had to ask. "Did you happen to mention to Pastor that it was my wish to not bring our relationship to the forefront?"

"No. How would that have mattered? I'm a grown man. I made a choice. I'm not Adam in the Garden of Eden, and you put the forbidden fruit to my lips and told me to bite it, then I turn around and tell God it was all your fault. My spirit felt differently about the situation, and I didn't obey it. That's my fault."

"Actually, that's why I'm here. I do feel as though I pushed you to go against your spirit, so I'm here to apologize. I also want to apologize for the way I acted yesterday. I was a maniac."

Tamarra waited on Maeyl to accept her apology, but all he did was stand there as if he were waiting for yet another apology. "What?" Tamarra asked.

"You don't have something else you want to apologize to me for?"

Tamarra thought for a moment, but couldn't come up with anything.

"Like accusing me of posting those pictures on the website in the first place? I mean, you didn't even ask me if I did it. You just assumed I did, and then didn't even give me a chance to explain."

"You're right, and I apologize for that too." Tamarra hoped Maeyl could forgive her.

"Apology accepted," Maeyl finally said, bringing a smile to Tamarra's face. "Now that's the face that belongs to the woman I love," Maeyl smiled in return. It was at the same time both he and Tamarra realized the words he'd just spoken.

Tamarra's heart melted. Here she stood before a man she'd only been dating a couple of months, but had known for several years. And he'd just confessed his love to her. Was it possible that there was life after divorce? That there was love after divorce? Everything in her told her that, yes, there was. But still, there was another part of her that hesitated to believe such.

Maeyl didn't know what else to say. He never expected to express his love for a woman without knowing for sure that she loved him too. He wanted to avoid an awkward situation such as this where the woman didn't say it back in return. Maeyl cleared his throat and asked, "Have you eaten yet?"

"Uh, no," Tamarra said.

"How about we go grab something to eat? We can drive to Columbus or something if you like," Maeyl suggested.

"Sounds good. But if you don't mind, I got a taste for Family Café." Tamarra smiled and winked.

"You got it!" Maeyl exclaimed. "Let me just go slip out of this church suit into something cooler. For it to be October, the weather is warm." Maeyl loosened his tie as he headed for the steps.

Tamarra knew Maeyl was the one. How could she have been so stupid and think he would set out to hurt her? It was time she put down her guards and let love in. That's just what she intended to do as the confession of Maeyl's love for her settled into her heart.

"Maeyl," she called out to him when he was almost all the way up the steps.

"Yes?" he asked.

"I—" Tamarra started before she was cut off by Maeyl's ringing cell phone that was on the table. "Uh, your uh, cell phone is ringing," she copped out.

"Just let it ring. I'll call them back," Maeyl said as he went on up the steps.

"Stupid phone," Tamarra said to herself.

"Did you say something?" Maeyl called down.

"Oh, I just said, nice phone," she lied, then repented.

"Oh, thanks," Maeyl said. "Oh shoot!"

"What's wrong?"

"I forgot that Pastor was supposed to call. That might have been the call. Can you check to see if that was Pastor's number that showed up on the caller ID?"

"Sure," Tamarra said, picking up the phone and checking to see if she recognized the most recent number that showed up under missed calls. "Yes, it was Pastor."

"Shoot, I'll just have to return that call before we head out."

As Tamarra heard Maeyl's footsteps above her head, she pushed a couple of buttons to exit out of the missed calls. In doing so, she accidentally ended up in downloaded pictures. When she pushed yet another button to try to get from that screen, she couldn't believe her eyes when a picture showed up on the screen; a picture that was none other than one that had been posted on the church website.

Tamarra couldn't believe she had almost fallen for the okey doke. Maeyl's cell phone ringing right before she could confess her feelings to him was divine intervention. That's how she saw it anyway. And then him asking her to check his phone and her stumbling upon that picture was no accident either. There was no good reason for him to have that picture on his phone unless his phone had been the one that had taken it. It hurt seeing the truth with her own eyes, but all of these things were supposed to be revealed to her before she got in too deep.

Her ringing phone interrupted her thoughts, and thank God too. She was seconds from going through a red light and into oncoming traffic. She looked down at her cell phone and saw just the number she had expected to see; Maeyl's. Tamarra rejected the call knowing exactly what he wanted. He wanted to know why it was that when he came downstairs from changing out of his church suit he found her gone. Hopefully when he picked up his cell phone he saw the picture she'd left up on the screen and knew exactly why she'd made an exit without telling him so much as good-bye.

Yesterday she'd gotten out of character quite a bit. But today, she didn't think the grace of God could keep her from losing her Christianity, albeit temporarily. She'd found proof that Maeyl was the culprit who'd somehow gotten someone to help him take the picture with his phone, and then post it to the website. She was no longer going to entertain him or his lies.

"How could I have been so stupid?" she asked herself, slamming her fists against her steering wheel, imagining how good it would feel to be slamming them upside Maeyl's head.

Tamarra knew that it wasn't a good idea to speak to Maeyl. Not right now. Not ever. And if he knew what was good for him, he'd keep his distance and not even think about trying to speak to her at church on Sunday, if she went. Sure this morning she was singing along with "Ain't no devil in hell gonna keep me from my Lord." But she had to admit that a devil on earth might be able to keep her away from New Day.

"Yes, that's exactly what I probably need to do," Tamarra told herself. "Get away from New Day and find a new church. Who needs all that drama anyway?" Tamarra turned on her radio, oblivious to the words that were playing: *"I'm so glad that God is not like man."*

"Don't worry, God," Tamarra spoke to God over the music. "I'm not going to let the devil stop me from going to church and praising you. It's just that New Day doesn't seem to be the place for me anymore. I need a fresh start somewhere else. Yeah, that's exactly what I need."

Tamarra's last comment was more to herself than God. She turned up the music and bopped her head at least two beats faster than the beat of the song itself. The music was so loud that she didn't hear her inner man warn her, *"You can run, but you can't hide . . . not from God."*

Chapter Twenty-one

Deborah had just finished editing a manuscript when her phone rang.

"Praise the Lord," Deborah greeted through the phone receiver.

"Praise the Lord," Mother Doreen replied.

"Mother Doreen . . ." Deborah hit the info button on her muted television in order to see what time it was. She knew it was late; after 8:00 P.M. She had been hardcopy editing the last few pages of a manuscript while comfortably lying in her bed, looking up at the television every few minutes to see any election coverage updates. Thus far, Obama was kickin' McCain's butt. Although 8:00 P.M. might not have been late for the average person, she knew it was for Mother Doreen. "Is everything okay?"

"Actually, I just got a call from my sister's doctor in Kentucky. She's had another relapse and is back in the hospital."

"Her sugar again?"

"Yes, dear," Mother Doreen stated. "We just can't seem to keep it under control."

"Well, God is still in the healing business, so I'm sure if we all keep praying, He will heal her."

"Oh, He's healed her already." Mother Doreen sounded so sure.

Deborah was puzzled. If God had already healed Mother Doreen's sister, then why was she still sick and in and out of the hospital?

"When my sister first fell ill," Mother Doreen continued, "we fasted and we prayed for that healing. Just the last time I was there I laid hands on that body and spoke to that illness. I rebuked it out of her body in prayer. And while we were praying, the praying turned into praise; praise for the healing that we knew was already done at that moment. Then the praise turned into worship. We couldn't help but bow down and worship the one who, with a single touch, answered a prayer." Mother Doreen let out a shout just thinking about what God had done for her sister.

Deborah knew her God was a healer and she believed in the healing power, but if this was the case with Mother Doreen's sister, why was the illness still attacking her body? "So what was it that God healed her of that time?" Deborah asked, choosing her words carefully. She didn't want Mother Doreen to think she was a doubting Thomas, but at the same time, she wanted clarity.

"Her diabetes," Mother Doreen confirmed. "See, God did His part. He healed my sister, only she didn't walk in the healing. She went right back to her old ways; eating Oreo's, fried chicken and drinking soda pop like it was going out of style. It's just like having the flu and God heals you from the flu; only you turn around and wash your hair, then leave it wet, put on shorts, and go outside barefoot in the dead of winter. How is that walking in a healing?"

"It's not," Deborah said, finally getting where Mother Doreen was going with things. "It's like praying that God heals you from lung cancer while puffing on a cigarette."

"Exactly, and that's basically what my sister is doing," Mother Doreen said, hiding the frustration she was feeling toward her sister's behavior. "Anyway, I have to head back down to Kentucky. I don't know how long I'm going to be there this time. You know my sister has those two babies; my fourteen-year-old niece and sixteen-year-old nephew. Their daddy is always on the road driving that truck, so he can't tend to them like teenagers need to be tended to. Sometimes he's gone a week or two at a time. And I know Satan is just lurking around for a crack to slither into and try to disrupt their lives. Not under my watch. So I'm going to head down in the morning."

"Did you need me to do something for you?" Deborah asked.

"Yes, that's why I called. I have an appointment on Thursday with one of the sisters at the church; just to go over some things regarding the Singles Ministry. I was wondering if you could meet with her for me. I want the ministry to continue to grow, and I don't want this sister to lose interest while I'm away. You're my backbone when it comes to running this ministry, so I knew I could call on you."

How could Deborah decline after those kind words? "Sure, Mother Doreen, I'd be glad to. What time is the appointment?"

"It's Thursday at 5:30 P.M. in the church conference room."

"No problem, Mother Doreen. I'll make sure I'm there. You be blessed, and I'll be praying, touching, and agreeing with you that your sister will begin to walk in her healing."

"Thank you, dear. God bless, and I'll talk to you later."

"Travel mercies and goodnight," Deborah said. "Oh, Mother Doreen, what's the lady's name that I'm meeting?"

"Oh, just a second. Let me pull my appointment calendar out of my purse." Deborah could hear some rustling in the background while Mother Doreen searched out her calendar. "Here it is. Helena Simmons. You know, that new child that came to the last meeting. Sister Helen, she goes by. All right then, dear. Goodnight."

Before Deborah could even come up with an excuse as to why she suddenly couldn't do Mother Doreen this one solid, the line was already dead. In two days she'd be face-to-face, alone, with Helen. She didn't know if all of God's armor in the world could shield her from this evil.

Chapter Twenty-two

When it was announced that the United States would have its first black president, Deborah thought she'd be celebrating for days, but waking up realizing that Thursday was now here, she didn't have a celebratory bone in her body. It was time to face her giant. She'd thought of a million and one reasons to cancel the meeting. When she had seemed to find the perfect excuse, she realized she didn't have Helen's number to call and cancel the appointment. The last thing she wanted was for it to get back to Pastor that she wasn't in position when she was supposed to be.

"The devil is always in position," Pastor would say. "You never have to worry about him not showing up for an assignment. You never have to worry about the devil showing up late."

That Thursday evening, Deborah prayed the entire drive to the church, wishing she could speak in tongues so that the devil wouldn't be able to decipher her request to God regarding her situation with Helen. But she'd never been filled with the Holy Spirit and received tongues. At first she used to think God saw something in her that made her unworthy of the tongues. That there was an area of her life she needed work on, and the fact that she couldn't speak in tongues was a dead give-away to everyone around her. She would always get embarrassed when Pastor would ask the congregation to pray in the Spirit and she wasn't able to. But after awhile, it didn't bother her much. She rarely even thought about communicating to God in an unfamiliar language. But now, more than ever she wished that she'd been blessed with the gift.

When Deborah pulled into the church parking lot, she saw four parked cars. One she recognized as the pastor's. Two of the other cars belonged to two members of the New Day Janitorial Ministry. They were probably cleaning up from last night's Bible Study. The remaining car Deborah didn't recognize and assumed it was more than likely Helen's. "I guess my prayer about her not showing up didn't work," Deborah said to herself. She then looked up and repented to God. She knew prayer worked and felt bad about the fact that she had just treated it like a magic trick gone wrong.

Upon entering the church, Deborah stalled going into the conference room by making a pit stop at the ladies room, even though she had just used the restroom right before leaving her home. "Holy Spirit, rise up in me, and take control of this meeting I have with Sister Helen," Deborah stood and prayed in front of the mirror. "Sit down my flesh so that you may stand. Decrease me so that you may increase. In Jesus' name. Amen and Amen." Deborah took a deep breath, and then headed into the conference room.

She was surprised to see that the conference room was empty. For a moment she wondered if maybe Helen thought she was a no show and had decided to leave. Deborah laid her purse down on the conference table as well as the notebook she'd carried in with her. She headed back toward the church doors so that she could look out and see if the mystery car was still parked in the lot. Peering through the glass church doors, sure enough, the car was still there.

"Hmm," Deborah pondered while rubbing her chin.

"Everything okay, Sister Deborah?"

The female voice behind Deborah startled her. She turned to see Nita, a member of the Janitorial Ministry, with a mop and bucket in hand.

"Oh, everything is fine, Sister Nita," Deborah replied. "How are you?"

"Blessed and highly favored," she said with sincerity and a smile.

Some people just recited that cliché to be saying it, but Deborah could always tell that Nita meant it. She knew some of Nita's testimony as a survivor of domestic violence. She could tell Nita felt that every day God allowed her to live and breathe and be free was nothing short of a blessing. Nita had said that she felt His favor upon her by allowing her to run her own cleaning company, where she did contracts for apartment complexes. She used this skill to head the New Day Janitorial Ministry. And every time Pastor took up an offering specifically for her ministry, she always sewed the seed right back into the church.

Deborah, although she didn't really know Nita all that well, was both inspired and moved by her perseverance and ability to obtain the victory in such an ordeal. Not many women would have made it after being abused physically, mentally, and sexually by their husband of seven years. It was a wonder Nita was still in her right mind. But God is able. He brought her through those last tormenting hours with her ex-husband, the father of her children.

For twelve hours straight, the man had beaten and raped her repeatedly while their two five-year-old twin daughters remained locked in their rooms. Nita had given a testimony that he'd abused her for their entire seven years together, and had threatened to kill her if she ever left him. He added even more fear by telling her that she'd see their daughters dead before he'd allowed her to take them from him. So Nita said she endured the abuse for the sake of her children. But on this dreadful day, her ex-husband would see his threats through by cutting each of his daughter's throats from ear to ear after slicing Nita's throat and stabbing her twenty-seven times all over her body.

Nita probably would have died hadn't the school gotten suspicious when the twin girls didn't show up for school that day. They knew of the abuse against Nita going on in the home from some of the things the twins would tell their classmates on the playground at school. To their knowledge, though, the children's father had never abused them. There wasn't much the police could do about the abuse against Nita without her cooperation. In addition, that was the day Nita was scheduled to volunteer in the school library, and she'd never missed a day she was scheduled to volunteer. If either she or the girls weren't going to make it to the school, Nita had always phoned and informed them. So the principal made the call to the local police and asked them to go check things out.

After three hours of negotiations, the police finally got her blood covered ex-husband to surrender and let them inside the house. When the police made it into the home, they were shocked to find such a massacre. They'd reported that all three stabbing victims were dead and awaited the coroner to arrive at the scene. To everyone's surprise, no sooner than the coroner was about to pronounce Nita dead, she took a breath and her eyes opened.

"A miracle," the coroner had told the media. "And I'm not a religious man by any means; never believed in all that God Almighty stuff before today. But I stand here a witness that this woman's survival was nothing short of a miracle. The police and EMTs didn't find a heartbeat or a pulse. I didn't find a heartbeat or a pulse, but yet we saw this woman rise up with our very own eyes. And thank God I had witnesses, or I'd commit myself to the nearest institution," the stunned coroner said before he concluded his interview with, "And if you want any more answers than what I've offered you, then you'll have to get them from God Himself."

Nita's survival had been a miracle. She'd lived through a twelve-hour attack, the slicing of her throat and twenty-seven stab wounds. And after weeks of healing and God restoring her, she'd have to live through the mourning of her two daughters, whose joint funeral she was unable to attend.

The town of Malvonia raised up, united and supported Nita by sending in their prayers, condolences, cards filled with money, setting up trust funds, and paying for counseling sessions for her. New Day held a one-month fundraiser which resulted in enough money to purchase Nita a condo and pay her bills for a year in advance. New Day's "Laborers Are Few" ministry helped her with some business courses that allowed her to find a trade, ultimately resulting in her owning her own business. So if anyone said they were blessed and highly favored and meant it, Nita was the one.

"Blessed and highly favored you are, Sister Nita," Deborah smiled. "By the way, have you seen the person who is driving that car?" Deborah pointed to the mystery car she had labeled as Helen's.

"Oh, yes. They are in the office with Pastor. It's a couple. I think they're doing marriage counseling or something."

"Oh," Deborah said confused. If it wasn't Helen's car, then that meant Helen hadn't shown up. "Thank you, Sister Nita," Deborah said as she turned toward the conference room to go retrieve her purse and notebook.

"No, problem, Sister Deborah. And you be blessed."

"Blessed I am, Sister Nita. Blessed I am." Deborah could breath again as she entered the conference room to collect her purse and notebook. She was so glad she'd repented to God for that comment about prayer not working. It obviously had worked as Helen was a no-show. "Thank you, God," Deborah said before scooping up her belongings, and then turning around to head out of the door. She'd taken only a single step before she froze in her tracks.

"Sorry, I'm late. It's something I'm working on, being on time that is." There stood Helen in the conference room doorway almost as surprised to see Deborah as Deborah was to see her. "I'm supposed to be meeting with Mother Doreen," Helen said, looking around. "Did she ask you to sit in or something?"

"Actually, Mother Doreen is not going to be able to make it and asked that I sit in for her," Deborah informed Helen, trying hard to hide her disappointment.

"Oh, is that so? And you agreed?" Helen picked.

"Of course, why wouldn't I?" Deborah swallowed hard, then pointed to a chair. "Please have a seat."

"Shall I close the door?" Helen asked.

"I was just going to go over some information regarding the Singles Ministry. You can leave it open unless you think you are going to speak on something confidential."

Helen thought for a minute. "I'll go ahead and close the door just in case. I mean, one never knows what might come out of my mouth," she taunted before closing the door and taking a seat at the conference table; two chairs down from where Deborah sat.

"Well, uh, why don't we start out with prayer?" Deborah asked.

"Sure," Helen shrugged, then followed Deborah's lead in standing.

Deborah made her way over to Helen and both hesitantly and nervously took the other's hands. To Deborah, Helen's hands were cold and slippery. Almost made Deborah want to gag. How could God put her in such a position to have to pray with this woman? It was so easy to do God's work when the package was wrapped up nice, neat, and pretty. Why wasn't it just as easy when the package didn't come looking like one thought it should?

"Dear Heavenly Father," Deborah prayed as the two women stood holding hands with eyes closed. After she finished, she made her way back over to her chair and sat down. Opening her notebook, Deborah began. "Well, first off, let me tell you a little bit about how the Singles Ministry was formed. Almost a year ago, Mother Doreen had a vision—"

Helen interrupted Deborah with a chuckle. "Are we really going to sit here and do this?" she asked. "Act like everything is gravy?"

"What do you mean?" Deborah asked.

"You know exactly what I mean," Helen spat, then leaned back in the chair comfortably. "So tell me, how are you and Mr. Chase coming along?"

"We're not," Deborah assured her. "Lynox and my relationship is strictly business."

"So you admit you did have a relationship?"

"Yes, I mean no, I mean . . . not like you think," Deborah stammered. Then in frustration she said, "I don't understand what this has to do with anything. You told Mother Doreen you were interested in learning about the New Day Singles Ministry, and that's what I'm here to talk about. Not anything else, especially not my involvement with Mr. Chase."

"Involvement? So you two are involved? I mean, why try to hide it? You don't want to end up like your little friend. What's her name, Tamarra? Look what happened to her when she tried to hide a relationship."

"For Pete's sake, I'm out of here!" Deborah stood, slamming her notebook closed, then standing.

Helen quickly blocked the conference room door. "Not so quickly," she told Deborah.

"Look," Deborah said, fed up. "I'm not playing your games any longer, Helen. As a matter of fact, I don't know why I've let you get to me this long. You are no better than I am." Deborah leaned in close to Helen and whispered. "Don't forget, you were there too." Deborah finally decided to fight fire with fire by reminding Helen that she wasn't such an innocent bystander all those years ago either.

"Yeah, but look at my situation, and look at yours. But anyway," Helen quickly decided to change the subject, "does Lynox know your dirty little secret?"

"Does he know yours?" Deborah shot back, straightening out her backbone.

"As a matter of fact, Lynox knows everything about me, and I him. I don't know what he's told you about me, but I've got that man's nose wide open. He still be ringing my phone. But I don't have the time of day for him. He's a dog just like the rest of them. That was obvious when I caught him sniffing around the trash." She looked Deborah up and down. "Anyway, don't be fooled, sweetie. He's a player. Whether you decide to hang around and get played is your business."

Deborah couldn't get past Helen insinuating that she was trash. "I'm sure a man like Lynox Chase can get any woman he wants, but rest assured, sweetheart, I am not that woman." Although it really wasn't necessary, once again Deborah wanted to fight fire with fire, and she did so by saying, "And I don't know when he has the time to ring your phone when he's constantly ringing mine."

"You trying to say I'm lying?" Helen said, pulling out her cell phone. She pushed a couple of buttons. She'd saved Lynox's number from the day he'd called her during the Singles Ministry meeting. She called herself pulling it up on her screen to tease Deborah. She held the phone up in Deborah's face.

Deborah's mouth dropped when she viewed the screen of Helen's phone. "So you're the one?"

"That's right. I'm the one standing in the way of you and Mr. Chase. But don't worry, honey. I don't want him anymore. You can have him. And when you're finished with him, I'm sure you'll throw him out too." A mischievous grin covered Helen's face. "After all, you know how we like to throw things out." A shrieking laugh escaped Helen's lips.

Deborah just continued staring at the cell phone screen, shaking her head. After a couple more seconds, she shoved Helen out of the way and stormed out of the conference room.

"I got the victor-victor-victory," Helen sang as she watched Deborah go storming out of the church. She'd expected to get a reaction from Deborah when she flashed Lynox's number on her phone, even though the message he'd left that evening was one last attempt to tell Helen that there was nothing between them, and to apologize if he had led her to believe there ever could be. But Deborah didn't have to know all that. Once again, Helen felt just showing Deborah proof that Lynox was still ringing her phone was enough, although she hadn't expected such a dramatic reaction.

Helen turned her phone back to her in order to put it back on its regular screen. That's when she realized why Deborah had reacted the way she had. With what Deborah had just seen on her phone, Helen knew she had to hurry up and think fast, or everything could blow up in her face.

Chapter Twenty-three

"I didn't see you in church this Sunday," Deborah said to Tamarra. "See, you're not the only one who can do drive-bys." Deborah smiled at Tamarra, then invited her into her humble abode.

"I'm not even going to lie to you and make up any excuses," Tamarra said, flopping down on her couch, wearing a night robe and scarf tied around her head. "I had absolutely no desire to be up in that place today at all."

Tamarra had a feeling someone was going to do a drive-by when she was a no-show at church today. Typically, Paige probably would have been right there on her doorstep too, but she had no idea that her best friend hadn't shown up for worship because she hadn't even been in church today. Today was one of those rare occasions where Paige had to go in to work. She'd made it a point to inform her superiors prior to their giving her a promotion that working on Sundays was out of the question. They honored Paige's wishes as best they could, but there were rare occasions, like today, when it was mandatory for her to be there.

"And to be even more truthful, I don't know if you'll see me up in that place next Sunday, or the Sunday after that either," Tamarra told Deborah. "The drama is just too much."

"Tamarra, don't say that." Deborah sat down next to her. "Don't even speak those words into the atmosphere for the devil to hear. That rascal will do every trick under the sun to make sure you keep good on that word."

"I can't help it. That's just how I'm feeling."

"Look, I know the whole thing with the pictures of you and Maeyl and the rumors and stuff are getting to you, but it soon shall pass. Troubles don't last always."

"But those pictures will. And so will the rumors and the lies." Tamarra beat her fist down on the couch. "And the hurt and the pain."

"Don't let church folks get to you. Don't let the people run you off. And don't hold the church accountable for the people inside of it. Remember, you're there for one thing; and that's to worship God." As the words spilled out of her mouth, Deborah knew that the message God was allowing to flow through her to give to Tamarra was for the messenger first. She, too, needed to take heed to those very words.

"It's not the people, Sister Deborah." Tamarra turned to look at her. "Not all of them, anyway. Just one to be specific." Tamarra shook her head. "I'm not really hurt about some of those diva-fied busy bodies up in New Day. It's Maeyl. I really wanted for him to be the one; not the one to hurt me."

"And he could be the one," Deborah assured her, resting her hand on her knee.

"Oh, no." Tamarra quickly stood up. "There is no way on God's green earth the good Lord would send someone to hurt me so bad; not twice. My ex did a good job of that himself. I didn't need Maeyl to pour salt in the wound. I mean, what could he have been thinking? I know he might have meant well; seizing the opportunity to let the world know he was kickin' it with a fine sista such as myself." Tamarra forced out a little joke to cover up her pain.

"Diva-fied," Deborah said. "Sounds to me like I'm sitting in the living room of a diva."

"Girl, I know . . . I'm just joking." Tamarra sat back down next to Deborah. "Trying to laugh to keep from crying. But I just don't understand what good Maeyl thought could possibly come out of posting those pictures of us on the church website. And on top of that, lying about it; saying that he's not the one who did it."

Just then, Deborah remembered the other reason why she was there. Not only to check in on Paige for not showing up at church, but to share with her the information she had regarding the pictures; information that initially she wasn't even going to tell Tamarra.

"About those pictures." Deborah stood up. "I know how they ended up on the church website, and I'm almost certain Maeyl didn't have anything to do with it at all."

Tamarra was all ears as she stood up as well. "Wha . . . what do you mean?" The thought that Tamarra had once again jumped to conclusions and shut Maeyl off for no good cause began to tug at her belly.

"I had a meeting with one of the members of the New Day congregation. She attended one of our singles meetings for the first time this past month and wanted to learn a little bit more about the ministry before officially joining. Mother Doreen was supposed to meet with her, but as you might know, she had to go back to Kentucky to see about her sick sister." Deborah paused.

"Yeah, but what does any of this have to do with me and Maeyl?" The anxiousness could be heard in Tamarra's voice.

"Well, during my meeting with the person, she accidentally showed me a display on her cell phone. I'm sure it wasn't the display she intended on showing me, but nonetheless, there it was, a picture of you and Maeyl. At first I thought, okay, maybe she just downloaded the picture from the website to her phone, but then I realized that it wasn't one of the pictures that was posted. But it was still you and Maeyl, nonetheless."

"But how can you be so sure she's the one who took the pictures?"

"Where else would she have gotten that picture? Besides, her character is a dead give-away. I have somewhat of a history with this woman. She has evil ways. I don't know; she could have even been trying to get to me by hurting my friends. Or maybe she's just trouble with a capital 'T'. I personally think she has some underlying issues." Deborah thought for a moment. "As a matter of fact, I know she has some underlying issues. She probably can't forgive herself about something, so she's taking it out on the world; on anyone who crosses her path."

"You sound like you know an awful lot about this person. Who is she?"

"Remember the woman who came into the last meeting late? Sister Helen?"

Tamarra thought for a minute. "Oh yeah. She's been attending New Day for a minute."

"Well, she's the one."

"But why? I don't understand. I've never said two words to that woman before," Tamarra pondered. Her emotions were that of confusion and curiosity. She had no idea why someone would do something so low. But then her emotions turned to anger. "I've got two words for her now though. Just wait until I confront Miss Thing and tell her a thing or two about herself. How she has perhaps destroyed the chances of me ever having a relationship with the man I love." Tamarra paused. Had she heard herself correctly? Had she just confessed her love for Maeyl? Not spending too much time on that thought, her anger arose once again. "I'm going to go slip something on, and then we're going to go hunt down Miss Helen." Tamarra began to untie her robe as she headed for her back bedroom.

"Wait! Tamarra, this has to be done decently and in order."

"I know," Tamarra agreed, still storming down her hallway. "I'm about to go get myself decent, so we can go bring some order to that crazy, deranged mind of hers."

"That's not what I mean, Tamarra." Deborah made her way toward Tamarra. "We can't operate off of our emotions and flesh. We have to address this situation correctly." Deborah studied Tamarra's facial expression to see if her words were sink-ing in. They appeared to be. "With the way you are feeling right now, how can you possibly hear from the Holy Sprit over your loud and boisterous flesh?"

Tamarra's shoulders slumped as she released some tension. "I suppose you're right. But Deborah, if you think I can just sit back and—"

"Turn the other cheek like the Bible says," Deborah finished her sentence.

"Let this go," Tamarra finished her own sentence. "I can't."

"I'm not asking you to let this go. I'm just asking you to let God. Let God guide you. First and foremost, I know we need to share it with Pastor. The church may have some type of procedure in place to deal with things like this; people like this. We don't know. So let's go to the shepherd of the house and see what Pastor has to say. Amen?"

Tamarra hesitated, but then reluctantly said, "Amen."

It was as if Deborah could breathe again. "Thank God. Because I haven't fought since Big Belina in eighth grade. And even then she kicked my butt. I did not want to have to have your back and chance another beat down."

The women erupted in laughter and embraced.

"Girl, you got my back in more ways than one. You just helped me to upper cut the devil and knock his tail right out." Tamarra pretended to be upper cutting an opponent in the boxing ring.

"Now that's the kind of fighting I can do," Deborah said as she shouted, "Praise God! Jab."

"Hallelujah. Low blow!"

"Worthy is the Lamb! Left jab."

The two women danced around the hallway punching the air and fighting the devil with their praise. Throwing blow after blow until they were confident that Satan was flat on his back and they could declare the victory.

***

After Deborah and Tamarra finished up their bout with the devil, they decided to go grab something to eat, since they'd both worked up an appetite. Tamarra was following Deborah in her car, as after their meal, she had some business to take care of.

Deborah led the way to the restaurant they'd decided upon, feeling as though she'd just defeated the heavy weight champion of the world. She was on cloud nine.

Ever since seeing that picture of Tamarra and Maeyl on Helen's cell phone, Deborah had thought long and hard about whether to share it with Tamarra. She knew what ratting Helen out could mean. It could mean payback on Helen's part. But Deborah had prayed on it, and in her spirit, she knew she couldn't just sit by and let someone sabotage the people at her place of worship, even if it meant sacrificing herself. So she made it up in her mind that she'd tell Tamarra what she knew at church on Sunday, then ultimately they'd have to take it to the pastor.

When Deborah didn't see Tamarra at church on Sunday, she suspected why. She, herself, had allowed people to keep her from the temple not too many Sundays ago. She knew she had to go see about Tamarra the same way Tamarra had come to see about her. On the way to Tamarra's house she'd prayed the entire time, non-stop, not allowing the devil any room to talk her out of doing what she knew was right.

As Deborah drove toward the restaurant, she felt relieved, in spite of what Helen might do once she and Tamarra took the incident to the pastor. "Hopefully she'll run back to the pits of hell where she belongs." Deborah chuckled out loud before repenting.

Meanwhile, following close behind Deborah, Tamarra was in total bliss as well. She was thankful the truth had been revealed, not just about who had posted the pictures to the church website, but the truth about her feelings for Maeyl. She couldn't wait to get to his apartment after she and Deborah ate.

Prayerfully, he could find it in his heart, once again, to forgive her.

Tamarra began to dig down in her purse when she heard her cell phone ringing. Without bothering looking at the caller ID, she answered. "Hello."

"Tamarra, honey, it's me, Mama."

"Hello, Mom," Tamarra said cheerfully. Not even a phone call from her mother could steal her joy today. "How are you today?"

"I'm doing good, sweetheart," her mother said, surprised at how courteous her daughter was being. Usually she had to press to get words out of her daughter's mouth, and when she did, they weren't always words spoken so kindly and gently. "You sound good today."

"Mother, I am good today, because God is good."

"Well, I'm glad to hear that. I need to talk to you about something. Maybe that God of yours has softened your heart enough to receive it. I need to talk to you about your brother." The line was silent with the exception of a far off crashing sound and brakes screeching, followed by a loud scream. "Tamarra? Tamarra, honey, are you all right? Tamarra, say something. Say something, please," her mother cried into the phone until it went dead.

Chapter Twenty-four

"Doctor, is she going to be okay?" Tamarra asked in a panicked voice. "I mean, we had just left my house not five minutes before it happened. I was following her, then all of a sudden she just went off the road. I slammed on my breaks and just screamed."

"Tamarra!" she heard someone yell out, then turned to see the face of the first person she thought to call. "How is she?"

"Oh, Maeyl, I don't know," Tamarra replied. "The doctor was just about to update me on her condition." Tamarra turned her attention back to the doctor. "I'm sorry, Doctor, this is a brother from church." The doctor shook Maeyl's hand. "You were saying, Doctor?"

"Well, like I was saying, Miss Lucas appears to be fine. She's lucky that the ambulance that brought her here was on route back to the hospital when the driver saw Miss Lucas's car veer off the road and into the ditch."

"I know, and I was in such a panic, I couldn't be any help to them. They ended up taking me back to my car just to get my praying, hooping and hollering self out of their way."

"Well, I'm glad you calmed down enough to be able to make it here to see about your friend. Anyway, besides a knot on her forehead and a busted lip, she looked fine. But the EMTs on the scene made the call to bring her in to X-ray the knot just to be on the safe side."

"And the knot?" Tamarra asked. "Is it serious? Does she have a concussion or anything?"

"Oh, no. Everything is fine. It's nothing a Ziploc bag of ice can't take care of. So in short, Miss Lucas is going to be fine."

"Thank you, Jesus!" Tamarra let out the breath she'd been holding for the last forty-five minutes and collapsed into Maeyl's arms. "Praise God."

"I do have some bad news though," the doctor added.

"What it is, Doctor?" Tamarra asked.

"Unfortunately, the squirrel she was trying to dodge didn't make it." The doctor winked, and then walked off after telling Tamarra that her friend was being discharged and should be out in about a half hour.

"God's grace and mercy is so sufficient. Yes, it is," Tamarra declared as Maeyl escorted her over to a chair in the waiting area. He then sat down next to her. "Thank you so much for coming."

"No problem. I called Pastor like you asked me to. As a matter of fact, I should call back since Deborah is already being discharged. No need in Pastor wasting gas to come up to the hospital." Maeyl placed the quick phone call, and then hung up the phone. "I tell you, I was scared to death when you first called me. All I heard were the words 'car accident,' 'Mount Carmel' Hospital, and 'come now.' I'm glad you called me back to let me know what was going on once you'd settled down. Until you did, I thought you had been the one in the accident."

"I was just so freaked out. I mean, she'd just left my house where we had been shouting and praising the Lord. I guess when praises go up, blessings do come down. Because it is a true blessing that she's okay."

"Well, I'm glad you got your praise on today after all, seeing that you weren't in church."

"Yeah, well, about that," Tamarra started, searching for the right words. "Maeyl, can I talk to you?"

"I think we do need to talk."

"I know you're probably starting to think that my first name is 'I'm' and last name 'Sorry.' But once again I have to humble myself and apologize for my behavior, when I stormed out of your living room without explanation. And then avoided your calls like the plague. I've really been acting like a part-time Christian lately."

"You've got that right."

Tamarra was shocked at Maeyl's stern response. But she knew his statement was nothing but more confirmation of what she already knew.

"And I'm sorry for that. It's just that when you had me check your cell phone to see if that was Pastor's call you had missed, I pushed a couple of buttons trying to clear the screen, and that picture of us that was on the website was on your phone. My mind started thinking up all kinds of things. I honestly thought without a doubt that you were the one who had posted the pictures. But then Sister Deborah came to my house today and shared with me that she'd found out the true culprit. You don't know how awful I felt."

"If you felt as bad as I did when I thought that, once again, the woman of my dreams had somehow slipped out of my life, then you're wrong. I do know how awful you felt."

"Maeyl, why are you like this? So forgiving? You don't even make me work for your forgiveness. I'd feel a lot better if you'd at least show some kind of a grudge."

"I'm only operating the way my Lord and Savior would have me," Maeyl reasoned. "Remember how many times the Bible says we must forgive a man?"

"Seven times seventy," Tamarra answered.

"And on top of that, God doesn't make us have to work for His forgiveness. It's automatic once we ask. And who has time to hold a grudge? As a man of God, I try my best to walk in love daily, and sometimes that means forgiving those who we don't even feel deserve forgiveness?"

"So are you saying that I don't deserve your forgiveness?" Tamarra asked softly.

"Would that make you feel better if I said you didn't?" Maeyl smiled.

"Perhaps," Tamarra teased.

"Well, sorry. I cannot lie; not even to make you feel good. You deserve forgiveness, Tamarra, and I forgive you."

"Thank you, Maeyl, and I really am sorry. I'm so sorry for once again jumping to conclusions."

"Once again, apology accepted. But tell me, who is the real culprit?"

Tamarra proceeded to give him the details. But with curiosity still getting the best of her, Tamarra asked, "But can I ask you one thing? Why did you have the picture on your cell phone?"

"Well, when the church secretary couldn't get me on either my home phone or my cell phone, she decided to send me a text message along with the picture to download. I simply had forgotten to delete it." Maeyl paused for a moment. "I take that back. That's a lie. I didn't forget to delete it. I didn't want to delete it. Heck, you looked kind of cute in that picture."

Tamarra blushed before planting a kiss on Maeyl's cheek. This was the first time she'd ever laid lips on him, and it felt good. "I'm gonna go over to the vending machine and grab a Mountain Dew. Would you like anything?"

"No, I'm good," Maeyl replied.

"All right," Tamarra said, then stood up with her purse in hand. That's when she saw Paige heading toward her. She'd forgotten that she had also called Paige and told her about Deborah's car accident. She realized that perhaps she should have called Paige back and told her not to come to the hospital when Maeyl called Pastor. It was too late now.

"I left work as soon as Norman showed up to fill in for me," Paige explained, hugging Tamarra. "I didn't have any business working on a Sunday no how," Paige fussed at herself. "Now God done made a way to pull me out of that place, although I wish it had been under different circumstances. How is Sister Deborah anyway?"

"She's fine," Tamarra replied. "Just a bump on the head

pretty much. The emergency squad just wanted to take precautions and bring her here for X-rays. Everything is fine."

"Thank God," Paige said as she hugged Tamarra. That's when she saw Maeyl sitting nearby. "Uh, hi, Brother Maeyl," Paige said, then looked at Tamarra in an attempt to study her face to make sure she was okay with Maeyl being there. Tamarra had told her about how she was really finished with him this time after discovering the picture from the website on his phone. But when Tamarra shot Paige the "it's okay" look, Paige figured everything had been worked out.

"Hello, Sister Paige." Maeyl stood, then looked at Tamarra. "I'm going to go now that Sister Paige is here."

"All right, Maeyl. I'll call you. And thanks again for coming." For the second time, Tamarra allowed her lips to rest on Maeyl's cheek. "Drive safely."

It was a toss up between Maeyl and Paige as to who was more shocked by Tamarra's show of public affection in front of someone they knew. Maeyl exited the hospital.

"Did I just see you plant a pucker on that man's face?" Paige asked.

"Yes, you did," Tamarra said proudly as she looked around the hospital. "And hopefully someone got a picture of that."

The women high-fived as they waited for Deborah to be discharged. Tamarra filled her best friend in on all of the past couple hours developments. She praised God the entire time, thanking Him that everything had worked out for her good in the end. But when Paige then turned the conversation to her and Blake and how quickly their relationship was moving along, Tamarra realized that *almost* everything had worked out for her good in the end—almost.

There was still a tad bit of information she'd withheld from Paige. It was information regarding what Paige referred to as her divine set-up. Hopefully everything would work out for good in that situation as well. Now if only Tamarra could find just the right time to tell her before things between Paige and

Chapter Twenty-five

"I was scared out of my mind. Your father and I were five minutes from taking the next flight to Ohio."

Tamarra had forgotten all about the fact that she'd been talking to her mom right before Deborah decided that a squirrel's life was more valuable than her BMW and ran off the road in a failed attempt at avoiding the little critter. With all of the excitement of being at the hospital, making up with Maeyl, and her issue with Paige, she'd forgotten to call her poor, worried sick mother.

"Oh, Mom, I'm so sorry," Tamarra told her, then filled her in on all that had happened. "I didn't mean to worry you or Dad." Although Tamarra was still trying to keep her spirits up, a part of her wanted to get indignant with her mother and ask her why she was so worried about her well being now when she should have been worried over twenty-five years ago.

"Well, is your friend all right?"

"Yes, she's fine. Only suffered a knot on her head. Her car even ended up being okay once the tow truck pulled it out of the ditch. I drove her to it once they released her from the hospital."

"Well, look at what God did for you."

"Yeah, He is something," Tamarra said. "Well, Mom, it's been a long, long day, and I have a brunch to cater tomorrow. I'd best lay it down and get some shut eye." Tamarra wasn't really tired. She was just attempting to keep her spirits up, and she knew that if her mother resumed the topic of conversation she was about to bring up prior to their phone conversation being cut short, Tamarra's spirit would pop like a balloon blown up beyond capacity, then deflate accordingly.

"Well, okay, dear. I understand." Tamarra could hear the disappointment in her mother's voice. It was evident her sweet hopes of resuming the conversation had just turned bitter. "Can you call me tomorrow after your catering affair?"

"Sure, Mom," Tamarra lied. "Talk to you tomorrow." Tamarra hung up the phone, then folded her arms in prayer. "Lord, I just got over one huge hurdle. Please spare me a little time to be refilled with your strength before I'm faced with an even bigger one; one that I know has been a long time coming."

On the following Wednesday after Bible Study, Deborah and Tamarra met with Pastor and reported the information about what Deborah had seen on Helen's cell phone. Pastor said that before any further steps were taken or before Helen was confronted with the matter, everything needed to be reported to and addressed with the New Day board members. Pastor then wanted time for the board to look into things further, see if they could find a way to confirm that the pictures had actually been posted from Helen's phone. There had to be some type of technology that could prove their claim.

In the meantime, Pastor asked Tamarra if she would be able to deal with attending services with Helen until the investigation was over. At first Tamarra was set on putting up a fight, thinking the pastor was just trying to save face and avoid confrontation with Helen. But then the Holy Spirit reminded her of how many mistakes she had made without properly looking into things. How she'd been falsely accused of things without anyone bothering to look into them on her behalf. She imagined she'd want the same type of respect.

She agreed that Pastor and the board members were

right to want to be clear on everything before they went accusing anyone of anything. So she decided to let things go and let God. After all, it seemed as though whenever she did that, things always worked in her favor. For once she wanted to know what it felt like to be out of God's way and in God's will.

Deborah purposely neglected telling Pastor about how Helen had been taunting her. Telling Pastor would more than likely mean revealing every little thing dating back to four years ago. She'd vowed she'd never do that. She'd never speak on it; not even with God. Besides, she didn't want Pastor to think she was going on some kind of witch hunt against Helen. If Deborah got her way, Helen would be so embarrassed and ashamed once Pastor and the board confronted her about the pictures, that she'd find a new place of worship anyhow. Then Deborah's little secret could stay swept under the rug just like it had been.

It all sounded like the perfect plan, but unfortunately, God's plan isn't always man's plan. This was one of those times. Sooner or later, it was God's plan for Deborah to finally face her past demons . . . and Him.

Chapter Twenty-six

Paige and Blake headed up Interstate 70 toward her parents' house for only the second time in their now almost six months of dating. Blake had practically insisted that Paige arrange for them to go up one Saturday and just hang out with her parents. He'd told her that two major holidays had passed since he'd met her parents, Thanksgiving and Christmas (three if counting New Year's), and he'd yet to spend some real quality time with her mother and father.

Although Paige could almost always bear to stay away from her father for as long as possible, she loved spending time with her mother. But no matter how much time she spent with her mother as an adult, she knew it couldn't make up for all the times she'd wanted to spend with her as a child . . . but couldn't. Usually she never got any alone time with her mother, but this time Blake had asked Paige to hint around to her father that he'd like for him to take him over to the construction company and show him the ropes a little bit.

Mr. Robinson was more than happy to oblige. Although retired, he still had a great deal of control over the company, making it a point to visit the establishment or one of its sites daily just to stay on top of things. For the first time since Paige could remember, this would give her an opportunity to have some alone time with her mother. No interruptions by her father's yelling out orders from another room.

"You nervous?" Paige asked Blake as he drove with her on

the passenger side. It was all like déjà vu; everything, right down to Blake's nervous silence.

"No," he replied without letting two seconds go by before recanting. "I take that back. I lied. I repent. I'm nervous as heck."

Paige laughed. "I knew it."

"It's that obvious, huh?"

"You haven't said two words in the last ten minutes. But this time I can't imagine why you'd be nervous. You've already met my parents, and they love you. My mom adores you, and my dad adores anyone who is willing to relinquish their Saturday afternoon to hear all about his thirty-five years in the construction business."

"I guess I'm just rehearsing in my head what to say."

"What do you mean rehearsing what to say? Just be yourself. That's the person who they already know and like."

"Yeah, you're right," Blake said with a smile as he tapped Paige's knee, then allowed his hand to rest on it momentarily.

Paige felt a tingling sensation throughout her body. She hadn't felt that way since the last time Blake had touched her; when she had finally confessed to him the secret she'd been keeping from him, which was the fact that she was still a virgin. Unbelievably, a twenty-seven-year-old virgin. She had been so embarrassed, initially not being a virgin by choice, but because she'd never dated a man long enough for him to get up to bat, let alone any bases. But after getting saved, Paige had been glad that she had not sinned against God with her body.

Ever since sharing such personal information with Blake, he had been very mindful not to do anything that might arouse either one of them in the wrong way. He wanted to respect both her Christianity and her virginity.

As soon as Blake pulled up in Paige's parents' driveway, her dad came barging out of the house with his jacket on. "You 'bout ready?" he said to Blake, shaking his hand.

"Dang, Daddy. Can we go inside and at least say hi to Mama," Paige asked him.

"Oh, she'll be there when we get back. Blake can say hi to her then." He then looked to Blake. "Ain't that right?"

Blake shrugged, wishing he could shake off his nervousness. He at least wanted to go inside and pray before venturing out with Paige's father, especially knowing that what he really wanted to discuss with the man had nothing to do with the construction business whatsoever.

While Blake and Paige's father had immediately headed off for her father to begin showing Blake the ins and outs of the construction business, Paige remained at the house with her mom. The two women were in the kitchen. Paige's mother stood at the counter placing the ingredients for a cake in the bowl. Paige sat at the kitchen table nibbling on a couple of slices of the ham her mother had prepared.

"Mom, why don't you come sit down and rest? That will give us time to talk. Besides, you said yourself you've been up since six this morning, and now you're over there slaving over some cake."

"Oh, I'm fine. I want to get this cake made before your father gets back."

"Figures," Paige mumbled under her breath as she sank her teeth into a piece of ham and yanked like a dog at feeding. She was more than just a little bit perturbed that even in her adult years she couldn't get her mother to pull herself away from doing something for her father long enough to have a five-minuteconversation.

"What was that?" Paige's mother asked.

Paige hadn't meant to make her snide comment as loud as she had. It was just intended for her ears; her own release. But obviously she hadn't expressed herself in a low enough tone. "Nothing, Mom," Paige said at first as she stood to go into the living room, but then decided she'd bitten her tongue long enough. She was a grown woman, and her mother would just have to accept it; that her daughter had an opinion, a voice, and that she'd never end up like her. "Actually, Mom, I did say something. I said 'it figures.'"

"What figures?" Her mother continued mixing without even looking up at Paige.

"It figures that you'd rather stand over there until you collapse just to please Daddy instead of take five lousy minutes to devote to a conversation with your daughter." Paige felt moisture running down her cheeks and couldn't believe she had worked up tears.

"Oh, honey, you sound like a spoiled brat," her mother said, still not looking up.

"Spoiled kids get doted with attention and everything they want. I grew up anything but spoiled. I couldn't even get my own mother to teach me how to use a tampon. You know who had to teach me how to use one, Mother? Sylvia from next door. And she was a year younger than me. She'd already had her period a year and her mother had taught her how to use one. I cried so hard that day in Sylvia's bathroom. She didn't know I was a virgin. That's when she told me I should use Maxi Pads. And you know what? I'm still a virgin. I bet you didn't even know that about me, did you, Mom?"

By now Paige had tears streaming down her face. She was sniffling and snotting. Shoulders heaving. Of course, her mother was now giving her daughter her undivided attention.

"Honey . . . I . . . I—"

"You're what?" Paige stood up in frustration. "Sorry you allowed Dad to force you to be at his beck and call. And while you were so miserable slaving for him you missed out on the time with your daughter?"

Mrs. Robinson dropped the mixing spoon into the bowl. "Force? Sweetheart, I don't know what you've been thinking all of these years, but I love your father, and I love doing things for him. He's never forced me to do anything a day in my life. I don't always say the words 'I love you' to your father, so my way of showing him versus telling him is doing things for him. I love pleasing my man," her mother assured her.

"Mom, you can save it, because I saw your face that day. I saw how good it made you feel the first time you all met Blake and he offered to get you a dinner roll instead of you jumping up and down like a jack-in-the box doing for everybody else."

"You're right, it did make me feel good. It made me feel good for you."

Paige was confused now, and it showed all over her face.

"Sit down, sweetie, and let me explain something to you," her mother said.

The two women sat down at the table. Mrs. Robinson took her daughter's hands into her own. "I know how you are. 'Spite the house you grew up in and how you witnessed my relationship with your father, I knew you'd never be like me. God didn't cut you from the same cloth as me. He cut you from the same cloth as your father."

"I'm nothing like Dad." Paige was appalled at the fact that her mother could even make such a comparison.

"Oh, but you are." Mrs. Robinson smiled while patting Paige's hand tenderly. "You're strong like your father. You're independent like your father, and you always know what you want like your father. And that's okay, honey. There is nothing wrong with that, but at the same time, you have to know your role as a woman. And from the bottom of my heart, I honestly thought that was the example I was displaying to you all those years. I had no idea you thought I was allowing myself to be some doormat. I love your father, and when God blesses you with a man whom you love the way I love your dad, you'll happily want to do all those things for him as well. And you'll do them cheerfully."

Paige could tell that her mother wasn't just feeding her a line. She could tell that she meant every word she was speaking. And come to think of it, Paige couldn't recall one time when she had ever heard her mother complaining about anything she did for her father. Seems like Paige had been the one doing all the complaining.

"I'm sorry, Mom," Paige apologized. "I guess I just never looked at things that way. I guess I was just too busy being jealous."

"But you had nothing to be jealous of, Paige."

"I was jealous of Daddy. He had you. Brandon had Daddy, and I had no one."

"Dear, you always had me. It's just that every time I invited you to do something with me, you declined."

"Yeah, but it was always domestic things. Wanting me to go grocery shopping with you to pick out a list of things Daddy had requested. Wanting me to help make dinner with you; something Daddy had requested. Wanting me to sew or stitch something up; something of Daddy's."

"But those are the things a mother is supposed to do with her daughter; shop, cook and sew. I just figured you were a tomboy . . . or gay," Mrs. Robinson added.

"Mom!" Paige said. "You didn't."

"I did," she confessed. "Now I know all that fasting wasn't even needed."

"I honestly can't believe you thought I was gay."

"Well, what was I suppose to think? Seemed like you wanted to spend more time with your brother, Brandon, than you did me. Heck, I have to admit, I used to be a little jealous myself."

"Why didn't you say something then, Mom?"

Mrs. Robinson paused for a minute. "I guess the same reason why you never said anything to me." She shrugged.

Paige shook her head. "Mom, I could kick myself. All these years wasted."

"Girl, please. We ain't wasted nothing. For all these years, I've loved you to death. For all these years, I've adored everything about my little girl. I love you, Paige."

"I love you too, Mom," Paige said as she embraced her mother.

"All right. Let me get back to this cake." Mrs. Robinson stood up.

"And don't forget to save me the bowl."

"No matter how old you get, you always gonna lick the cake bowl, just like—"

"I know," Paige finished her mother's sentence with a smile, "just like my father." Paige's mother winked, then turned her attention back to the preparation of the cake.

Paige sat at the table and came to the conclusion that the person she had tried to avoid finding in a man; demeaning all their characteristics as flawed, just happened to be the person whom she was . . . her father.

When Blake and Mr. Robinson came through the front door, Paige and her mother had just finished their conversation and were putting icing on the cake.

"You two back already?" Mrs. Robinson called out from the kitchen.

"What do you mean already?" her husband replied. "We've been gone for hours."

Paige looked up at the kitchen clock. "It's only been a couple of hours, Daddy."

"Well, it seemed like forever." He excitedly rubbed his hands together, and then threw Blake a look. "I couldn't wait to get back home so that . . ."

Blake shot Mr. Robinson a stern look and tried to inconspicuously shake his head.

"Couldn't wait to get back for what, honey?" Mrs. Robinson curiously inquired.

Paige's father looked over at Blake for help. He figured that since he had cut his sentence off, he should be the one to finish it, and that's exactly what Blake did.

"Uh, he couldn't wait to get back to get some of that cake," Blake stammered, pointing at the two-layer cake with cream cheese icing. "He kept going on and on about the generational recipe for that cake."

Both Paige and her mother glanced at each other with peculiar looks on their faces.

"Samuel, you know darn well I make cakes from the box," Mrs. Robinson said. "There ain't no family recipe for cakes; not that I know of anyway."

This time Blake looked at Mr. Robinson for help. Paige and her mother suspiciously watched them exchange looks.

"Okay, that's it," Paige said, laying her rubber spatula down. "What are you two up to?"

The men looked at each other, and almost as if Mr. Robinson was going to burst wide open, he blurted, "Blake's got something to tell you, sweetie," he said to Paige. "Or should I say, ask you?" He elbowed Blake a couple of times, putting him on the spot.

Everyone's eyes were frozen on Blake. "Well, uh, Paige, the real reason why I wanted to come visit your parents was so that I could spend time with your father. I'm a traditional, old school man in some ways, and I believe in one tradition that's worth keeping. I know the day we have a daughter together, I'd want the guy she's serious about to show me the same respect." Blake looked at Mr. Robinson who gave him a nod and another elbow to hurry him on. "With that being said, Paige, with the blessing of God first, and now your father . . ." Blake paused as he dug a small box from his inside coat pocket.

"Oh, dear," Mrs. Robinson gasped. It was now very clear the purpose of Paige and Blake's visit.

"Blake . . ." were the only words Paige could get out of her mouth before she choked back tears.

Getting down on one knee, Blake opened the box. "Paige Renea Robinson, the woman who I know, that I know, that I know I found only through the grace of God, the woman who I know, that I know, that I know was formed from my rib . . ." Now Blake was choking back tears. "Would you mar—"

"Yes! Yes!" Paige screamed before Blake could even get

the full question out of his mouth. "Yes, I'll marry you, my Boaz." Paige got down on her knees and threw her arms around Blake's neck, squeezing tightly.

Blake steadied to keep his balance as well as hold on to his new fiancée. "Sweetheart? Sweetheart?" he spoke in between Paige's cries. "Calm down. Calm down." Blake managed to peel Paige's arms from around his neck and look her in the eyes. "Let me finish the question." He took the ring out of the box and held it with his index finger and thumb. "Paige, sweetheart, will you do me the honor of being my wife?"

This time Paige didn't respond at all. She was too fixated on the two-carat diamond ring that Blake held.

"Paige? Paige?" Her mother had to call her name two more times, and then walk over and nudge her before she was brought out of her trance. "Answer the man," Mrs. Robinson instructed her daughter with furrowed eyebrows.

Paige tore her eyes from the ring long enough to look up at Blake and reply, "I will, Blake Dickenson. I will honor both you and myself by being your wife. In Jesus' name, I will," Paige cried as Blake slid the ring on her finger.

Blake wiped Paige's falling tears as she stared down at the ring, shaking her head as if she couldn't believe this moment was happening.

"Now how about we eat some of that cake your father was so anxious to get home to," Blake joked as everyone laughed.

"I'll get some plates," Mrs. Robinson said.

"No, Mom, you all sit down," Paige insisted, "I'll get it." Paige walked over to her father who was taking his seat at the table. "And, Dad, I'll get you the biggest piece so that I don't have to get up twice to get you another one." She leaned down and wrapped her arms around her father and kissed his cheek.

"You know your pops like a book, huh?" Mr. Robinson said, lovingly patting his daughter's cheek.

"Why shouldn't I? After all, I'm just like you." Paige looked over at her mother and winked, then made her way over to the cabinet to get some plates.

"I'll help you," Blake stated.

"Knives are in that drawer right there." Paige pointed and Blake followed her directions and retrieved a knife to cut the cake.

As the two stood over the cake, Blake slicing and Paige holding the saucers for him to put the cake slices on, Mr. and Mrs. Robinson sat at the table holding hands. Paige couldn't remember the last time she'd seen her father show her mother that type of affection. She surmised that she probably couldn't see it before because she was too blinded by the log that was in her eye while trying to pluck the splinter from her father's eye.

"I can't wait to tell Tamarra, Deborah, and the women at the Singles Ministry," Paige said with excitement as Blake cut a huge slice of cake, for Paige's father. He placed it on one of the saucers.

Blake didn't reply. He cleared his throat before saying, "Paige, your father was right; I had something to both tell you and ask you."

Paige was uncomfortable with the tone of Blake's voice. "What is it, Blake?"

"It's about a question your father asked me the last time we were here. About my purchasing two tickets to the movies."

Paige placed her finger over Blake's lips. "Baby, that is the past. I don't care about the woman you had arranged to meet that night. All I care about is the woman God arranged for you to meet that night."

"But—"

"Hey, what's the hold up on that cake?" Mr. Robinson shouted. "You love birds snap out of it. You'll have plenty of years for that mess."

"Coming, Dad, coming," Paige said as she walked her father's piece of cake to him, then returned to Blake to get the other pieces. Unbeknownst to Paige, who had carried a secret she'd kept from Blake hoping it wouldn't interfere with the progress of their relationship, Blake now stood with a secret of his own, praying that it wouldn't interfere with them moving forward with marriage.

Chapter Twenty-seven

"Hear my cry, oh Lord. Don't turn your face far from me."

From the very second Deborah heard those words from Micah Stampley's CD fill the sanctuary, she gasped. The girl representing the New Day dance ministry with a solo performance was interpreting every word of the song with arm and leg movements as well as facial expressions.

Deborah watched intensely as the girl beckoned God to hear her prayer and not turn His face from her in her time of trouble. There had been so many times Deborah thought God had turned His face from her, and with good reason; starting with the obvious reason she gave Him over four years ago. How could He even stand to look at her when most days, whenever she thought about that dreadful act of her past, she couldn't even stand to look at herself? She was sure He'd turned His face from her . . . she was sure of it. But even so, she wasn't going to turn her face from Him. It had taken her long enough to make this decision, but it was final. She would spend the rest of her days repenting somehow, someway, to her Father in heaven. There were so many times she had wanted to beg and plead with God, just as the dancer seemed to be doing before her.

"You okay, sister?" a gentleman sitting next to Deborah asked as he kindly rested his hand on top of her shivering hand. He'd noticed her slight trembling. He'd even noticed the tears spilling down her face and staining her silk top before she had noticed it herself.

Deborah looked down, for the first time realizing how out of control her limbs appeared to be. Her hands were shaking. Her knee was bouncing and she felt as light as a feather. She looked at the man. She wanted to tell him that she was okay, but the words wouldn't come out. Besides that, it would have been a lie. She wasn't okay. She hadn't been okay in years. She'd only made things appear as if they were okay. But now, as a chill ran through her body and she trembled even more, she felt cold; like the covers were being pulled off of her on the coldest night of the year.

"Lord, in the name of Jesus, give this sister whose hand I hold peace in her mind. Peace in her body," the man automatically began to pray when he saw that Deborah was too moved to verbally respond to him.

While the man closed out his short, whispered, but powerful prayer, Deborah turned her attention back to the liturgical dancer who was now begging and pleading with God to deliver her from the hands of her enemy. The girl's head was bowed and her arms were extended as if she herself were nailed to a cross. She jerked her body from left to right as if the enemy was on each side of her pulling, tugging, and consuming her. Then all of a sudden the girl broke free and raised her arms up to heaven in victory. It was her sign of the deliverance she had received as a result of her cry out to the Lord. The girl repeated the movement again and again, as if there was more than just one thing, more than just one situation and stronghold, she had to be delivered from. On the fourth time around, the music got stronger, the pleas of Micah Stampley got more demanding, and this time when the dancer broke free and raised her arms to heaven, so did Deborah.

"Glory!" Deborah began to shout as she stood straight up from her seat. "Deliver me, Lord," she cried out. "Deliver me from my enemies. Deliver me from my pain. Deliver me from my guilt. From my shame. Glory! Thank you, Lord. Thank you, Lord. You heard my cry, oh Lord. I know you did. I know you did." Never had Deborah cried out in such a manner before. She had always gotten her praise and worship on; handclapping, shouting, and stomping, honoring God in spirit and in truth, but never had she just given up control of herself and turned her spirit over to the Lord.

"Cleanse me, oh God!" Deborah pleaded. "Hide me and protect me from my troubles, God. Don't turn away from me. Help me, God! Please come see about me, Heavenly Father. Forgive me, Lord. I repent to you, oh God. I took a life, oh Lord, and I'm not the author of life, God; you are. I'm sorry, God! Please forgive me!"

Some members of New Day began to shout and praise God right along with Deborah. They couldn't help themselves as they witnessed the deliverance the dancer had only interpreted actually manifest itself before their eyes. Others shot each other looks as if to say, "Did she just say she took a life?"

Tamarra stood behind Deborah with a prayer cloth, waiting to cover her once she began to rest in the Spirit. Tears of joy flowed down Tamarra's face. There was nothing more she enjoyed witnessing than one of her brothers or sisters in Christ getting their breakthrough. And there was something about a breakthrough that was contagious as other members began to release and cry out to God. The Holy Spirit was definitely filling the temple.

"Thank you for my sister's breakthrough," Tamarra cried out. "Thank you, Lord! Hallelujah! Hallelujah! Thank you, Lord. I love you, Lord. I praise your name." Tamarra was filled with so much joy. Whatever it was that Deborah had been keeping inside of her, she was now finally releasing it. Like the song said, she'd cried out to God and He'd answered her prayer speedily. She'd received an instantaneous breakthrough. And even though Tamarra was excited and happy for Deborah, she was even more excited for herself, because deep down inside she knew that if God would do it for Deborah, then He would do it for her. Her breakthrough was coming too; of that she was sure

Chapter Twenty-eight

"I made a complete fool of myself," Deborah said as she paced back and forth in front of her living room couch. "I'm never going back to that church again. Any church for that matter."

Deborah couldn't believe she had acted in such a manner in front of the entire congregation. She didn't remember much about the last half hour prior to her arriving back home, but she did remember collapsing on the ground with her skirt flailing in the air. And when she awoke, Pastor was preaching, and she was lying in the middle of the aisle with a prayer cloth covering her. She had sat up, and two people helped her stand. She didn't even look up to see the faces of the persons who had come to her aid. She was too embarrassed. She'd felt like a fool. Here she was lying out on the floor. No telling how much of her business the church had seen or heard, and church seemed to be going on as usual.

She'd seen people fall out in the Spirit before. She'd even been one of those helping hands to get them to their feet after they had rested in the Spirit, but for it to have happened to her; Lord have mercy. Was she that bad off in life? Deborah had always thought that those people who fell out in the Spirit like that were just doing too much. Although Deborah never condemned them in any way, she just felt as though it didn't take all of that to get a praise on, or a breakthrough for that matter. But then again, what Deborah experienced wasn't just a praise. It wasn't just a breakthrough. It had been deliverance. She had to admit that she felt a hundred pounds lighter, as if she'd left weight back at that altar.

While at the altar, she'd felt like someone had taken over her body. Like someone had taken a shovel and begun to dig down to the roots, removing every part of her flesh and emptying out the excess body fat. It was unexplainable as far as Deborah was concerned, and then there was the fact that she didn't even remember hitting the ground.

"It at least had to hurt," she said out loud as she immediately began to rub her head, checking for any sign of a lump. She closed her eyes and tried to remember exactly what had taken place just a little while ago in the New Day Temple of Faith sanctuary. She tried to remember falling, but the only thing she could recall was a feeling as if someone had lifted her off of her feet and laid her peacefully onto the ground.

She squeezed her eyes tighter, willing herself to remember. Suddenly her eyes jammed open upon remembering something. Something she'd said. *"I took a life . . ."*

Deborah gasped, buried her face in her hands, and once again, collapsed; only this time she landed on her couch. "Oh God!" she panicked. "Oh God! What did I do? What did I say?"

There was a pounding at the door that startled Deborah so badly that she jumped to her feet. Her heart began to beat just as loudly as the pounding on the door, almost as if they were in competition with each other. There was more pounding from the door. Instantly, Deborah thought about the words she'd said back in the sanctuary, *"I took a life,"* and assumed someone was coming for her. Although she'd only meant to be confessing those words to God, others had heard, and now someone was coming to hold her accountable.

Her first instincts were to run upstairs to her room and hide. While in her room she'd pack her bags and prepare to go away in hiding once who ever was at her door left. But where would she go? And who would she be hiding from? God? Adam and Eve had tried that little stunt in the Garden of Eden, and it hadn't worked. So Deborah knew it wouldn't work for her either.

She dropped her arms in defeat and went to answer the door. When she opened it, there stood Mother Doreen. Deborah looked over Mother Doreen's shoulders to see if she was alone.

"It's just me," Mother Doreen assured her. "I came alone." She brushed by Deborah, inviting herself into the house which was uncharacteristic of Mother Doreen, who always made it a point to never intrude on someone. But this morning there was something different about Mother Doreen's demeanor, like she was on a mission or something. An assignment. She meant business. And on this day, she was about her Father's business indeed. "I know Pastor tells us when we do drive-bys that it should be at least two or more because you never know what type of situation you'll be walking into. But God equipped me with a legion of angels for this one. So I'm good."

Mother Doreen walked over to Deborah's couch and took a seat without being offered one. Deborah closed the door behind her, then focused her attention on the woman sitting on her couch. A woman, who in the past, she'd known to be very calm and settled. Yet the woman she was looking at now seemed to have a no nonsense aura about her. And one thing Deborah immediately noticed was that there were no sweat beads.

Mother Doreen picked up on Deborah's perception of her and spoke on it. "I know . . . I know you're not used to seeing me in such a forward state, but my God told me to come to you. Pastor wasn't even finished giving the Word. Church wasn't even over yet, but the Lord said, 'Go see about my daughter now.' And He said for me to come to you boldly and to walk in the authority in which He's graced me for such a time as this. An authority that I had not exercised until this very moment." She looked up and mumbled, "To God be the glory."

Deborah stood silent, taking in her sister in Christ's words. Mother Doreen even sounded different. She had such power in her tone. And again, there was no sweat. Whatever fear Mother Doreen might have walked in in the past when it came to confrontation, she had been delivered from. She had been delivered today, right along with Deborah, when she decided to say yes to God and embark upon her assignment. With the way God had moved at New Day, no one would probably leave that sanctuary the same way they had come.

"Come sit down, child." Mother Doreen patted the spot next to her.

Deborah walked over and sat down next to the church mother of New Day. She was timid like a little girl about to have "the talk" with her mother.

"God said you ain't finished," Mother Doreen told her.

"What?" Deborah was puzzled as to what Mother Doreen was getting at, and it showed on her face.

"God says you ain't finished yet. You have more to tell Him." Mother Doreen twitched her bottom to get comfortable as she faced Deborah. "You were about to say too much back there in the sanctuary. God said what you have to say is to Him. For His ears only right now. Later, it will be your testimony. It will be your ministry, but right now, you have to give it to God first. He ain't gon' let you give it to nobody else until you give it to Him first. Whatever this thing is inside of you that you are holding back, give it to Him, child." Mother Doreen placed her hand on Deborah's stomach. "You've got to birth it out of you. God said He's been trying to push it out of you Himself. He's been using people and situations to get you to push it out, but you won't let go. What you have inside of you is taking up space. See, God wants to birth something new in you, but you won't make room for it because you're protecting that thing that's still-born inside of you. God says what you have in there is dead. Push that dead thing out, so He can birth new life into you."

Deborah had been in the book business for years, but never had she been read like one. And somehow Mother Doreen sat there speaking into her life as if she were an open book. But down to the very last minute, Deborah insisted on protecting that thing inside of her. "I . . . I don't know what you're talking about," Deborah lied. "You or God for that matter." She gave off a slight chuckle that didn't amuse Mother Doreen the least bit.

"Yes you do, dear." Mother Doreen's tone had softened back to its normal pitch as she placed her hands on top of Deborah's. "God had to lay you out in the Spirit. He had to allow you to rest in Him. You were about to lose it. The time or the place wasn't there, at church, in the sanctuary." Mother Doreen cleared her throat. "See, some church folk with that religious spirit think the only place one can be saved and delivered is at the church altar. That's why you got the same folks running down to the altar every Sunday with the same old stuff. God said you can give Him your stuff right in your own living room. Right in your own secret place." Mother Doreen released Deborah's hands and pointed to the floor. "Your time is now. Your place is right here. Go boldly to His throne of grace and give Him what you owe Him."

Deborah all of a sudden heard a wailing noise. A cry out as if someone was in pain. When her knees hit the floor, she realized it was her. "I can't. I can't do it, Mother Doreen."

"Yes, you can. God is calling you higher, but you can't even excel because something is weighing you down. Something is keeping you from what God has for you. He wants to use you mightily, but He can't because you are holding onto something that you feel makes you unworthy of being used. Give it to God, child. Take authority over this thing and give it to God."

"Jesus!" Deborah cried out. That was the only thing that would flow from her tongue. "Jesus!"

"That's all right, baby. Let it out. When you can't say anything else, call Him! When your brain can't relay the words that are on your heart, just call Him! Call on Jesus!" Mother Doreen stood up and began to pace and speak in tongues. This was something Mother Doreen rarely did outside of her secret place, but she needed to stand in the gap for Deborah right now.

She needed to send up a prayer to God that the devil couldn't interpret.

"Jesus!" Deborah continued to cry out. "I'm sorry. You died for me, and yet I've been holding on to something you took to hell for me already; my sins. I'm sorry. Lord, help me! I'm sorry for the sin of fornication, and I'm sorry that instead of covering the sin with Jesus' blood, I tried to cover it by killing my baby."

"That's right!" Mother Doreen shouted, then followed up with some tongues. "The accuser been standing up there telling God all about it. Now is your time to shut the accuser up. Send him back to hell, Deborah," Mother Doreen ordered with authority. "Send the accuser back to hell with nothing more to say to God about you that you haven't already told Him yourself."

"I killed my baby, God. Not my baby, but yours. You give life. I had no right to take it. I repent from the depths of my soul, oh Lord. I'm sorry. Forgive me. I'm sorry that I couldn't even forgive myself. I'm sorry that although I know what your Word says about forgiveness, I didn't believe it to be true for myself. I'm sorry for what I did that day, and for holding onto it for so long." Deborah's cries were uncontrollable as she thought back to that day in the abortion clinic.

Most of the women in the clinic waiting to abort their babies, hardly looked pregnat at all, especially the girl who sat next to Deborah. Her stomach was as flat as a washboard while the fact that Deborah was with child couldn't be denied. She'd wished she'd invested in just one more "fat suit" to wear to the clinic. Fat suit is what Deborah referred to as all of the oversized clothes she'd worn to hide her pregnancy. Deborah could sense the woman next to her stealing periodic glimpses of her belly. Finally, Deborah looked in the woman's direction and caught her staring down at her belly. That's when, cold busted, the woman decided to speak to Deborah in order to play it off.

"Hi, how are you?" the woman had asked.

Deborah had merely nodded and smiled. A nervous, mental wreck is what she was. But back then, just like she'd done for all those years in between, she hid her true feelings with a smile.

"I'm Helen," the woman had said, extending her hand to Deborah.

"I'm—"

"Pregnant," Helen had finished Deborah's sentence. "Very pregnant." She rubbed Deborah's growing round belly. "Did it just kick?" she asked Deborah in surprise.

Deborah ignored the girl's comment and simply shook the woman's hand, fighting back tears at the thought that maybe her baby had kicked. According to the medication the doctors had given her to take, there is no way that baby inside of her should be in any condition to move. But what if the meds hadn't worked? What if what Deborah was about to do was no better than burying her baby alive? Why had she waited so long? Why? Why? Why?

Now, once again, Deborah was full of regret, she regretted waiting until her fiancé, Elton, had come back home from playing basketball overseas to tell him that she was pregnant. She was pregnant with his child, whom she'd learned was a son. She'd wanted to tell him face to face. He'd always made his five-year plan clear. It included playing basketball overseas, tightening up his game so that the NBA couldn't deny him a place in the league, marrying the girl of his dreams, who was Deborah, and then having 2.5 kids and a dog . . . all in that order.

He'd been successfully playing basketball in Chile for a full season and things were looking good. He'd proposed to Deborah right before he left the states to let her know that no matter how many miles were between them, she was his girl. Deborah had been attending New Day at the time, and the women of the church even threw her and Elton an engagement party. Pastor had blessed them and even given them a counseling session before Elton left the country. Deborah felt so blessed that

God's anointing was truly on their pending marriage. Elton and Deborah even agreed that they would abstain from sex until they were married, which they felt wouldn't be so hard considering they would be living in two different countries. Deborah even stopped refilling her birth control prescription, since she no longer had a need for them.

After a few months of living in Chile, Elton flew Deborah down to visit him. It was that one trip where things had gone a little too far, and Deborah, unbeknownst to her, left Chile pregnant and unwed. Engaged, but unwed all the same. There was no in-between in the Bible as far as Deborah could find.

At first, Deborah couldn't understand why all of this was happening to her, but then she realized why. After praying and crying, crying and praying for days in and days out, she heard this voice telling her that it was her punishment for tainting her relationship with Elton. She just couldn't keep her legs closed while visiting him, and now look. She'd gone down to another country and practically seduced Elton. Her jeans didn't have to be so tight. Even if it was hotter than water boiling a pot of spaghetti noodles, she didn't have to wear all those backless and strapless halter tops, enticing Elton with her smooth skin. After all, he was a man. He was a man of God, but he was a man first and foremost. She'd not only sinned, but she had caused Elton to sin. The baby growing inside her belly was nothing but a result of her sin. She knew it was a sin or else she wouldn't have gone through the extremes of spending more money than she had on big clothing in order to hide her pregnancy from those around her.

Deborah had allowed that voice to convince her that Elton was right; she had to get rid of the baby. How could they possibly repent for their sins and call themselves moving on with the result of their sin constantly staring back at them? They couldn't. She couldn't. Not stopping for a moment to decipher whether or not the voice that had been leading her was the voice of God, she agreed with Elton that they should abort the baby. Before heading back to Chile, he'd left her the necessary monies to get the procedure done. It had cost a pretty penny considering that by the time Deborah had met face-to-face with Elton to share the news of her pregnancy, she was already well into her second trimester. The procedure wouldn't be cheap, and it wouldn't be easy. And it hadn't been. The only thing that had been easy was lying to people when they questioned her about her weight gain.

To this day, Helen rubbing her belly in the clinic, causing her to think for one second that the child that had been developing inside of her for a little over five months was still alive, ached her very being. Helen had confessed that she was only six weeks pregnant at the time and had done all sorts of research on how at only six weeks it really wasn't a baby, etc . . . etc . . . , but that she didn't know how Deborah had the courage to abort a child that already had all of its organs and everything.

"You're better than me," Helen had said, rolling her eyes, "but then again, maybe not. After all, that's a real live baby you're about to take out." On that note, Deborah's name was called, which ended the short conversation she'd had with Helen. A woman who she never thought in a million years she'd ever see again.

As Deborah cried out on her living room floor, she thought back to something Mother Doreen had said to her about God using people to push this thing out of her. All this time while Deborah thought Helen had been sent by the devil as one of his advocates, God Himself had been using her to get rid of, how had Mother Doreen had put it, the stillborn baby . . . the stillborn issue.

"Jesus!" Deborah cried out as she hunched over in a fetal position. Her muscles tightened and her body tightened for a moment as if she were in pain. As if she were a mother in labor. And she remembered what labor pains felt like, as the day of her abortion the doctor had given her something to induce labor so that she could give birth to the baby that lay lifeless in her womb. She was now feeling those pains all over again. Now, though, it was as if she were pushing out the afterbirth; the mess that had her bound. Now she would be free. Now she would finally be free.

Hours later, Deborah stood to her feet and turned her attention to a cracked front door. That's when she realized that Mother Doreen must have let herself out. She walked over to the door and opened it, confirming that Mother Doreen's car was in fact gone. Just like an angel sent by God, Mother Doreen had come and gone after serving her purpose. No conversation about what she'd witnessed. No questions asked.

Deborah closed the door and locked it. Just like the last time a couple of saints from New Day had decided to make a drive-by visit to her house, she leaned up against the door and looked up to the heavens. "Lord, I declare that I am clean by the blood of your son. That I am restored by your love. That I am whole because of your grace and your mercy. Have your way in my life, Lord, as from this moment forward I completely surrender myself unto you. Use me for your good, for the glory of your Kingdom. I'm ready to be used!"

God had used Mother Doreen to push her toward complete deliverance. She was no longer broken, but healed. She couldn't wait to see just how God planned on using her now.

Chapter Twenty-nine

"Nobody blames you for leaving your husband, Tamarra," Deborah told her as they sat in the classroom holding the Singles Ministry meeting. Initially, Deborah wasn't going to show up, and not because of Helen. Oh, she was more than ready to face that giant. Better yet, she knew she didn't have a choice. She was done running. Like Mother Doreen had told her; it was time to send the accuser away packing. The real reason why Deborah wasn't going to attend the meeting was because she didn't need to anymore.

Deborah was able to admit that her membership and involvement in the ministry had just been another cover up; a bribe to God to get Him to acknowledge her, forgive her and not turn His face far from her. The more she thought back over things, the more she had realized that she had Martha syndrome; that she'd been doing hands-on busy work thinking God would see her works and show more favor toward her. More forgiveness even. All this time God really wanted her to seek Him. All this time she had actually been the one who had turned her face far from God, too humiliated to face Him due to her past guilt and shame.

It was time for Deborah to take on the characteristics of Martha's sister, Mary, and sit at Jesus' feet and receive the Word. To meditate on it and be clear on the revelation of the Word as it applied to her own life. But even with all that, Deborah still came to the meeting as it would be one of the last with Mother

Doreen. Mother Doreen had decided that in the next couple of months she would prepare to relocate to Kentucky in order to be there to help take care of her sister. Deborah promised Mother Doreen she'd finish off the duties with her as a new leader of the New Day Singles Ministry was assigned.

Somehow, as always, instead of taking care of the initial items on the agenda, the women began to talk about relationships. Once again, Tamarra found herself speaking on her marriage with her ex-husband and their divorce. Tamarra had just expressed how awful she felt about having a divorce under her belt, and Deborah was comforting her.

"Knowing your husband was never fully committed to you a day in the marriage, and on top of that had a child outside of the marriage," Deborah had continued, "surely God understands that was too much for you to bear. Most of us in here can probably honestly say that we would have done the same thing ourselves. After some illegitimate child fathered by our husband outside of our marriage showed up on our doorstep, we'd have made a beeline to the courthouse too."

Several women backed up Deborah with a couple of "Amens" and "You know that's right."

Tamarra just sat there the entire time taking in their undeserving support. For months these women had been supporting her, and all the while she'd let them believe a lie. She was so tired of living a lie. She'd witnessed Deborah, along with so many other people at New Day, be delivered from so many situations. She'd witness them just let go of old junk and become new creatures in Christ. She wanted it. She wanted deliverance, but she knew it was up to her to take the first step in achieving it.

"So don't beat yourself up about leaving your husband," Deborah said. "Besides, the Word says—"

"I didn't leave my husband," Tamarra blurted out, interrupting Deborah.

There was silence as the women looked among each other with puzzled faces. Then the whispering started. Finally a bold sister shouted out, "Don't tell us you got back with that sorry son of a gun."

"Yeah, what about Brother Maeyl?" one of the women questioned. "He's a good man of God. I know you didn't kick him to the curb for someone with a track record of being a cheat."

The fact that Tamarra and Maeyl were an official couple was now common knowledge. They didn't dare do things such as hug up in church, hold hands, or anything else that would offend God being that the two were not married, but they no longer purposely hid their relationship. They frequently shared rides to Bible Study, and they ate out at Family Café at least once a week. But what they didn't do was play husband and wife without the ceremony. Tamarra had even invited Maeyl to join the Singles Ministry. She felt they each could use the support as well as learn valuable information to aid them in their courtship.

Maeyl was unable to attend tonight, but he assured her he'd be joining her for the future monthly meetings. Knowing how Maeyl would soon be a male in a room that usually consisted of women where she could moan and harp on her past relationship, she knew that would have to come to an end. The last thing she wanted for Maeyl to have to endure was an hour of hearing about her past. Besides, her past and her separation from her last husband wasn't really what she had allowed everyone to believe it was, including her best friend, Paige. And now that there might not be such an opportunity where she felt she could speak on it as openly, she decided tonight's meeting was the perfect time to reveal the truth and put closure on her past marriage once and for all.

"Brother Maeyl and I are a couple," Tamarra said proudly. "And there's no way under the sun, unless God Himself showed me His face and I saw His lips moving telling me to let Maeyl go, would I trade that man in for the world."

"Then if you didn't leave your husband," Deborah couldn't help but ask, "does that mean you never divorced him, and all this time you've still been married?"

Tamarra took a deep breath, attempting to retain the courage she needed to tell these women the truth. Only if they'd keep quiet long enough to let her. "No, I'm not still married. I am divorced, but like I said, I didn't leave my husband. He left me. I didn't want the divorce. He wanted a divorce from me."

Tamarra allowed the women a minute to take in her words and for them to register in their heads. Once their gasps of surprise subsided, she continued.

"Yep, that's right; he left me," Tamarra reiterated. She looked about the room, observing the shocking stares from the group. "He left me, and yeah, I was angry, mad, and upset in finding out that my husband had been living a lie, only I was the lie. That other woman and his child, that's the life he really wanted. Not the life he pretended to have with me."

Tamarra's eyes watered. Once Paige noticed, she quickly grabbed a couple of tissues and handed them to Tamarra.

"No," Tamarra refused the tissue. "I'm tired of holding back these tears. It's about time I let them out. Maybe then they won't keep fighting to come out." Tamarra blinked, and for the first time since the night her husband packed his bags and left her, she cried.

"Now, now," Mother Doreen stood up and said as she walked over to Tamarra and patted her on the shoulder. "It's all right, dear."

Tamarra quickly stood, jolting Mother Doreen's hand from her. "It's not all right!" she exclaimed. "I'm sorry, Mother Doreen. I know you are just trying to help, but it's not all right. I'm not all right!" Tamarra declared.

Mother Doreen slowly made her way back to her seat as Tamarra continued.

"I'm a mess, y'all," Tamarra confessed.

"Now don't say that," Mother Doreen stated. "God don't make no mess."

"I didn't say God made this mess. I said I'm a mess. Everything God gives us is without sorrow, but then we go getting in His way and making a mess out of things."

"Well, I agree with Mother Doreen," the young twenty-something woman in the group stated. "I ain't no mess. Now I got some things that need to be fixed and things God needs to deliver me from, but I ain't no mess. God don't make no mess. So if you want to claim that you're a mess, go ahead and do that. But I'ma do me."

"By all means," Tamarra told her, "you go right ahead and do you. And while you are doing you, I'm going to be doing God, because He's the only one who can fix my mess. I've tried to do me in the past. And that got me nowhere."

"Amen!" a woman stood up and shouted, followed by several others. "I'm a mess, too," the women began to proclaim. Some began to lift their hands to heaven and plead to God to fix their mess. Some repented and apologize for getting themselves into the messes they were in by not following God's commandments or just simply being disobedient by going left when He'd told them to go right.

For the next few minutes some deliverance took place. Even the young twenty-something woman found herself crying out, "I am a mess, God. I'm the one who chose to sleep with man after man unprotected. To have child after child, each with different daddies. You didn't create my body for that purpose. This body was supposed to be yours, dear God. A living sacrifice, holy and acceptable. And I made a mess out of it," she confessed. "Forgive me, Lord." The woman cried out and collapsed on the floor.

Mother Doreen, who had been comforting quite a few of the women, made her way over to comfort the young lady.

"See, ladies," Tamarra stated. "I wasn't claiming the title of a mess, I was confessing it. You can't quit it until you admit it. God wants to hear you call those things out. The accuser is already up there tattling on you. That's the accuser's job."

Mother Doreen nodded her head in full agreement, as she, too, had just recently told Deborah that very same thing.

"But God doesn't want to hear it from Satan," Tamarra

stated. "He wants you to confess it. To man up. Well today, I'm manning up." Tamarra looked up and shouted out at the top of her lungs. "Lord, I'm a mess. Help me! Heal me! Mend me! Fix me!" She then looked to the women. "Some of the messes I've gotten myself into I don't even know how I got into them. But one thing is for certain and two things are for sure; I don't know how I'm going to get out of it, but I know who is going to get me out. God is good; hallelujah!"

Several women co-signed Tamarra's hallelujah with one of their own. All of this support and praise gave Tamarra the courage to continue with her testimony.

"My husband left me, y'all, and I've been running around here like I let him go," Tamarra admitted, "too ashamed and embarrassed to speak the truth. But the truth is going to set me free from my mess. But guess what? It's all right that my husband left me. It's all right that I begged him not to go the day he packed his bags and headed out the door." Tamarra's mind went back to that awful night she'd never forget.

For the two weeks after Tamarra's ex-husband's secret of infidelity was revealed, she gave him the silent treatment. She wouldn't cook for him or clean the house, let alone show him any signs of affection. She needed to heal, but she was too busy cursing God to seek Him for His healing power. She blamed God for allowing her to walk around like a fool for so many years. She blamed God for not revealing her husband to her for who he was prior to fifteen years of marriage.

"I've served you all these years," she had fussed at God. "I've praised you. I've worshipped you. I've given you the last of my last in tithes and offerings. Where's my harvest? This? This mess right here?" she cried out. "Even when I couldn't get Edward to go to church but twice a year, on Easter and Christmas if it fell on a Sunday, even when he got copies of the returned checks from my tithes and offering and we argued, I still praised you, Lord. I was obedient to you, Lord. I kept all my promises to you, Lord, and you couldn't do the one thing I asked of you; to bless my marriage."

In the middle of Tamarra's outpouring, words her pastor had shared with her came to mind. "God don't bless no mess. Now He will take your mess and make it a blessing to the rest of the world to keep someone else from getting into that same type of mess, but in the end, your mess is simply your testimony. Your ministry."

Back then, Tamarra had just brushed those words off. The God she served was a big God and could turn any situation around, which is why she had gone on and married Edward in the first place. He was a good man, had been raised in the church as a child, but as an adult, he had strayed away and never went back. Tamarra, on the other hand, hadn't been in the church very long herself. But she was on the road to becoming a true practicing Christian when she and Edward met. Listening to him talk about growing up in the church, Tamarra had just assumed that Edward was still a churchgoer. He would frequently talk about his current work in the church, so once again, Tamarra made the assumption that in reference to his work, he meant his ministry.

After only two months of dating, Tamarra was already head over heels in love with Edward. She was in love with the surface of Edward, so a few months later when she found out that Edward's work in the church was as an accountant, simply keeping church books, but that he hadn't attended church since childhood, she felt stomped. A prayer that should have gone something like this: "God, your Word says that one should not be unequally yoked, so if Edward is not the equal that you have sent to find me, remove him from my life speedily in the name of Jesus," went something like this instead: "God, you know I'm already in love with Edward, so please let me have him." Well, she got what she asked for.

It wasn't even a year after meeting him that Tamarra and Edward were married. For some reason she thought she could eventually change Edward; get him to get back into church and all, but try as she might, only one person can change someone, and that's God. But even then, they have to want God to change them. So Tamarra spent years often compromising who she was for the sake of her marriage. Once a faithful Bible Study attendee, when Edward decided to make Wednesday night his night with the boys, something about that didn't sit right with Tamarra. She decided to cut down going to Bible Study to every other week, making the opposite Wednesday her and Edward's date night. This meant a decrease in his time spent with the boys. This was just one of many occasions Tamarra would find herself putting God on the back burner.

Tamarra came to the conclusion that God got fed up with running a close second to Edward, so He eventually just had to move him out of His way altogether. This truth was something Tamarra had determined she'd take to her grave, but while living, it would eat her alive.

Now, Tamarra felt so much relief in getting out the fact that her husband had left her. All of that anger she had bottled up was finally being sent to the pits of hell where it belonged. It was anger that Tamarra really had toward herself, but felt better aiming it at her ex-husband. Anger that this evening, when the sun went down, would disappear; for good. And even though Tamarra was blessed to have one less burden to deal with, she still knew that she needed to pray for the strength to unload that one last burden that was weighing her down.

Chapter Thirty

"Mother Doreen, I sure am going to hate to see you go," Deborah told her as the two of them remained in the classroom, straightening up after the meeting had come to an end and everyone else had left.

The meeting had gone over by a full hour after the sudden release of praise, shouting, and worshiping, thanks to Tamarra sharing her testimony. Chairs had been moved to make room for the dancing and shouting. Tissues were all over the place from the tears of joy the women had shed. Lo and behold, the major issues on the agenda, such as leadership replacement, hadn't even been touched upon. So all of the women agreed that they'd hold two meetings that month, the next in two weeks. It would also be a goodbye potluck for Mother Doreen's departure.

"I sure am going to hate to go," Mother Doreen replied. "But God's calling me down there to take care of my sister."

"But doesn't she belong to a nice sized church there in Kentucky? Seems as though with such a large church family to look out for her, you wouldn't need to move there."

"Oh, her church family takes care of her just fine," Mother Doreen assured Deborah as the two got the classroom back in order. "Matter of fact, some of them take care of her almost too fine." Mother Doreen stopped what she was doing and stared with a far away look in her eyes.

"You say that as though there's something wrong with that," Deborah commented after noticing Mother Doreen's expression.

Mother Doreen picked up a tissue from the floor and pitched it into the trash can. "Umm, I could be wrong. But there is just something about that church's assistant pastor. He's always up at the hospital when she's in there. Always calling and coming by the house when she's at home." That far away look returned to her eyes as she stood over the trash can.

"Mother Doreen, I don't think that's anything to really be concerned about. Surely nothing to pack up and move out of the state about. After all, your sister is what, around forty years old, and you said yourself that y'all were raised in that church. She's probably like a daughter to them."

"To some, yeah, but that assistant pastor ain't been there but five years. I understand it's the church's duty to be there for the sick and the shut-in, but like I said, I just got a strange feeling."

"Well, if the feeling is strange enough that you have to pack up and move across the country and leave your own church family, then so be it," Deborah said, intentionally trying to make Mother Doreen feel guilty and change her mind about relocating.

"Across the country? Child, please. Kentucky ain't nothin' but a hop, skip, jump, and swim across the creek from Ohio."

Deborah laughed. "I know, I know, but I thought I'd make one final attempt to talk you out of it."

"No, you can't do it, my sister. Like I said, I believe God is sending me down there to intervene on something. I can't say no to God. It's just like when Willie's job with the railroad brought him here to Ohio." She looked up. "God rest my Willie's soul." She drew an invisible cross across her heart with her index finger, and then continued. "As much as I loved my home in Kentucky, I knew I had to come here. Although Willie and I had only been dating for not even six months, God had showed me that Willie was the husband He had for me. I had to come. Well, now I've got to go back. But hopefully I won't face all the trials and tribulations I faced going back home that I did leaving home." Mother Doreen shook her head.

"Oh, come on now, Mother Doreen. Things couldn't have been that bad. I've heard you say that you wouldn't have traded that Willie of yours for nothing in the world."

"And I wouldn't have, but at the same time, I wouldn't have wished my Willie upon anybody in the world either."

"Mother Doreen!" Deborah had shock all through her tone.

"I'm serious, child. It took me a minute, almost not until his death, but I understood why God chose me to be Willie's wife; because He knew I could handle it. He knew I was a strong enough woman of God that not even Willie's cheating, drinking, gambling, lying, and what have you, could turn me away from believing in who my God was." Mother Doreen sat down in a chair as she shared things about her marriage with her late husband that she'd shared with no one but the pastor, and that was usually during the counseling Willie would agree to have every time she had threatened to leave his behind.

"Then why did you put up with it?" Deborah asked out of curiosity. "I mean, the same way God gave you Willie, He would have given you another husband, one that didn't drink, gamble, and cheat. The verdict is still out on the lying thing. I think that's just something that men can't help."

Both women let out a chuckle before Mother Doreen got serious and continued.

"That may be true, but God had work to do in Willie, and He did that work through me," Mother Doreen told her. "Most women probably would have run off and left his tail in a heart beat, and don't think for a minute that I didn't want to, but I was very tuned in to what God was telling me. I was very tuned in to God when He'd tell me when to run and seek shelter, when He'd hide me, and when to stay and fight. Well, when it came to Willie, He told me to stay and fight. Just like David in the second book of Samuel, He'd let me know when He'd deliver the enemies to me, and that's just what He did."

"How so?" By now Deborah was sitting and hanging onto Mother Doreen's every word.

"God used my faith to allow me to hold on, to believe that He could do a new thing with my husband. Man says once a cheater always a cheater. God says He was once a deliverer and He's still a deliverer. Always will be a deliverer. I believed in Him to deliver my Willie. I prayed. I laid hands on my husband. I oiled up my husband's personal belongings and prayed over them. I visited the inner and the outer courts-not the courthouse-to take care of my marriage. I prayed for the Jezebel spirits of the women my Willie would run around with. When I caught them in a hotel room, I didn't take off my earrings, kick off my shoes, and look for the Vaseline. I removed my flesh, and put on my armor of God, and pulled the anointed oil from my purse. I didn't scream and cuss out Miss Thang. I called out to God and prayed for her." Mother Doreen stopped and laughed.

"What? What's so funny?" A confused look crossed Deborah's face.

"I'm just thinking about how God's got jokes. Do you know one time He even had the nerve to use me to bring one of these women to salvation? This woman had never been to church a day in her life, and now she goes faithfully." A proud look covered Mother Doreen's face.

Deborah was in awe, not at Mother Doreen's actions, but at her obedience in the Lord. She was in awe of the God in Mother Doreen. When Mother Doreen said 'Yes' to God, she meant it. Not too many women can say that they caught their husband in a hotel room with a woman, and then led the woman to salvation (eternal life) instead of beating her down (ending her life).

"Mother Doreen, I had no idea that you had gone through so much in your marriage. Every time I saw you in church you always had a praise in your mouth. There was always joy on your face and peace on your mind." Deborah shook her head. "I guess there are a lot of us Christians running around here wearing what's called a church face."

"Hold up, dear." Mother Doreen put her hand up. Her tone was kind, but firm. "I never once had to put on a church face. If there was a praise in my mouth, it was an honest praise from the depths of my soul. A praise as a result of God being who He is. If you saw joy on my face, again, it was the joy of the Lord. And if my mind was at peace, that was because the peace of the Lord surpasses all understanding. I mean, sometimes I'd drive to church feeling all woe is me. Face dragging. Can't even part my lips to sing along with the Marvin Sapp song playing on the gospel radio, let alone send up a praise. But during the entire drive, the Holy Spirit would be beating my flesh down, and by the time I hit the church doors, I was in complete awe of God. God was bigger than any situation and problem and man." She leaned into Deborah and nudged her. "Dear, you'll get to a point where instead of telling God about all of your problems, you'll tell all of your problems about God."

"Amen, Mother Doreen. I hear what you're saying, but at the same time . . . and not that misery loves company or anything . . . but sometimes it helps to be able to look around and know that the person you think has got it all together really doesn't. Then you don't always feel like such a mess, which was how Sister Tamarra so eloquently put it."

"I know, but had I come in here looking all broke up just so folks would know that I go through too, that would have been a mask. That would have been wearing a church face. I believe the reason God always fixed me right before I walked through that door was because He knew that the God that people like you saw in me, was sometimes the only God they'd ever see. If I said it once, I've said it a thousand times: It ain't always about the preacher preaching or the choir singing. Sometimes that ain't even God. Sometimes certain choir members be singing in the flesh and preachers be preaching in the flesh. But honey, when you can show up to church with God already in you, what the church folk do doesn't even matter."

Deborah had to agree with Mother Doreen. Perhaps

knowing that she wasn't perfect and going through things might have been a comfort to Deborah some days, but always seeing God's love and anointing on Mother Doreen had proven to be even more ministering; it let Deborah know that there was hope. It let Deborah know that there was a God.

"So I never take for granted, whether I'm at church or on the streets, that I'm a witness," Mother Doreen said. "That the God in me is sometimes the only God a person might see ever."

Deborah shook her head. "I'm in awe of you, Mother Doreen."

"Don't be in awe of me, child. No one has it all together. Nobody but Jesus. But like Paul said in the book of James, I'm not perfect. I'm not where I need to be, but I'm still pressing forward."

"Wow. Thank you, Mother Doreen. Thank you so much. You have no idea how free I feel after talking to you."

"Don't thank me, child. You ain't no babe in Christ. You know you got set free the minute our Lord and Savior died on that cross for you."

"I know, but thank you for always letting God use you."

"No problem, dear." Mother Doreen stood up. "Well, it's getting late, so we better get going."

"All right, Mother Doreen. And I know I never thanked you for doing a drive-by on me that one Sunday, but I sure was blessed by your obedience. I was delivered that night, Mother Doreen. You were one of the people God used to push that thing out of me." Deborah had never got to thank Mother Doreen because by the time she was able to get up off of her knees that night, Mother Doreen was nowhere in sight. Deborah had no idea when Mother Doreen had left or how many hours she had cried out to God. All she knew was that she was a new woman in Christ.

"Oh, don't thank me, dear. I was just letting God use me. I'm always just letting God use me," were Mother Doreen's last words to Deborah before they tidied up one last bit, then headed out of the church.

Deborah drove toward home not doubting one bit that God wouldn't continue to use Mother Doreen. As much as she would miss her elder, she knew she had to let Mother Doreen go to do God's work in Kentucky, but something in her spirit told her to pray constantly for the equipping of that particular saint as she moved into foreign territory. Not foreign territory as far as the state of Kentucky, considering that's where Mother Doreen had been born and raised, but foreign territory as far as the situation she was about to walk into.

"Sweet, Mother Doreen," Deborah whispered to herself as she drove. "I got a feeling that what you are about to face with your sister goes beyond anything you've ever had to experience with your Willie." Deborah looked up. "God, be with her."

Chapter Thirty-one

"You said what?" Tamarra exclaimed, nearly spitting out the sip of bottled water she had just drank.

"I know, can you believe it?" Paige said, full of excitement. "I've been holding this in for three weeks. I wanted to surprise you when I announced it at the party this weekend, which is really our engagement party, but I just couldn't. I can't believe I've kept if from you this long. For a minute I even thought about announcing it at the last Singles Ministry meeting we had, but you know we ended up having a Holy Ghost party up in there."

Paige continued to talk while Tamarra sat there, almost in a daze. Instead of going out to the buffet after church service today, Paige invited Tamarra over to her house where she wanted to try a new recipe out on her. When Tamarra began to question why her best friend, the eat out queen, was all of a sudden taking up an interest in cooking, Paige couldn't hold it in any longer. She just had to share the news about Blake's marriage proposal with Tamarra and how she'd been beefing up her kitchen skills for her future husband.

"My cousin is going to be catering the engagement party we have planned," Paige said. "And before you get it twisted, the only reason why I didn't have you do it was because I was trying to wait and surprise you about the whole thing. I mean, can you believe it? I'm getting married."

Tamarra finally found her voice. "But how could you

not say anything? I mean, why didn't I know? Where's the ring?" Tamarra grabbed Paige's left hand that was free of any jewelry.

"Oh, just wait until you see it. It's beautiful. I pick it up in a couple of days. We had to have it sized." Paige's eyes began to fill with tears. "Oh Tamarra, I can't believe this is actually happening, can you?" Paige waited on a response from her friend, one that she never got. "Hello, Tamarra." Paige snapped her fingers. "I shared with you the best news of my life. I'm not saying you should be doing back flips, but I thought I'd at least get a congratulations out of you."

"Well, uh, congratulations . . . I guess."

Paige snapped her neck back and gave Tamarra the sista-girlfriend-oh-no-you-didn't look. "You guess?" Paige stood up from the couch where the two had been sitting, waiting for Paige's first stab at homemade lasagna to come out of the oven. "Perhaps I shouldn't have shared my good news with you. Then again, I'm kind of glad that I did. I'd hate for you to have put a damper on my engagement party. Guess now I know better."

Tamarra felt bad that her reaction wasn't as cheerful and congratulatory as Paige would have liked, but how could it have been, knowing what she knew? Tamarra, in all honesty, had meant to get around to telling Paige all about her and Blake's connection, but she had been too caught up in her own issues. She was happy that Paige had finally found a man that passed the test of time, and the test of being nothing like her father. She was even happier that it was Blake. She'd had every intention on telling Paige absolutely everything, but who knew the two would be getting hitched so soon?

"I'm so sorry, Paige," Tamarra apologized. "I didn't mean to make you think that I wasn't happy for you. Because I am. It's just that . . . " Tamarra's words trailed off as she hurried to come up with a way to put her words. "It's just that . . . well . . ." Quick on her feet, Tamarra came up with yet another cover up. "Well, look at you. The man's got you cooking for Pete's sake. You've spent more time in the kitchen lately than your prayer closet, I bet. And you said you'd never end up like your mother, slaving for some man."

"Things have changed now, Tamarra. I had a long talk with my mother about that, and things weren't exactly how I made them out to be. My mother taught me that when you love some-one, when you really love someone, doing those things is a part of showing just how much you do love them." Paige smiled. "And I really love Blake.

Well, that excuse didn't work, Tamarra thought to herself. She lowered her head and tried to think of something else.

Mistaking her being in deep thought for sadness, Paige sighed sympathetically. "Oh, I get it." She walked over and sat back down next to Tamarra. "It's because Maeyl hasn't yet pro-posed to you."

"Huh?" Tamarra replied, the thought of Maeyl propos-ing to her being the last thing on her mind.

"There's no need to be jealous of my engagement. Your day will come, especially now that you've been honest with your-self and everyone else about your past marriage." She hugged Tamarra. "You've buried it once and for all. Now God can give you that new thing Pastor is always talking about."

Tamarra couldn't contain it, so a chuckle slipped from between her lips.

"What's so funny?" Paige asked, releasing her.

"Oh, Paige, honey, it's not that," Tamarra assured her.

"Now, now. No need to stop lying to yourself again. Just admit it; you're jealous of Blake and me."

For some reason, Paige's misconception had gone from making Tamarra laugh, to making her angry. "Paige, trust me, I'm not jealous of you."

"You can't keep doing this to yourself, Tamarra. I mean, you let one lie go only to start living another one. It's okay that you're jealous; after all, even though you and Maeyl didn't really hook up until around the time Blake and I did, you two have still known each other much, much longer."

"Paige, I said that's not it." Now Tamarra stood to her feet, trying to control her rising flesh.

Paige ignored her friend as she went right on with her own theory as to why Tamarra wasn't happy for her. "Blake and I have only known each other for a little over six months while you and Maeyl have known each other for what, a little over six years? But the length of time you've known a person plays no part in how much you love someone."

"Well, good," Tamarra snapped, "I'm glad you don't seem to be too concerned about how long people have known each other, because if you must know, I, my friend, have known Blake even longer than you have."

Just then, the smoke alarm went off in the kitchen. Paige had forgotten all about the lasagna. The cheese had probably boiled over into the oven, causing the smoke to form, setting off the alarm. Paige glared at Tamarra without saying a word. For now she had to go tend to the kitchen; leaving one smoking situation to go take care of another. And everyone knows that where there is smoke, there is fire. Paige headed to the kitchen knowing that she could only put out one fire at a time, but as she exited the living room, she shot Tamarra a look letting her know that she'd be back to put out the one in her living room as well.

After turning off the smoke alarm and airing out the place by opening several windows, Paige returned to the living room where Tamarra nervously awaited. Tamarra had thought about pulling the same stunt she'd pulled at Maeyl's, leaving without saying a word, but she'd brought this on herself, and it was time to come clean.

"So . . ." Paige said, feigning cheerfulness. "Where were we?" She cleared her throat and sat down at a chair across from where Tamarra sat on the couch. "Let me recap. I just told you that Blake had proposed to me and that I said yes." Paige feigned a smile. "I looked at Blake dead in his eyes and without even thinking twice I said, 'Yes, Blake, I'll marry you'."

"Look, I get that, Paige, but you've only known him a few months," Tamarra tried to reason. "I've known him . . ." she paused, "well, like I said earlier, I've known him longer than you have."

Ignoring the fact that Tamarra had so graciously informed her of such prior to the smoke alarm going off, Paige decided to continue without taking that into consideration. While in the kitchen she had tried to reason over and over in her head why it should make a difference that Tamarra knew Blake long before she did without telling her. It could have been an oversight, but then Paige couldn't help but think that perhaps the two of them had known each other on a more intimate level. Maybe that's why Blake insisted that they not talk about their past relationships; he didn't want anything regarding him and Tamarra to come up. But Paige had quickly swept those thoughts under the rug and rebuked the devil for trying to plant them there.

"I know I've only known Blake for a short while by most people's standards, and had it been any other man under any other circumstance, I would think I was going crazy by agreeing to marry him so soon. But I know in my heart I was destined to be Blake's wife. It's God ordained, right down to how we met. I mean, nobody can dispute that regardless of anything. So the fact that you've known Blake for some time means nothing." Paige hoped she sounded convincing, because she wasn't fully convinced herself.

For the past thee weeks Paige had imagined how she'd stand up at the Singles Ministry meeting and give her testimony about how Blake had proposed to her. She thought it would be a wonderful change of scene at the meeting. Instead of a war story, she finally had a story with a happy ending. But after seeing how her best friend was reacting, and the tad bit of information she'd shared with her, Paige herself was almost beginning to second guess her engagement. When Paige first saw Tamarra's reaction to the news, she thought perhaps she was just acting that way because Paige hadn't shared the news with her immediately. But

Paige couldn't focus on Tamarra. She had to keep this a God thing.

"My being Blake's wife was a spiritual set up by God if I ever witnessed one. Right down to how we met. It's just like in the book of Esther when she was destined to be Queen." By now Paige's eyes were filled with tears. "I know I'm no Esther, but for the first time in my life, I feel like I'm worthy of this blessing of God, and I'm not going to miss my blessing. I'm not going to let you or anyone else steal my joy," she declared as tears began to stream down her face.

Tamarra looked around for a box of tissue and located one on Paige's end table. She grabbed a couple, then handed them to Paige, remembering how just a few weeks ago, Paige had been there to wipe her tears when she first told the group the truth about her broken marriage. Now her own heart was broken as she looked at her friend knowing the secret she had kept from her about Blake.

As far as Tamarra was concerned, because of the secret she'd kept, her friend might be making the biggest mistake of her life. She couldn't have that on her conscience. She had to let her best friend know the truth, the whole truth, and there was no better time than now.

"Paige, can you just sit down and let me talk to you, please?" Tamarra asked, pleading with her eyes.

"Sure," Paige agreed as they both walked over to the couch and sat down.

Although Paige agreed she'd listen to what Tamarra had to say, she didn't want there to be any beating around the bush. "Tamarra, just tell me straight up exactly what's going on."

"I will, Paige," Tamarra assured her, "and I should have done it that day in the church parking lot when you first told me about you and Blake. But then I decided to wait until you went on a real planned date versus the one you thought was spontaneous that night at your job."

"What do you mean that I thought was spontaneous?"

Paige was defensive. "There was no thought about it. Like I said, God had everything to do with it."

"No, he didn't, Paige," Tamarra insisted, "and that's what I'm trying to tell you. It wasn't spontaneous. It wasn't by chance, and it wasn't a divine set up. It was a set up, but not by God." Tamarra's tone lowered as she practically mumbled the next sentence. "Blake and I planned the whole thing."

"Excuse me? What was that?"

"Blake and I planned the entire thing. See, Blake is the same guy I told you I met at a catering affair that I tried to get you to go out on a blind date with, but you refused. I just knew that if you would only give him the time of day, the two of you would hit it off just fine, but you adamantly refused. Then I watched you go on date, after date, after date. Paige, the folks at New Day were starting to talk. I felt like I had to do something."

Paige's cheeks turned red with fury. "Talk? Talk about what?"

"About you and all of your dates. Members would see you out with a different man almost every week. That's uh, that's why I, uh, initially talked you into joining the Singles Ministry. Pastor thought that it might be of some value if—"

"Pastor? You mean you had a talk with Pastor about me?" Paige stood up again in anger. "And you didn't say anything to me about it?"

"Paige, you know when Pastor speaks with someone, the same level of confidence is expected out of them just as we expect a level of confidence with Pastor."

"But this is me we're talking about."

Tamarra didn't care. She'd always prided herself for making sure that anything someone put in her ear didn't come out of her mouth and into someone else's ear. The last thing she wanted to do was have Pastor thinking she wasn't trustworthy and that people couldn't share things with her.

"I'm sorry, Paige."

"Well, did you at least tell Pastor and everyone else that

I wasn't the Holy Hoe they thought I was? That I was still a virgin?"

"That wasn't my information to give."

"So you just let folks talk about me?"

"Get over yourself," Tamarra snapped. "Folks are always going to talk about you regardless. Who are you not to be talked about? So don't start thinking more highly of yourself than you ought. And anyway, we've gotten off subject here. We're supposed to be talking about you and Blake."

"Ha!" Paige said. "Me and Blake? There is no me and Blake. I've been living a lie, unbeknownst to me, but he's been sitting back letting me. I mean, I really love this man. I took him home to meet my parents for crying out loud. Most men I've dated never even got to see a picture of my parents." Paige thought for a moment, and then something came to mind. "He knew you were a caterer."

"Huh?" Tamarra was confused.

"On the way to my parents' house, his first time meeting them, he mentioned that you were a caterer. For the life of me, I couldn't recall ever telling him that about you." Paige bopped herself upside the head. "He played me. Stupid me. I can't marry that man. I can't even date that man. It's over!" Once again, the floodgates opened and tears poured from her eyes.

"Hold up, Paige. I'm not saying that you shouldn't date Blake. Heck, I'm not even saying that you shouldn't marry him. I just didn't want you to not know the truth. I didn't want you to base everything on this so-called divine set up."

"The truth is supposed to set one free, but all I'm getting from the truth is a bunch of hurt. Thanks a lot, Tamarra."

"I'm so sorry," Tamarra said as she got up and hugged her sobbing friend. "I was so selfish to do something like this. I mean, I know had I just told you in the beginning everything would have been fine. But again, me being selfish—worried about my own issues—I just didn't think."

"Oh, don't worry about it, girl," Paige said, wiping her tears with the worn tissues. "We're even."

"What do you mean, we're even?"

"Well, folks were talking about me and all my dates on a search for my husband, when I should have just kept my tail standing still so that my husband could find me. Like you said, what did I expect you to do? Folks are always going to talk. And like I said, we're even. I'm no better than you. I don't remember doing too much of nothing when folks got to talking about you and Maeyl."

Tamarra hadn't thought about that. "Yeah, you're right."

"Oh, forget you, girl," Paige said, playfully shoving Tamarra before the two embraced.

After a few moments of hugs and a couple more mutual apologies, Tamarra finally asked, "So what are you going to do about Blake? I mean, it's not like the man doesn't really love you. He told me so."

"Oh, he did? When did he tell you that?"

"He told me on one of the thousand times he called me to let me know that you two were getting serious and that he wanted to come clean about you guys' chance meeting. About me telling him where you worked and what time you got off. You'd been complaining about working in that ticket booth all week, so I knew everything would work out as planned." Tamarra thought for a minute. "Maeyl was right; playing cover up with a good thing somehow makes it seem bad. The same way I forced Maeyl to hide our relationship, I forced Blake to basically do the same thing with yours and his. And look how things turned out with me and Maeyl."

Paige thought for a moment. "Yeah, look how things did turn out for you and Maeyl," she smiled. "I mean, at first, child, it was like a soap opera. But in the end, everything worked out just fine for you two."

"So are you saying that perhaps everything could work out just fine with you and Blake?"

"Perhaps." Paige shrugged with a knowing look on her face right before the phone rang. She walked over and looked at the caller ID. Taking note that it was Blake, she looked at Tamarra, smiled, winked, and then repeated, "Perhaps."

Chapter Thirty-two

Tamarra could barely walk she was so stuffed. The lasagna Paige had made was delicious. She'd told her it was her grandmother's recipe. Not that Tamarra had too many requests for lasagna at her catering affairs due to how expensive it was, but the next time she did, she'd be sure to ask Paige if she could use her grandmother's recipe.

"Who would have thought it?" Tamarra asked herself, flopping her body that she was sure held two extra pounds of lasagna, onto her sofa. "Paige Robinson, getting her cook on for her husband-to-be."

After Paige's phone call with Blake, that eventually Tamarra herself took part in once Paige put her on the line as well, Tamarra knew that despite her interference in Blake and Paige getting together, those two were definitely meant to be. Tamarra had to give all glory to God for connecting those two soul mates.

She watched Paige be just as forgiving to Blake as Maeyl had been to her. And it was Tamarra who had brought it to Paige's attention that Blake really hadn't lied to her. He just simply withheld the truth.

"But you told me you were outside of that theatre meeting another woman," Paige had said to Blake while all three were on the phone line.

"Actually, dear, you are the one who said that I was meeting another woman," Blake corrected her. "I simply said that I was meeting someone."

Eventually both realized how childish it was to go back and forth, and ended up laughing at how ridiculous they sounded. By the end of the thirty-minute phone call, the engagement was on and a wedding date had been set for a year from now. All's well that ends well.

When Tamarra heard her phone ring, she slothfully went to answer it. Staring at the caller ID, she thought twice about answering the call. But she knew that it was time for her to stop feeling like an ant and become a giant to every and anything that might try to hinder her in the future. It was time, she felt. If after all these years, Paige could finally confront her mother about how she felt, surely Tamarra could finally confront her own.

"Hey, Mom," Tamarra answered, returning to the couch.

"Well, the devil must be freezing his buns off for the first time in life, because your father said hell would freeze over before I'd get you on the phone," Tamarra's mother joked.

"That's Daddy, full of jokes," Tamarra stated. "How are you, Mom?"

"Splendid, splendid, and more splendid," she said.

"That's good to hear." Tamarra paused for a minute. "Sorry I haven't returned any of your calls. There's just been so much going on in my life. You know I'm seeing someone now."

"You don't say. Well, good for you."

"Thanks, Mom. He's a wonderful God-fearing man. He attends New Day. We've known each other for years, but we've only been seeing each other for a few months."

"Well, you know your father and I would love to meet him . . . get to know all about him, the same way he knows all about us, I'm sure."

Tamarra picked up on the fact that her mother was really asking if she'd told her new beau about her family. "He knows a little about you all, but not everything."

"And not everyone, I'm sure. I mean, after all, you were married to what's his name for umpteen years, and he never knew about Raymond. Every time you two came to visit, which wasn't often, you'd call ahead to make sure I'd removed Raymond's pictures from the mantel and put away any photo albums. It saddens your father and me how you act as though Raymond doesn't even exist. Speaking of Raymond—"

"Mom, are you serious? It saddens you and Daddy that I act like Raymond doesn't exist? What about how I felt about you and Daddy acting like the entire incident didn't exist. And now you want me to acknowledge that monster?"

"You know you really shouldn't talk like that. Whether you like it or not, Raymond is your brother."

"And those girls he raped that landed him all these years in prison were somebody's daughters."

"It's molested," Tamarra's mother corrected.

"What?" Tamarra looked down at the phone as if she couldn't believe her mother was trying to downplay the reasons behind her brother being in jail.

"He was charged with molestation; not rape."

"Well, he should have been charged with rape," Tamarra snapped, "because that's exactly what he did. That's exactly what he did to those girls. He raped them, Mom. The same way he raped me!"

"Look, your father just walked in. I have to go."

"Yeah, you run off and take care of Daddy the same way he ran off to take care of Raymond."

"I don't know what you're talking about," Mrs. Evans stammered.

"Like heck you don't!" For the first time during their conversation, Tamarra realized that she was raising her voice at her mother. She took a deep breath and lowered her tone. "I'm sorry, Mom. I didn't mean to disrespect you, but how much longer are we going to live this lie?"

"I'm not going to sit here and listen to—"

"Yes, you are!" Tamarra demanded, realizing that once again she'd raised her voice at her mother. She swallowed and lowered her tone. "Yes, you will listen. You owe me that much."

Tamarra took a second to think about the words that she was about to let come out of her mouth. They were words that she had longed to speak over the years, but never had. But she wanted answers. She needed answers.

"Raymond raped me, Mom. He raped me for four years before I ever told you. And hadn't you realized the stains on my sheets weren't from me peeing the bed, and questioned me about it, it might have gone on longer. Heck, we might even be living together as husband and wife instead of brother and sister."

"That's sick," Mrs. Evans said.

"No, what he did to me was sick. What you and Daddy did to cover it up was sick. I'll never forget that day you sat me in my bedroom and badgered me about the stains on my sheet."

"Well, if you had done your laundry like I'd told you to, I never would have had to do it myself and noticed them."

"Are you serious? Are you serious?" Now Tamarra was well aware that she was loud talking her mother, and this time, she didn't care. "You're blaming me? But why should that surprise me? As quiet as it's kept, you've always blamed me. Why, I don't know."

"I'll tell you why," Mrs. Evans decided to shoot back. "Your brother told me how you used to come in his room wearing just a sleep shirt with no pants. Sitting on his bed Indian style with your panties showing."

"They were Wonder Woman panties, Mom; Underroos. I was only ten years old when Raymond started raping me. Raymond was thirteen. He knew better. But then again, if Daddy had done a better job hiding his porn tapes, then maybe this could have been prevented. Maybe Raymond wouldn't have watched them, and then had the desire to come try all that sick stuff out on me."

"Now that's enough. Your father had no idea that Raymond was sneaking into his private things. Quit trying to blame everybody else. You have to take some blame yourself, too, you know. Have you ever asked yourself what part you had in all this? I mean, you did allow it to go on for four years. And I can only imagine how much longer it would have gone on if I hadn't pressured you into telling me."

"Believe me, Mom. I've asked myself that same question. But not more times than I've asked myself how you and Dad could cover it up and act as though it hadn't happened. I mean, the performance we all had to put on. You and Dad faking a divorce just so no one would question why the family wasn't living together. Dad took Raymond all the way to Maryland, and you kept me here in Ohio. Then as soon as Raymond turned of age and was able to move out on his own, you and Dad suddenly reconciled. And the entire world bought the whole charade. All of that just so Raymond and I wouldn't be living in the same house together, and he wouldn't sneak into my room at night."

"Well, what would you have suggested?" Mrs. Evans had the most indignant tone ever in his voice.

"How about calling the police?"

"What kind of parent puts their own child in jail?"

"The same kind of parent who protects their child. Funny thing is, I was the one who you and Dad should have been protecting, but instead you protected the rapist."

"He's your brother!" Mrs. Evans scolded.

"No, mother, he's your son. He's no brother of mine. He's dead as far as I'm concerned, and you know what, Mom? That's exactly what I tell the very few people who actually know that I ever had a brother; that he died. But then again, I didn't have many friends considering I was home schooled."

"Is that what that so-called New Day church of yours teaches the Christians to do down there? Lie? That's exactly why I stay as far away from church as possible. Some of those denominations are like cults. Brainwashing folks."

"You should talk?" Those words seethed through Tamarra's teeth. "You brainwashed me into keeping quiet and living a lie. I believe we took 'what goes on in this house stays in this house' to the extreme."

This was a conversation that Tamarra had dreamed of having for so many years. So much so that she used to practice in the mirror exactly what she would say. Of course, those lines went out of the window the minute her mother tried to shift the blame on her about what her brother had done to her. She hadn't foreseen that happening. No. The script she wrote ended with her mother and father apologizing to her and telling her how much they loved her. She never thought in a million years her mother would have accused her of enticing the rapist.

"Like I said, you might want to take a look at yourself and see what role you played in all of this," her mother reiterated. "I really thought by you being involved in church and all, it might help you, but I see it's doing just the opposite. You won't even confess to having a part in it."

"I don't care if I used to go in Raymond's room butt naked," Tamarra screamed. "I was only ten. I was only ten." Tamarra became angry with herself as tears threatened to fill her eyes. No, she told the tears. *No, you will not fall.*

Tamarra had cried enough over what her brother had done to her. She cried every night he had come into her room and assaulted her. He'd made her do all the disgusting things he'd seen on the porn tapes he'd watched; the tapes that belong to their father that he'd sneak and watch only moments before assaulting her. The day her father packed up her brother and moved out of town, she vowed she'd never let another tear fall over the once sweet boy who would do anything for his little sister, to the now monster who would do anything to hurt his little sister. No more tears for what he'd done to her. Ever. That included now.

"Look, Mom, I've been really asking God to help me work on myself, and in the past few months, He's delivered me from a lot of things. He's helped me to face and cope with some things."

"Well, tell me, Tamarra, in these past few months, has this God you serve put forgiveness before you?"

"I, uh . . . what do you mean?" Tamarra didn't think she liked what her mother was getting at.

"Have you done anything that you needed forgiveness for, and God put it on a person's heart to forgive you?"

"Mother, here lately, more times than you can imagine."

"Then why is it you have no problem seeking forgiveness, but you can't forgive others?"

"I do forgive others. I forgive others all the time, but this is different." Tamarra choked back tears. "I couldn't even give my husband a child because of what your son did to me."

"My son? You say it as if I'm responsible for Raymond's acts."

"Well, I'm sorry you took it that way, Mother, even though that's not how I meant it. Perhaps you're experiencing a dose of conviction."

"How dare you, Tamarra?" her mother spat, on the verge of tears. "Your father told me that bringing up your brother with you was useless."

"Well, this time I'd have to say Daddy was right. I know God's grace and mercy has been upon me. I know I'm blessed that He put it on others' hearts to forgive me for my wrongdoings, but this mountain just seems to be unmovable right now."

"But if you'd just say move mountain—"

"Mom, it's not that easy! And don't be one of those non-Christians who are always trying to quote scriptures to those of us who are! If you can quote the scripture, then you should be able to live by the scripture!" Tamarra yelled, leaving dead silence on the line. "I'm sorry, Mom. I'm sorry I yelled at you. I'm sorry for disrespecting you in any way, it's just that, I guess God ain't done with me yet. I've come such a long way these past few months, and yet I'm still not where I need to be."

Mrs. Evans exhaled. "I understand, honey. In spite of what you think, really, I do understand. And I'm going to hope

that your God works on you, and soon," her mother said, almost
as if there was a sense of urgency. "Anyway, just know your father
and I love you, Tamarra, we really do. I'm sorry for the choices
we made that hurt you. I never wanted to hurt my baby girl." Her
mother began to sob.

"Please, Mom, don't cry."

"Tamarra?"

"Yes, Mom."

"While you're seeking God to help you with forgiving
your brother, can you please ask Him to help you find it in your
heart to forgive your father and me too?" she cried. "I'm so sorry."

This was the first time in all these years her mother had
ever apologized to Tamarra for how they handled the situation.
Although she knew that it might take a minute and some prayer,
she could find it in her heart to forgive her parents. What would
take work was finding it in her heart to forgive her brother. In
all honesty, that's something Tamarra felt she would never be
able to do. But according to Philippians, she could do all things
through Christ who strengthens her.

"Okay, Mom. I will," Tamarra assured her.

"I love you, Tamarra."

"I love you too, Mom," Tamarra said to her mom for the
first time since she was a little girl. Looks like Jesus was moving
pretty fast. "Bye, Mom," Tamarra said, then ended the call. She
let out a long breath. "Yep, Tamarra," she said to herself, "you
aren't where you want to be in this whole forgiveness thing right
now, but at least you ain't where you used to be."

Getting up to prepare for bed, not only did it feel as
though the weight of the lasagna had fallen off, but the weight
of a heavy burden she'd carried for years had fallen off also.
And even though some weight of the burden remained, God
wouldn't place more on her than she could bear. And she knew
that with His help, one day she'd be even further along than she
ever imagined. But for now she would take things one day at a
time.

Chapter Thirty-three

The New Day Singles Ministry meeting/pot luck was about to start. Deborah had arrived an hour early to help set up for Mother Doreen's farewell. The members had agreed to allow non-members to participate as well so that they could say their goodbyes to Mother Doreen, who was heading for Kentucky first thing in the morning.

"Everything looks so delicious," Tamarra said to Deborah as she and Maeyl entered the classroom. People were starting to arrive.

"Thank you." She looked around the room. "I'm thinking I might have to set out some chairs and pull another table out from the storage room."

"Oh, don't worry about that, Sister Deborah," Maeyl told her. "I'll take care of it." Brother Maeyl proceeded to do so.

"What's that you got there?" Deborah inhaled the aroma, trying to figure out the dish covered in foil that Tamarra held.

"Mac n' cheese. Maeyl's favorite." She leaned in and whispered. "It's the only time he gets it. You know how I am about cooking for a man like he was my husband when he ain't."

Deborah shook her head. "You still a mess . . . but in a good way."

The two women laughed as Tamarra then went to find a place to set down her dish.

"Mrs. Lucas?"

Deborah heard her name being called. She turned to face a woman of who she did not recognize. "Hello, my sister," Deborah greeted anyway.

"I thought that was you. The last time I saw you, it was so quick and brief that I wasn't sure it was you."

"We've met before?" Deborah questioned. "I'm sorry, I don't remember."

"We never really got a proper introduction, although we did talk on the phone. I'd called you up some time ago regarding my manuscript. I'd wanted you to do some editing work on it prior to my leaving out of town. I came up to Family Café to meet you, but you weren't in the best of moods. You practically ran me down leaving the café."

Deborah almost wanted to die. She thought back to that day Lynox had showed up at Family Café. She'd just assumed there was no real client; that he had set the whole thing up. Now the evidence that she had been wrong, very wrong, stood before her.

"My apologies," Deborah said. "I thought I had been set up by an author who I had declined to represent. I was a little upset."

"I'd say you were more than a little upset. But I understand. I have days when I'm going through it as well. So I won't hold that against you."

"Thank you, sister, I appreciate that."

"Good. I hope that means we can still get together regarding my work."

Deborah smiled. She was blessed that the woman would still even consider working with her. "I'd love to. And I appreciate your willingness to work with me."

"Oh, I'm not quick to jump to conclusions about folks. I let my spirit guide me. My spirit says that you're good people. Just like Doreen. She's the one who had recommended you to me in the first place, you know. I couldn't remember her name back then because I'd only met her in a long checkout line at the grocery store. We exchanged numbers, and not too long ago, she called me with an invite to church. She was letting me know that she would be leaving, but that I was still welcome to visit New Day. She even invited me to the potluck."

"Well, I'm glad you could make it."

"Thank you."

Deborah apologized once again and thanked her for coming before she had to excuse herself to go take care of some things. She was glad that she hadn't ruined witnessing to someone and that God was giving her a second chance. But she couldn't help but think about Lynox. He'd made a last ditch effort at the café to get back into her good graces, and being the persistent man that he was, had even called her several times after that. Eventually she wore him down with her blatant neglect, and he'd seemed to have given up. But Deborah knew his kind. He was no quitter. And maybe, just like God had given her a second chance to make an impression, Lynox, too, was deserving of a second chance. Hmm . . . she'd have to pray about that.

The following Sunday morning, New Day was on fire. The praying, praising, and worshiping were deep. Took them to another level. Another dimension in God's spiritual realm. So many people rededicated their lives to the Lord or got saved for the first time. It was an awesome experience, an experience Paige was grateful that Norman had gotten to witness.

She'd finally gotten around to inviting him to church, and reluctantly, he showed up. She knew that God would be pleased at her evangelism spirit, but not so pleased at how she'd actually gone about finally convincing Norman to come.

"New Day is a mixed church. There are people of all races and ethnicities; talk about your melting pot of women," Paige had said, and that's all that needed to be said to pique Norman's interest. And although in his heart he hadn't really come

E.N. Joy

211

to New Day for an encounter with the Lord, that's exactly what he got.

Norman didn't go to the altar and get saved, prayed for, join the church, or anything, but Paige was almost certain she saw him lift his hands and mouth the words, "Thank you, Jesus." She didn't know if he was thanking Jesus for the experience, or because of the two beautiful women he was sandwiched in between who practically fought over who would share their Bible with him. Nonetheless, Paige just hoped his experience at New Day would allow him to see her in a new light; God's light.

Chapter Thirty-four

Tonight was Deborah's last time attending any of the New Day Temple of Faith Singles Ministry meetings. As expected, with the hoopla over the potluck and all the kind words everyone took the time out to say to Mother Doreen, they never got around to actually having a real meeting. With Mother Doreen in Kentucky, she'd gotten with Pastor via telephone on prospects to head the ministry in both her and Deborah's absence. As always, Pastor trusted Mother Doreen's judgment and left it in her hands.

Before entering the classroom, Deborah stopped off into the bathroom. After using it, she exited the stall only to find Helen entering the bathroom. This was the first time since that day in the conference room that the two women had been alone face-to-face, and now, as Deborah stood boldly and with authority staring Helen in the eyes, it appeared as though the table was now turned.

Helen was the one with eyes cast away, head bowed. Deborah couldn't help but to feel good, relieved. Not because Helen felt the need to now steer clear of Deborah, but because Helen no longer had anything over her. The accuser had nothing to accuse her of. Deborah had confessed her sins and released her burdens to the Lord, and He had forgiven her. Now, no devil in hell or earth, could bind Deborah, could keep her from her God and being used by God in whichever way He saw pleasing.

"Helen," Deborah greeted.

"Uhh, Sister Deborah, I was hoping I'd run into you tonight."

Surprised, Deborah replied, "Is that so?"

"Yes, I uh . . ." Helen searched for words. "I, uh, just wanted to know uh, how are you?" Helen found words, but Deborah could tell that they weren't the ones she'd been originally searching for.

"I'm blessed and highly favored," Deborah replied, the same way Nita would have replied. And just like Nita, she meant it.

"That's good."

Silence.

"Look," both women started at the same time.

"You go first," Deborah told her.

"No, you go," Helen said.

Deborah cleared her throat, and then slowly took Helen's hands into hers. *If Mother Doreen can pray for a woman who had just climbed out of bed with her husband, surely I can pray for this one,* she thought. And with that thought she began to pray The Lord's Prayer. For some reason, that was the prayer that dropped into her spirit. She prayed the prayer as if she was singing the song. Her voice soft, moving, and sincere. When she finished, she opened her eyes to see tears flowing down Helen's face. With no more words to say from within, she simply pulled Helen to her and gave her a Holy Ghost hug.

Once the women came out of the embrace, Helen sniffled. "Pastor had a word with me the other day about those pictures of Sister Tamarra and Brother Maeyl that were posted on the website. I confessed that I placed them there."

"Oh, you did?" Deborah was shocked by Helen's confession.

"Yes, but I just told Pastor that I'd taken them with the thought of promoting the Singles Ministry in mind."

Deborah sighed. "Now, Helen, you and I both know that that's probably not the truth."

"Look, I confessed at least. That was a start."

Deborah nodded her head. "Yeah, and we all have to start somewhere, I suppose."

"But don't worry, I plan on telling Pastor the whole truth . . . eventually."

Deborah nodded again. "Anyway, I'm glad that's out in the open. And I'm glad you decided to join the Singles Ministry after all. I'm sure it will be a blessing to you." Deborah stepped past Helen to exit the bathroom.

"So are you going to tell anyone?" Helen called out. She'd found the original words she'd been searching for.

"Tell anyone what?" Deborah turned and asked.

"About me." Helen looked down. "I had one too, you know. And I know I taunted you that day in the clinic. I just felt that if I could make your situation seem worse off than mine, then I wouldn't feel so bad." Helen paused before saying, "A friend of mine invited me to Bible Study at her church last Wednesday, and the Bishop there preached on Paul; how Paul was honest enough to admit that he still struggled in certain areas of his life and how he faced and dealt with them, unlike those with a pharisaical spirit who condemn others for doing the very things they do themselves. I guess I was one of those people with a pharisaical spirit that the Bishop was talking about."

Deborah knew exactly what scripture the Bishop must have taught from. "Paul says, 'I know the law but . . . can't keep it . . . sin . . . keeps sabotaging my best intentions, I . . . need help . . . I decide to do good, but . . . My decisions . . . don't result in actions. Something . . . gets the better of me every time' (Romans 7:17-20 TM).

"Yep, that's the one," Helen recalled.

"Well, did it work?" Deborah wanted to know.

Helen looked puzzled. "Did what work?"

"You making my situation seem worse off than yours; did it make you feel less bad about what you had done?"

Helen shook her head.

"Then why keep taunting me like you did? If you honestly came to realize that what you and I did, no matter who was further along than whom, was the same thing, why keep dangling it over my head?"

"I felt that as long as I could keep making you feel bad about it, making it something you'd be ashamed of forever, that you'd keep it a secret forever. As long as no one knew about you, then they wouldn't know about me."

Deborah nodded as if she understood, although in all honesty, she just couldn't grasp Helen's logic about the entire situation.

"Well . . .?" Helen asked.

"Well what?"

"Are you going to tell? I mean, look at you." She pointed to Deborah's head all the way down to her feet. "You don't even look the same anymore. It's like you have a faith lift. God's made you over. Obviously He's forgiven you. You're standing here looking at me, your nemesis," she chuckled, "straight in the eyes. No more downcast looks. It's like you're staring the devil down for the first time and not backing down." Helen choked on tears and lowered her head.

"Don't you do this to yourself, Helen." Deborah said as she walked over to her with authority and placed her hand on her shoulder. "You are not the devil. Now you might have let the devil use you at one time, but you are not the devil. Don't let Satan tell you that you are one of his. Know who you are and whose you are." Deborah pointed up. "You belong to God. And God loves you the same way He loves me. If He forgave me, then you know He'll forgive you. So instead of hanging on to the past, let go and let God."

Helen looked into Deborah's eyes as she wiped away a tear that had fallen down her face. "Yeah, I'm sure God will forgive me . . . someday. After all, I hear He has a sense of humor. And it certainly would be funny for Him to forgive someone like me," Helen said as she made her way over to the bathroom sink to get herself together.

"He already has forgiven you," Deborah whispered as she made her way down the hall and into the classroom. "He already has."

With Mother Doreen, the voice of reason, no longer a part of the Singles Ministry, Deborah knew she'd be up next in line to be appointed leader of the New Day Singles Ministry. She knew deep inside that it wasn't her calling though, and had shared such with the pastor. She didn't believe in taking a position at church just because it needed to be filled. She knew that God had just showed her her calling, and that was to minister to women like Helen. To women like herself.

Deborah entered the classroom just in time to hear the newly appointed New Day Temple of Faith Singles Ministry leader be announced by the pastor.

"As you all know, it's unfortunate that Sister Deborah will no longer be a part of this ministry as God has called her to focus on other things. But it is with great pleasure that I present to you Sister Lorain, the new New Day Singles Ministry leader," the pastor announced.

Before Deborah knew it, everyone was staring at her as she stood in the doorway laughing uncontrollably. She couldn't help but think back to the words Helen had just spoken about God having a sense of humor. And her thoughts traveled back to the night Lorain won the raffle at the Singles Ministry dinner. *Maybe if tight clothes, make-up wearing Lorain did join the Singles Ministry, then men would join as well . . . God would have to have a crazy sense of humor to use Lorain in that capacity.*

"Is everything okay, Sister Deborah?" Pastor asked worriedly.

"Oh, I'm sorry," Deborah apologized. "It's just that something that someone just said to me was on the money."

"Oh? And what was that?"

"That God has a sense of humor. He has a sense of humor in deed," Deborah said as she continued laughing, not being able to fathom what exactly God had in store for New Day Singles Ministry with Lorain now in charge. It would be a new day all right. A new day indeed . . . .

Reader's Group Guide Questions

1) Although the title of this book is *She Who Finds a Husband*, it was evident that God's Word is sovereign, which states "He Who Finds a Wife." Do you believe once the women let go and let God's Word prevail by allowing their husbands/mates to find them, things turned out better?

2) Paige had a problem with one of her co-workers who she felt ignored the fact that she was now a Christian, since he was used to dealing with the old, worldlier Paige. How do you feel a born-again person should deal with those types of situations; be it co-workers, family, or friends? Have you ever found yourself in a similar situation? If so, how did you deal with it and was it effective?

3) Deborah carried around guilt and shame because of an act she'd committed years ago that she regretted. Instead of confessing the act to God, she felt as though she was hiding it from Him, then got angry with Helen for threatening to reveal it. Do you think that is what the accuser is doing to so many Christians today in order to keep them in bondage; in God's ear accusing, while all the time God is simply waiting on His child to confess the sin to Him directly so that healing and deliverance can begin?

4) Some of the women at New Day put on a church face and assumed Mother Doreen had been doing the same. Do you agree with Mother Doreen; that just because a person is going through something, they don't always have to appear broken? That an experience with the Lord and even the mere anticipation of a move of God can be magnified over the problem or situation?

5) Helen had committed the same act herself that she taunted Deborah about having committed. Do we as Christians some-

times try to justify or cover acts we've committed that might not have been pleasing to God by pointing our finger in the direction of someone who we feel did something even worse?

6) Because of Deborah's actions that day in Family Café, Zelda made a decision that she didn't want to attend New Day Temple of Faith. Do you believe that the actions of the members of a church play a role in whether people decide to attend that church, or are a reflection on the kingdom as a whole?

7) Deborah blamed herself for ending up in the predicament she did with Elton. Do you agree, somewhat agree, or totally disagree that she was to blame?

8) Paige had allowed her mother's role in the marriage to her father to shape her thoughts on relationships. The last thing Paige wanted to do was to find a man that was like her father in order to avoid ending up like her mother. Do you think Paige might have missed out on a man God had for her because of her way of thinking?

9) There were a couple of unfortunate mishaps at New Day Temple of Faith regarding the use of the Internet. Do you believe the Internet can be used as a weapon of the enemy to attack Christians and mankind in general? How should we protect ourselves from the enemy's use of this form of technology?

10) Were the issues that Paige needed to be delivered from less significant than those of some of the other characters in the book? Why or why not?

11) Tamarra carried around loads of baggage from her past. Even though she seemed to be delivered from so much, there always seemed to be even more issues she had to face. Have you ever felt that way? That you'll never be able to shed all the burdens laid upon you?

12) What biblical story can you relate Tamarra and her brother's situation to?

13) Which characters, whether main characters or background characters, would you like to see in future installments of the New Day Divas series?

14) Were there any particular characters, issues, or situations that you could closely relate to?

15) Although Tamarra's mother didn't attend church or believe God to work in her own life, she always questioned Tamarra about church and God in hers. Why do you think that is so? Do you know non-Christians like that? Ones who won't allow God to operate in their own lives, but keep you under the Christian microscope?

About the Author

E.N. Joy is the author of *Me, Myself and Him*, which was her debut work into the Christian Fiction genre. Formerly a secular author writing under the names Joylynn M. Jossel and JOY, she decided to fully dedicate her life to Christ, which meant she had to fully dedicate her work as well. She made a conscious decision that whatever she penned from that point on had to glorify God and His kingdom.

The *New Day Divas* series was incited by her publisher, Carl Weber, but birthed by the Holy Spirit. God used Mr. Weber to pitch the idea to E.N. Joy; sort of plant the seed in her spirit, of which she prayed on and eventually the seed was watered and grew into a phenomenal five-book series that she is sure will touch readers across the world.

"My goal and prayer with the *New Day Divas* series is to put an end to the 'Church Fiction versus Christian Fiction' dilemma," E.N. Joy states, "and find a divine medium that pleases both God and the readers."

With book one, *She Who Finds a Husband*, launching the series, readers will agree that this project is one that definitely glorifies God in every aspect, but still manages to display in a godly manner that there are "Church Folks" (church fiction) and then there are "Christian Folks" (Christian fiction) and come Sunday morning, they all end up in the same place.

E. N. Joy currently resides in Reynoldsburg, Ohio where she is continuing work on the *New Day Divas* series, as well as working on the anthology series titled *Even Sinners Have Souls*.

You can visit the author at www.enjoywrites.com or email her at enjoywrites@aol.com to share with her any feedback from the story as well as any subject matters you might want to see addressed in future New Day Divas books.

Urban Christian His Glory Book Club!

Established in January 2007, *UC His Glory Book Club* is another way to introduce **Urban Christian** and its authors. We are an online book club supporting Urban Christian authors by purchasing, reading, and providing written reviews of the authors' books. *UC His Glory Book Club* welcomes both men and women of the literary world who have a passion for reading Christian-based fiction.

UC His Glory Book Club is the brainchild of Joylynn Jossel, author and Executive Editor of Urban Christian and Kendra Norman-Bellamy, author and copy editor for Urban Christian. The book club will provide support, positive feedback, encouragement, and a forum whereby members can openly discuss and review the literary works of Urban Christian authors. In the future, we anticipate broadening our spectrum of services to include online author chats, author spotlights, interviews with your favorite Urban Christian author(s), special online groups for *UC His Glory Book Club* members, ability to post reviews on the website and amazon. com, membership ID cards, *UC His Glory* Yahoo! Group and much more.

Even though there will be no membership fees attached to becoming a member of *UC His Glory Book Club,* we do expect our members to be active, committed, and to follow the guidelines of the book club.

UC His Glory Book Club **members pledge to:**

- Follow the guidelines of *UC His Glory Book Club.*
- Provide input, opinions, and reviews that build up, rather than tear down.
- Commit to purchasing, reading, and discussing featured book(s) of the month.

- Respect the Christian beliefs of *UC His Glory Book Club.*
- Believe that Jesus is the Christ, Son of the Living God.

We look forward to the online fellowship.

Many Blessings to You!

Shelia E. Lipsey
President
UC His Glory Book Club

**Visit the official Urban Christian His Glory Book Club website at <u>www.uchisglorybookclub.net</u>

Coming Soon

Been There Prayed That:
New Day Divas Series Book Two

Mother Doreen has left New Day Temple of Faith in Malvonia, Ohio in order to move to Kentucky to help her diabetic sister care for herself and her family. With her sister's husband, a truck driver, pretty much living on the road, Mother Doreen feels in her spirit that she's needed to intervene on her sister's behalf, especially when certain members of her sister's church family, namely the Assistant Pastor, seems to be there for her sister just a little bit too much. Mother Doreen's suspicions really start to grow when her sister's belly does too. Is it Mother Doreen's spirit of discernment warning her that things in her sister's home and church aren't what they seem, or is Mother Doreen just a busy body church mother sticking her nose where it doesn't belong?

Back in Malvonia, Tamarra and Maeyl's relationship is moving along nicely. She even has a feeling that the man she knows God placed in her life is going to propose to her. But will all of that change when suspicions begin to rise when someone from Maeyl's past shows up at New Day Temple of Faith unexpected and unwelcomed?

Follow the New Day Divas series by E. N. Joy as this soap opera in print brings back these and all of your other favorite blessed and highly favored characters, as well as some folks who claim to be saved, but due to their actions, others might beg to differ.

Chapter One

"What the Jacks Daniels was Mother Doreen thinking when she vouched for this woman to be the new leader of the New Day Single's Ministry?" Unique spoke in a loud whisper to the woman next to her who responded with a shrug, wondering the same thing herself. "Better yet, what was Pastor thinking to approve such a thing?" Rolling her eyes she added, "Heck! For that matter, they could have named me leader, seeming just any ol' everybody can lead a ministry around here these days. Do you even have to be a member of this church to be a leader anymore?" Once again, the woman she was venting to shrugged.

The room was full of hushed whispers, teeth sucking, neck snapping and eye rolling as Sister Lorain took the podium in front of the twenty-five members of the New Day Temple of Faith Singles Ministry. She appeared oblivious to all that was going on around her. Instead, she was delighting in the fact that she was doing God's kingdom work. She was a leader in a church; a place not too long ago she thought she'd never step foot in, let alone be operating a ministry. But here she stood, holding the torch, or as church folk would say, the mantel, passed down to her from Mother Doreen as the former leader of the New Day Single's Ministry.

It was a new day all right. With this being only her third meeting since taking over as the new leader, several men had joined the ministry, which was something the past leader had been unable to achieve. Up until recently, the ministry had consisted of nothing but single women. Today, although the men remained out numbered, there were at least seven of them no less.

Lorain credited this now co-ed ministry to God for moving her to personally invite the single men of the congregation to join the ministry. But some of the other women . . . most of the other women . . . okay, all of the other women, credited her short skirts, three inch pumps, and low cut blouses for the sudden increase in male attendance. And that Mary Kay cosmetics she sold on the side and tried to push on the women at every church function was partly to blame as well.

Although all the women thought these things about Lorain, only Unique was bold enough to say it out loud, with the intent of Sister Lorain over hearing her. But Sister Lorain seemed completely unaware of all the negative energy and comments being made around her . . . about her. So Unique figured the next time she'd have to say it even louder.

The young twenty-two year old, Unique, was raised in a project in Columbus, Ohio that was now called Rosewind Terrace, but would always be known as the former Windsor Terrace. A mother of three children with three different fathers, Unique was one of the less diplomatic members of the ministry. And it had nothing to do with the fact that she was raised in the projects, but had everything to do with the way she was raised by her single mother of five children with five different fathers.

It was only two years ago when Unique moved to Malvonia, Ohio with her sister, who was also a single mother of two children with two different fathers, who began to change her ways for the better. Prior to moving in with her sister, Unique had been evicted from her apartment for nonpayment of rent, which had only been $25 a month thanks to her Section 8 Housing voucher that paid the bulk of the rent. But between her drinking, smoking weed, and paying babysitters while she went out partying, Unique never even had $25 left over from her welfare check to pay the rent.

Unique's sister took her and her kids in with opened arms the day the Sheriff came with an order that allowed for all of her and her children's belongings to be placed on the sidewalk.

Now two years later, the seven of them were still making the best of the three bedroom finished basement house her sister was leasing.

Unique was still on welfare. She was no longer partying like she used to, although she'd hit the club every now and then if one of her girlfriends in Columbus called her up and talked her into doing so. These occasional nights out with the girls sometimes led to a little bit of smoking and a drink or two. But since getting saved, joining New Day and getting baptized a year and a half ago, she'd made great strides toward giving up old things. With her occasional backsliding, she was nowhere near where she needed to be in Christ, but she was far from where she used to be. But no one judged her then and no one judged her now. Nope, nobody at New Day judged anybody . . . with the exception of Sister Lorain that is. So it was probably safe to say that things were about to change up in New Day Temple of Faith.

As Sister Lorain opened up the meeting in prayer, invisible stones shattering glass house after glass house, hurled through the room.

Yes, indeed . . . judgment day was near.

ORDER FORM
URBAN BOOKS, LLC
78 E. Industry Ct
Deer Park, NY 11729

Name: (please print):_____

Address: _____

City/State: _____

Zip: _____

QTY	TITLES	PRICE
	A Man's Worth	$14.95
	Abundant Rain	$14.95
	Battle Of Jericho	$14.95
	By The Grace Of God	$14.95
	Dance Into Destiny	$14.95
	Divorcing The Devil	$14.95
	Forsaken	$14.95
	Grace And Mercy	$14.95
	Guilty & Not Guilty Of Love	$14.95
	His Woman, His Wife His Widow	$14.95
	Illusion	$14.95
	The LoveChild	$14.95

Shipping and Handling - add $3.50 for 1st book then $1.75 for each additional book.

Please send a check payable to:

Urban Books, LLC

Please allow 4 - 6 weeks for delivery